SECRETS
in the
WOODS

Beyond the Darkness

Dragana Stjepić

To: John & P. J.

DRAGANA STJEPIĆ

ISBN 978-1-64191-218-1 (paperback)
ISBN 978-1-64191-219-8 (digital)

Christian Faith Publishing, Inc.
832 Park Avenue
Meadville, PA 16335
www.christianfaithpublishing.com

Printed in the United States of America

CHARACTERS

Arfabele Land—Witches World
Emily Landar—Main character
Gabby—Mother
Allen—Father
Briana—Jealous Girl
Mitti—Briana's Friend; easy to be manipulated
Adriana—Briana's Friend; hard core one
Megan—Briana's Friend; follower
Nikki—Emily's Friend
Mike—Emily's Lover
Pete—Mike's Best Friend
Alex—Mike's and Pete's Other Friend
Aza'el—Main Evil Witch
Gary—Book Store Owner/Magic Man
Jack—Nikki's Boyfriend
Mayla—Good Witch Leader
Kayla—Jack's and Nikki's Daughter
Alona—Gary's Wife/the good witch who placed Aza'el into the deep
    sleep
Mahu—Great Evil Leader; who died about one thousand years ago
Lin—Mayla's Assistant
Eliot—Good Witch/Klexon Witch Warrior
Abe—Klexon Warrior
Saga—Dark Zal; Aza'el's destiny
Hank—Football Coach

Sam—Football Player
Roger—Football Player
Brian—Football Player/Brutal Rapist

Chapter 1

THE BEGINNING

It had been a very long drive to Philly. Emily Landar was a new member to the town. She moved out of New York City into a smaller town in Philadelphia. Her mother Gabby and her father Allen have decided to move for work. There was a better job offer, and plus, they all thought they could use a fresh start.

Emily was a very beautiful young woman. She was about 5'7" and weighs about 150 lbs. She looked very healthy and had very attractive features. She had very long black hair, and it was usually wavy. She had green eyes, which stand out with her black hair, fuller lips, and a very attractive smile. Emily was going into her first year of college. She was eighteen years old.

The family arrived at their new house and was settling in. The night before school, Emily got all her school things ready, even her clothes. She could not believe they moved from the greatest city ever. Her mother and father called her down for dinner. Emily sat at the table along with her parents. Gabby asked her if she was ready for school and how she was feeling. Emily nodded and continued eating her food. Allen told her that if she did not try to have some type of friendship with people including her own mother, there were going to be some issues that needed to be discussed as a family. He also told Emily to open up a little more to the world and communicate better with her mother. Emily looked at her dad.

"Open to the world, Dad? Really? Mother has been the one always turning her back on me, working all day long and gone every time I needed her. Not to mention that all my friends are in NY," she said.

Emily stood up and walked off to her bedroom. Gabby looked at Allen. Allen told Gabby to let it go.

"Emily just needs some time to accept that you had to work and it has nothing to do with you not loving her," said Allen to his wife.

At seven in the morning, Emily's alarm clock went off. She woke up, got ready for school, ate breakfast, and started walking. As she was walking up to the school, she noticed a guy. He seemed handsome to her and was driving a nice car. "Some people just have it so easy," she told herself as she saw him having fun with two other boys.

Walking up the stairs into the school, she also bumped into the cheerleaders. One of them looked at Emily and sighed.

"Already bumping into me and don't even know me yet," said the girl.

Emily ignored her and walked passed them. Emily kept on walking toward her class. When she entered her classroom, she noticed a lot of the college students messing around and the boys messing around with the girls. They were trying to be nice but also a little sexual, grabbing the girl's buttocks as the girls laughed it off. Emily took a seat and smiled at the crowd. A young man approached her seat and sat on top of her desk.

"Who are you, beautiful?" he asked her. "I have not seen you in this neighborhood before."

"I'm Emily and I am new to this town," she replied.

Another boy stated, "I like having pretty girls in my classrooms. It keeps it interesting."

The boys laughed and got themselves seated. A female sat down next to Emily and introduced herself as Nikki. Next thing she knew, the nice, handsome man she noticed outside walked in her classroom as the two boys from earlier approached him giving him dap.

Nikki noticed Emily looking at him and said, "That's Mike, and the two goofballs that are with him are Pete and Alex. They have been like best friends forever. In high school, they played football. I'm not sure if they will play again for college."

As Mike sat down in his seat, he looked back at Emily. They locked eyes on each other for a second and Emily turned away. Also in the classroom was a girl named Adriana. She noticed Mike's and Emily's gaze and did not like it. Adriana was a cheerleader, along with her friends Briana, Mitti, and Megan.

Mike was a football player in high school and now will play for college as well. He was tall, about 6'2", had dark hair and low haircut, was a white male, and loved to work out. All the girls wanted him, and he was able to have anyone he wanted.

The bell rang. Emily and Nikki walked into the hallway. As Emily hit the corner, Briana bumped into Emily knocking her books down.

"So you're the new girl in town. I heard about the way you looked at Mike. Yes, I get notified by phone quickly of what goes on in this school, and just an advice from me to you, you might want to stay away from him. Everyone here knows he is my man," she told Emily and walked away.

Adriana walked along with Briana and looked back at Emily and smiled. Briana walked up to Mike and the rest of the crew. They were talking loud and laughing. Emily was picking up her books, and Nikki helped her.

"Don't worry about her. She is a bitch," Nikki said to Emily.

"Yeah, I see that. What's the big deal about her and Mike?" Emily asked her.

"Well, she and Mike used to date in high school. She cheated on him, and he left her. It was like the biggest story in school since no one has ever broken up with Briana before. But ever since, every other girl he dates, Briana gives her hell," Nikki replied.

"What does Mike do about it?" Emily asked.

"Well, not much. He does not believe that she can be evil and he really never cared enough. Let's go to lunch. I'm starving," said Nikki.

After school, Emily and Nikki went to stop by in a coffee shop. Nikki pretty much showed her a little bit around the neighborhood. At the coffee shop, Nikki's friend was working there.

"This is Jack," Nikki introduced him to Emily.

"Nice to meet you," said Jack.

"I have not seen you in school," said Emily.

Jack told her he was not interested in school anymore, and he was going to take over the coffee shop from his father. After high school, he was tired of school. Emily nodded her head.

"So are you going to Briana's party?" Nikki asked Jack.

"Probably not, but if you go, I'll go with you," he replied, and Nikki smiled.

Emily could notice there was something going on between these two, and she just smiled. Emily got up and said she had to get going she still had unpacking to do. Nikki asked her if she knew her way back home. Emily replied that she did and she will see her tomorrow at school.

"It was nice meeting you. Come back, buy some coffee," said Jack to Emily as she was leaving out.

As Emily was walking home, she passed by a creepy old bookstore. She slowly walked past the window looking in and noticed a book that looked like something from old centuries. She saw it had a big ring on the cover. While she focused on the book, an old man appeared on the window. Emily looked at him, and he looked at her. Emily backed away from the window and continued her walk. About five minutes into the walk, a car started to slow down next to her. It was Mike.

"Hey, I don't think we met yet," said Mike.

"No, we have not," Emily replied.

Mike was slowly driving his car while she was walking, talking to her out of his window.

"You're the new girl, right? Where do you live? Maybe I could give you a lift," said Mike.

Emily told him she did not need a ride, and she did not live far.

"Are you sure? I'm heading this way anyway," he told her.

Emily stopped walking and looked at him with a smile. Mike nodded his head telling her to get in and stop playing around. Emily got in the car. She was feeling nervous. She knew she was starting to like him.

"Well, I'm Mike. What's your name?" he introduced himself.

"I'm Emily, but I'm sure you already heard my name," she replied.

He told her he did hear about her, but he wanted to introduce himself to her the right way. Emily smiled.

Mike pulled up at her house, and she thanked him for the ride.

"I'll see you at school tomorrow," said Mike.

Emily waved to him and went into the house. As Mike drove off, Emily ran up to the window watching him. She felt a very strong connection toward him.

"Is everything okay?" her father asked her.

"Yes, Dad. Everything is going fine," Emily replied. She left to her room and started unpacking. However, all she could think about was Mike.

Allen knocked on her door asking her if she needed some help. She said no and continued to unpack.

Chapter 2

MEANWHILE AT HOME

G abby and Allen were making dinner together while discussing Emily's future here in the new town.

"Maybe we should have a family camping or something. We have not done anything as a family in a very long time," Gabby said to Allen.

"You really think Emily wants family time? She is eighteen years old. I think we are the last people she wants to be with right now," Allen replied.

Emily came downstairs with a happy face. Her mother asked her what was new as she remembered that smile from when she was a teenager. Emily looked at her mother and shook her head.

"Nothing," Emily said to her mother.

Emily sat down on the couch and started to read a book. Gabby knew her daughter did not like talking to her much, so she left Emily alone. The following day, Emily left her house to explore the town some more. Emily stopped again by the creepy bookstore. Only this time, the old man was not there. There was something about that bookstore that Emily found interest in. As she continued her walk, the four girls from her new school pulled up in Briana's car. Briana was driving, and all of the windows were down. Adriana was in the passenger side. Briana drove her car so close to Emily that Adriana grabbed Emily by her skirt and Emily jumped back. The girls in the car laughed. Emily ignored them and continued to walk.

"Oh, what's the matter? You don't like to be touched?" said Adriana.

Emily was quiet but then stopped walking and stood still. Briana stopped the car, and the girls hopped out. Briana walked up to Emily's face and asked her where she was going. Emily did not respond. Briana slapped Emily in the back of her head and told her friends to get back in the car and leave the freak alone. Emily was hurt by those words, but she did not say anything. The girls sat back in the car and drove off. Emily ran back home. She stormed into her room crying. Her father asked her what was wrong, but she would not open the door. Her mother was at work. Emily knew she was eighteen years old, and she could run away and go wherever she wanted. She did not have to go back to school, but she wanted to make her father proud.

The following morning, Emily did go to school. The four girls passed right by Emily as she was putting some books into her locker. Briana stopped and called her a freak. The football players heard Briana calling Emily a freak, so they joined in besides Alex and Pete. Emily did not listen to them anymore. She left her locker and walked away. Alex and Pete watched Emily walk to her classroom. Pete turned to Briana and asked her why she had to do that? He told her that Emily was neither ugly nor a freak so what she was doing was stupid. The other football players got quiet. Alex and Pete then walked away from the group.

Emily sat in her classroom right next to Nikki. Nikki told Emily that she saw what happened in the hallway, and she told Emily not to pay them any attention.

"The more you allow them to upset you, the more they will do it," Nikki told Emily.

Emily looked at Nikki and asked her why they were doing that. They don't even knew her. Nikki explained that Briana does not care. She wanted to run everything, and she gets her way; and if she does not like you, then that's what she does. Emily turned her head away. She was very upset. After the class, Mike ran up to Emily and walked her down the hallway and out the school. Briana and Megan saw them together. Emily told Mike she was walking home today and she did not want a ride. Mike said okay, but next time, he will give her a ride. She smiled as he walked away and into his car. When Briana saw Mike leave in his car, she walked up to Emily and bumped her.

"What do you think you are doing?" Briana asked her.

"I don't know what you are talking about," Emily replied.

"I will not tell you again to stay away from Mike. If you don't, then you will have to deal with me," said Briana.

"I do not care about Mike," said Emily even though she had strong feelings for him.

Megan walked up as well and stood by Briana's side. Then, the two girls walked passed Emily with an attitude and left the school. Emily watched them drive off as she started to walk home.

It was a weekend, and the school was having a welcome-back party for the students. Everyone was invited. Mike decided to stop by Emily's house. He knocked, and her dad opened the door.

"Who are you?" Allen asked.

"I am Mike. I go to the same college as Emily," Mike replied.

"So what do you want?" Allen asked.

"Well, there is a welcome party at the school, and I was wondering if Emily wanted to go," replied Mike.

Allen thought about it for a second. However, he knew she needed new friends especially after what happened to her best friend back home.

"I will go get her," said Allen.

He invited the boy in and told him to wait by the door as he went upstairs to get Emily. A couple of seconds later, Emily came down to the door.

"You know this is just a little creepy," said Emily to Mike.

They both smiled. Emily asked him to step outside for a little privacy, and they did. Mike asked her if she would like to come with him to the get-together at their school. It was just a welcome party to the New Year. Emily told him she was not interest to go, but he insisted. He made her say yes. Emily went back in the house, changed clothes, and left out with Mike for the night. She wore a short, blue dress with a V-cut on top and some heels. Mike looked at her like he had never seen anything so beautiful before. He held her hand, walked her to his car, and opened the door for her. When they arrived at the school, everyone stared at them at the entrance. Emily felt uncomfortable. Briana was bursting on fire out of rage. Mike walked over to a table and grabbed them two drinks. Emily told him she was not drinking today. He respected that and put her cup back on the table. Alex and Pete joined in with them.

"You are the new girl," said Alex to Emily.

Emily nodded but did not look at his face. Alex thought she was a little awkward.

"Okay, let's go dance and have some fun," said Pete as he walked into the dancing crowd and Alex followed.

Pete found his girlfriend, Mitti, who was friends with Briana. Pete grabbed Mitti, and they ended up dancing. Mike pulled Emily onto the dance floor as well, and they danced too. He twirled her around and spun her around, picked her up, and held her tight. Briana was watching the whole time. She felt like she was about to explode or throw up.

Emily however, felt loved. She has not felt this way in a very long time, ever since she lost her best friend. Briana and her three friends left the scene and into the bathroom. Briana threw her little handbag against the mirror, and the mirror broke.

"How could he? How could that asshole do that to me right in front of everyone?" Briana yelled out loud.

There was a girl in the stall. She walked out and tried to wash her hands, but Briana pulled her aggressively by her arm and told her to get out. The girl did and Briana slammed the door behind her.

"Calm down. We will make them both pay for it," said Adriana.

"You don't understand. This is embarrassing," said Briana.

Briana grabbed her handbag and walked back out. Adriana shrugged her shoulders, and along with Megan, they followed after Briana.

Emily was starting to drink a little. She was getting comfortable. She was getting more and more drinks from Mike's friends. Emily tried to avoid them. However, they were pushing them at her so she couldn't resist. The football players noticed she was getting drunk. At that moment, Adriana managed to get Mike away from Emily. She asked Mike if he wanted to join the football players and the girls for a night ride to the lake tonight. Mike was thinking about it, but he was not sure if Emily would want to join. Mike tried walking away to get back to Emily, but Adriana held onto him. She continued to question him and beg him to go on the night ride. He told her again he was not sure if he will go, but Adriana would not let it go.

Meanwhile, across the room, there were four football players who did not want to leave Emily alone. Emily was searching with her eyes for Mike, but he was nowhere to be found. Emily started freaking out, and she ran away from the party. She ran outside. She was stumbling because she was a little tipsy. One of the football players tapped the other one and nodded his head toward Emily's way.

"Come with me, man. Let's go have some fun," he told the other player.

However, all four players ended up going after Emily. Emily was outside calling out for Mike, but she heard no response. One of the players named Brian grabbed Emily form the back. Emily screamed, and he dropped her to the floor. The other three players started messing with her as well.

"What is wrong with you? Get up. We just want to have some fun," said Brian.

"Leave me alone. I did not do anything to you guys. Why are you doing this?" Emily replied.

Other students only walked passed them not acknowledging what they were doing to her. Brian tried to grab her by her arm, but Emily stood up and ran off and they followed. Emily ran into the woods across the street from the school. She thought maybe she could lose them in the woods. It was very dark. Emily hid behind a big tree. She could hear their footsteps and calling out for her. Emily felt them nearby. She tried to run again, but Brian caught her.

"Let me go!" Emily screamed.

Brian picked her up, and her heels fell to the floor. Brian told her to be quiet. The other three players laughed. Brian took out a bottle of liquor and sipped it. He passed it to his other friends. Emily was now crying and screaming at them to let her go. But they refused. Brian threw her on the ground and sat on top of her. He ripped the top of her dress exposing her bra. Emily was trying to close her top back up, but Brian did not allow her. The other players laughed. Brian started kissing her on her neck. She tried fighting him off but was not strong enough. Brian started lifting her dress up. Emily was begging him over and over again to stop it, but he refused. He ripped her panties off and threw them to the side. Emily managed to kick him with her knee. He felt that pain and slapped her for it. Brian lifted her legs up and unzipped his pants. He pulled out his manhood and slid himself inside of her. As Brian was fucking her harder and harder, Emily let out a scream of pain. One of the other players was touching her breast while Brian was fucking her. He was laughing. Emily looked at the third guy who was drinking the bottle. Emily then turned her head toward the fourth guy and noticed it was Pete, Mike's best friend. Emily looked at him and asked him for help while Brian was fucking her, but Pete just stood there watching. When Brian was finished, he stood up and the second guy who was touching her breast took over. He then slid his manhood inside of her and fucked her as well. Emily gave up fighting. She just laid there and took the pain. When the second guy was finished, the third guy tried to fuck her next but Pete stopped him. Pete placed his hands on his head and told the guys to leave. They did not want to at first, but Pete convinced them that everyone was probably looking for them at the party. Brian looked at Emily and told his boys to come on and to leave the bitch there.

The three boys started walking back to the party as Pete tried to stay behind and help her. However, Brian pulled him and told him to come with them and he did. Emily laid there, alone, half naked. She slowly stood up and covered herself the best way she could. She started walking home holding her shoes in her hands. Her makeup ran down her face. There was blood between her legs and dirt all over her body. She snuck in her house without her parents seeing her. When she entered her room, her father called out for her. She said she was fine and she was going to bed. Emily took her clothes off and threw the dress away in the garbage. She took a shower and sat down in the tub crying.

Back at the party, Mike finally escaped form Adriana. He asked Pete and the rest of the crew if they have seen Emily and they said no. Mike was looking everywhere for her, but he was not able to find her. Then, Briana approached him.

"Hey, sexy, the night is still young. You want to go dance?" Briana asked him.

"No, I do not. Have you seen the new girl?" Mike asked her.

"Why are you looking for her when I'm right here?" Briana replied with a question.

Mike looked at Briana but did not have anything to say to her. He then turned around and stepped outside. He called Emily on her cell phone, but she did not answer. Pete came out and asked him if he was still looking for her. Mike nodded. Pete convinced him that she probably left home or was somewhere else having fun. He told Mike to come in and celebrate with the players. Mike believed him and so he returned to the party.

The following day, Emily did not make it to school. She needed a day to herself. She did not want to face the people at her school. After class, Mike came to visit her, but she did not want to see him. A couple of days passed by, but Emily stayed to herself. She did not want to communicate with Nikki either. One day, when Emily was walking home, Mike caught up to her. He asked her why she has been hiding from him. She continued walking ignoring him. Mike grabbed her and asked her to talk to him.

"Why did you leave me at the party?" Emily asked him.

"I did not leave you. Adriana needed me for something, and it turned out to be nothing; and when I came back to look for you, you were gone. I thought you left home," Mike replied.

Emily was ashamed of what happened in the woods, and she did not want anyone else to know. She decided to keep it to herself and move on. She will deal with the pain on her own just how she has been her entire life. Emily told Mike it was fine and continued to walk home. Mike asked her if she was sure that there was nothing she wanted to talk about. Emily told him no. He asked her if he could give her a ride home and she said yes.

School became a little tough for Emily. Every time she passed by the guys at school who raped her, she puts her head down. She was too scared to even look at them. Mike was at practice with the other football players. Emily was passing by the football field, and Mike saw her. He ran up to her and asked her if she wanted to watch him. She told him no. At that moment, Brian walked up to them and looked at Emily.

"Why do you hang out with this chick, man?" he asked Mike.

Mike told him to fuck off. Brian walked back onto the field. Mike apologized to Emily for Brian's behavior. Emily had nothing to say. She just walked away. Mike saw Emily was hurt. He walked angry into the football field passing all the players. The players were asking what the hell he was doing and so did their coach. Mike ignored them all and walked straight to Brian.

"What the hell are you doing, man?" Brian asked him.

Mike did not respond. He punched him in his face cracking his nose. Brian fell to the ground, and Mike was going to punch him again, but the other players held him back. The coach told Mike he was not allowed to play for the next two weeks. Mike said that was fine and walked off the field. The other two players, who were with Brian that night, watched Mike as he walked away angry.

"Yo, do you think he knows?" one of the players asked the other one who was there that night.

"I don't think so," his friend replied.

Later that evening, Emily met up with Nikki. They went to the coffee shop again. They talked, joked around, and had fun. Jack asked Nikki out on a movie night. Emily nodded to Nikki suggesting to her that she should do it. Nikki told him that she would love to go and told him to pick her up at seven. He told her he would. Before the girls left the coffee shop, Jack asked them if they were going to Briana's party since everyone in the school was invited. Emily quickly said no.

"We will see. It is the biggest party ever. She does it every year," said Nikki.

"I don't care," said Emily and the girls left the shop.

Back at Briana's house along with Megan, Mitti, and Adriana, they were getting ready for their party. All the drinks, decorations, and everything else was ready.

Mitti has long brown hair. She looked Asian and was a short girl, friendly, but very easy to be manipulated. Briana has long blond hair, was very aggressive, and always wanted to be in control. Adriana has short hair to her ears, was a tough girl, has tattoos, and did not put up with nobody's crap. Megan admired Briana. She was a follower and wanted to do everything that Briana does. She as well has long blond hair and was a very attractive young woman.

"I am very excited for tonight's party," said Briana.

"I'm sure you are excited, especially when Mike comes," said Megan.

"I am going to make him remember me tonight. You know, girls, the goods, goods he used to get," said Briana.

The girls laughed.

As the girls are getting ready for the party tonight, Pete comes over bringing more liquor. Pete walked into their room and dropped off the liquor. He grabbed Mitti's hand and walked her into the living room.

"I miss you, baby," said Pete.

"I miss you too," replied Mitti.

"I just wanted us to have like five minutes alone. We don't seem to spend any time together anymore, and I was thinking if we could maybe start doing some things alone. You know, we are in college now, and I think we need to work on our relationship more. You know, improve it," said Pete.

"Oh yeah, like what?" Mitti replied as she kissed him.

"Well, how about I come and pick you up tomorrow and you come over," said Pete.

Before she was able to answer him, Briana walked in. Pete rolled his eyes. Briana sits right next to them on the couch asking Pete if Mike was coming to the party.

"Yes, he is. He also told me he will invite the new girl to come as well. What's her name?" asked Pete.

"Oh, the new girl, Emily," said Mitti.

Briana got pissed off, stood up, and looked at Mitti and Pete.

"You guys think this is funny? He is bringing her here, and you guys know I still like him and we used to date last year," said Briana.

"Look, girl," said Pete as he stood up off the couch, "Mike has moved on and you need to as well."

"Oh, maybe you're right," said Briana as she stormed out of the living room back into her room where she was getting dressed.

"Is everything okay?" Adriana asked Briana while she was still working on her makeup.

"Yes," Briana responded. "I have a plan for tonight."

Emily was in her room as her cell phone rang. It was Mike and she was nervous to answer it.

"Hello," she said.

"How is my princess doing?" Mike asked her.

"Oh, I am far from a princess," she replied.

"Hey, listen. I was wondering if you would like to go to the party with me tonight at Briana's," he asked her.

"Oh no, thank you. I don't like her," said Emily.

"Oh, come on. Ask Nikki to come along as well. I don't mind. It would be a good opportunity for us to hang out a little more and me show you a good time since you are new to the town. The first party did not go so well. Maybe in this one, I can fix things with you," said Mike.

Emily thought about it for a second. She hated Briana, but at the same time, she did not want to be the looser here.

"Okay. I will ask Nikki, and if she goes, then I might," said Emily.

"What? Are we in high school still?" Mike laughed. "That's fine. I understand. So I will see you tonight?" he asked her again.

"Maybe," Emily replied.

"Did you want me to pick you guys up?" Mike asked her.

"No, thank you. I said maybe I will be there," Emily made it clear to him.

"Okay then, bye," said Mike.

"Bye," Emily replied.

Emily was scared to go to the party due to the fact she would see those three football players again. She could not forget what they did to her, but at the same time, she wanted to move on with her life. Emily found some courage and called Nikki. Nikki answered the phone, and Emily told her the whole story of how Mike was calling her and asking her to go with him to Briana's house party and how she really likes him. Emily asked Nikki to go with her, and Nikki agreed to go. Nikki told her she would go so Emily could spend some time with Mike. Emily thanked her. However, Nikki did remind Emily that she was putting gasoline on fire when it comes to Briana. Emily kind of ignored that statement.

Chapter 3

THE PARTY

Emily and Nikki were on their way to Briana's party. While they were walking, Emily told Nikki the story about her best friend who had a car accident back home. It was a male, and they were very close. She thought he was her first love. One night, he was on his way to pick her up and was running late, so he decided to speed up because he did not want to keep her waiting. It was raining that night, and he had a car accident. When the police found him, there were flowers and a letter expressing his love to her. He never had the chance to tell her himself. The entire time, they were best friends and he loved her too. But Emily never knew nor did she have the opportunity to find out. Emily told Nikki that she thinks about him every day. Nikki understood where she was coming from, and she felt bad for Emily. That is the reason why Emily lost interest in meeting new people. Then, Emily's mother moved to accept a new job, and they thought it would be good for Emily to start over.

"Well, I welcome you with open arms," Nikki said hugging her.

As they walked up to Briana's house, they heard music and saw a lot of people.

"Wow, I'm not sure if I should go in there. I mean, she really does not like me," said Emily.

"Oh, come on. Who cares about her? I was not going to come either, but since Mike wants you here, now I'm glad you're going.

This should be interesting. Plus, everyone is invited to her annual parties," said Nikki.

As they were walking inside the house, Mike saw Emily right away. He was having a conversation with Pete, but when he saw her, he just walked away.

Pete smiled and yelled out, "Go get her, man!"

Mike walked right in front of her.

"Hey, I see you made it. I'm surprised you showed up," said Mike.

"Why is that?" Emily asked.

"Well, you know about the incident at school. Briana can sometimes come off the wrong way," said Mike.

"Oh, I can't let little things like that get in the way now. Can I?" Emily replied and smiled.

"Okay. Well, I will leave you guys alone for a little bit, and I will be back to find you," said Nikki pointing at Emily as she walked away backward.

Mike and Emily were having a conversation. Mike leaned forward and gave Emily a kiss on the cheek. Megan across the room, who was watching them with a drink in her hand, tapped Briana's shoulder and pointed across the room at Emily and Mike.

"So she comes to my house and gets on with my man? I don't think so," said Briana.

The four girls walked to the back of the house. They took their clothes off to be in bathing suits. Briana jumped into the pool with the rest of the girls following.

Pete screamed out, "Yeah! Let's go. Now, this is what I'm talking about!"

Pete jumped into the pool in his boxers and swam toward Mitti. Other guys and girls started to join them. More people leave the house to go outside and party by the pool. Emily and Mike noticed that everyone was leaving toward the pool, so they followed as well. Mike saw Briana swimming and hugging another guy. She smiled at Mike, but he turned away.

"I believe he saw you," said Megan.

"Good. I hope he did. Let's have some fun," said Briana.

They continued to be loud and naughty in the pool. However, Mike and Emily did not get separated. They continued on with their conversation. Briana nodded to Adriana, and she got the clue. Adriana knew what to do. She got out of the pool and grabbed Emily. She told her to get in the pool with them. Emily said she did not bring a bathing suit. Adriana pulled Emily away from Mike and continued talking to her. Meanwhile, Briana got out of the pool as well and walked up to Mike. She asked him if he could help her bring down some drinks from upstairs. He told her he could. She started walking into the house, and Mike followed. Pete watched Briana and Mike go in the house and walk upstairs. Briana took Mike to her bedroom. They walked in, and she closed the door.

"Where is the liquor, Briana? What are we doing here?" Mike asked her.

Briana did not respond. She walked up to him slowly and touched his chest. Mike asked her to stop, and he tried to walk out of the room, but Briana stopped him.

"Oh, come on. You remember how much fun we used to have in this room. You used to make great love to me," said Briana.

"Stop, Briana. What's in the past is the past. You know why we broke up and that's the end of it," Mike replied.

Briana pushed Mike onto the bed. He tried to get up, but she sat on top of him. She took her top off. He pushed her off of him and stood up. He tried to walk out of the room, but she grabbed him and hugged him topless. Mike grabbed her by her waist and told her to put her top back on. She refused.

Downstairs, Adriana and Emily were still having the conversation about going into the pool.

"Well, if you want, we can go upstairs and see if Briana has any bathing suits that might fit you," said Adriana.

"Oh no, thank you. I don't think she would like that," Emily replied.

"Don't be silly. We started off on the wrong foot, but I think you are pretty cool. She does not mind. Trust me," said Adriana.

Emily and Adriana started walking into the house and upstairs toward Briana's room.

"I'm out of here, I do not understand why you keep playing these games, and they need to stop," Mike said to Briana as he was trying to walk out.

Briana then grabbed him, jumped on him, and started kissing him. At the same time, Emily opened the door and saw them. Mike pushed Briana off of him, and Emily closed the door. She ran downstairs passing Nikki.

"What's wrong, Emily?" asked Nikki.

Emily ignored her, storming out of the house with Mike rushing right behind her. Briana and Adriana stayed in her room.

"You think that worked?" asked Adriana.

"I'm not sure," Briana replied.

The two girls laughed and went back to the party. Pete was asking Mitti if she knew what Briana was up to. Mitti confirmed their plan to Pete, and he got upset with her. Pete got out of the pool to support his best friend. Mitti ran after him telling him to stop walking away. Pete stopped, turned around, and asked her why she has to be evil like Briana. Mitti explained to him that she had nothing to do with it.

"I really do not like you hanging out with her. I don't understand why you keep being around her. She does not mean any well toward anybody," said Pete.

"She's my friend, okay. Just cause this new girl comes to town does not mean things have to change, and you know Mike and Briana are meant for one another," said Mitti.

"But that's it. You are wrong. Mike has moved on. This is not high school anymore. He does not want anything to with Briana. She cheated on Mike big time. She stole money from his house and tried to make it look like she was pregnant by him so he could stop playing football. You know I'm only here because I want to be with you," said Pete. Pete then walked away leaving Mitti alone.

"Where are you going?" Mitti asked him, but he was already halfway out the door.

Mitti left to look for Briana. Pete mostly wanted to help Mike because he felt guilty for what he did to Emily. Emily ran out of the house, across the street, and into the woods. She felt very hurt and embarrassed. As she ran, she started to cry as well. She ran into the woods deeper and deeper trying to get away from people. She finally stopped at a cliff. There was nothing to see after that cliff. It was a big fall. She stood there, crying, thinking if she should just jump. She decided she couldn't do it and took a couple of steps back. She slowly walked over to a tree, leaned against it, and sat down to the ground. Pulling her knees upward and resting her forehead on her knees, she continued to cry. Lifting her head up, she started to ask herself why these things were happening to her; why can't she just have a good family, a mother that actually cares more about her and not work; and why she had to lose her best friend, her first love. Why did she have to come to this new school just to be taken as a joke? She hated this new town and wanted to go back to NY. She sat there and cried and cried.

Meanwhile, Mike was walking around yelling her name and looking for her. Pete approached him and told him to calm down.

"What's wrong with you, man? Relax," said Pete.

"She's out there somewhere, and it is midnight. I have to find her," Mike said with worry.

"All right, I'll help you, but you can't be out here yelling around like your some hillbilly from the mountains. Get in," Pete told him and opened the doors to his car.

They both hopped in Pete's car and left to look for Emily. Emily stopped crying and noticed something shining on the ground. She slowly realized where she was and that it might not be so safe to stay there. She ran so far into the woods where it was too dark to see anything. After seeing something shiny, she approached it closer and closer and saw that it was a ring. It's a beautiful ring. It looked silver and shiny. Emily tried it on her finger, and it was a perfect fit. Once she placed the ring on her finger, it grasped tightly onto her skin and a white wave shot from the ring toward the rest of the woods knocking Emily to the ground. The branches from the trees were knocked down, and some of them almost fell on top of her. She tried to avoid getting hit by the branches and started running back home. She was scared.

When Emily placed that ring on her finger, a portal opened up between the human's world and the witch's world. An evil witch has awakened from her long sleep. This witch was in her castle under a big rock. When Emily placed that ring on her finger, the evil witch gasped for air, broke the rock, and stood up on her feet. She examined her body slowly as she was naked. She looked up at herself in the mirror and laughed. "Game time," she said.

Emily stopped running and looked around. Nothing, everything has calmed down. "What the hell was that?" Emily asked herself. She then tried taking the ring off but did not succeed. She pulled and pulled, but it was not coming off. It started to rain, and she decided to leave it on and started walking home. When she walked out of the woods, Pete and Mike spotted her.

"Stop the car!" Mike yelled and Pete stopped.

Mike ran out of the car yelling at Emily to get in the vehicle.

"Emily, stop. Are you crazy walking home alone at this time of the night? And where were you? We have been looking for you?" Mike asked her.

"Go away. Why do you care? Why are you out here? Now, you want to come after me like you care. Go back to your bitch," said Emily.

"Come on, Emily. It's raining. Get in the car. We can talk about this. She asked me to go up there and help her bring some more drinks down. If I knew she was up for that, I would have never went," Mike said to her and grabbed her by her arm.

"Stop walking away. I'm serious. Since I saw you the first day in school, I was interested in you. Briana is history, and if we could get out of this rain, we could talk about it," he said to her.

"You people in this town are all the same, assholes," Emily said to him as she stood there angry in the rain.

"Get in the car and let me at least take you home. I will not allow you to walk home alone," said Mike.

"Fine. Just don't talk to me," said Emily.

Emily then started falling to the floor, and her chest started to hurt, but Mike caught her. She grabbed her chest and screamed in pain. Mike held her.

"Are you okay?" he asked her with worry.

She screamed one more time as she held onto her chest. Mike screamed out asking her if she was all right again. The pain then went away, and she stood back up onto her feet.

"Yes, I just want to go home," she said to him.

She walked to the car and sat in the back. Pete looked at her in his mirror. Mike sat in the passenger seat. Nobody talked.

Chapter 4

AT HOME

When Emily arrived at home, she was very tired and wet.

"Are you okay, hon?" her dad asked her.

Emily walked up the stairs.

"I'm fine, Dad. Where's Mom?" she asked him.

"She's asleep," he replied.

Emily rolled her eyes and stormed into her room. She knew her mom would not stay up to make sure she got home safe. She looked down at her hand and noticed the ring was turning into a dark color. She tried taking it off again, but it did not work. Emily started talking to herself.

"Damn, what is this? What am I going to do? I can't keep it on forever."

Emily tried washing it in the sink hoping the soap would help it slide off, but nothing worked. She started to worry, but she did not want to tell her father. He did not need to worry about her, not that she would even think about telling her mother who was never available. She then ran from the bathroom back into her room locking her door. Emily looked into her mirror, and she noticed her eyes were changing colors. They looked darker. Emily knew something was wrong, but she did not know what. She thought to herself maybe it will be all over by tomorrow morning. Not that she wanted to face her school tomorrow, but she had no other choice. If she does not go, then her father would get involved.

Back in school, Emily bumped into Nikki in the hallway. As they walked together to their class, they passed Pete and Mitti. Emily gave Mitti a stare as they passed each other creeping Mitti out. For some reason, Emily felt better. Even though she felt hurt last night, she woke up feeling better and stronger. She did not care what people had to say about the party or her. She told Nikki she will meet her in the classroom. She was going to use the ladies room first. Nikki nodded and left. Emily went to the bathroom and walked over to the sink. She looked at herself in the bathroom mirror and wondered why she was feeling the way she did. She could feel that she was not being her usual self. Her moods were changing, her personality was changing, and her behavior and thoughts were changing. She felt like she wanted revenge. In a way, she liked it. She felt more in control of situations. Staring at herself in the mirror, she lifted up her hand examining the ring. "I wonder if this has anything to do with it?" she asked herself. Picking up her book bag, she straightened her back and lifted up her head; and with a smile, she walked out.

Back at home, Allen watched his wife getting dressed for work. He walked up to her and hugged her from behind and gave her a kiss on the cheek. She slowly backed away. Allen got upset.

"You know what. Maybe the thing Emily is feeling is true. I don't know what else to do to make this marriage work or for you to start paying some closer attention to your daughter. You're in and out of her life. All you focus on is your job," Allen said to his wife.

"Don't you dare. I raised her, she is grown now, and I have to work. Unlike you with a part-time job remodeling houses, I have to bring in the real money," said Gabby.

"Is this what this is all about? The money? Don't forget who stood by you all those times you had nothing. Who put you through school before we had Emily?" he questioned his wife. He stepped closer to her, so close to where she could feel his breath on her face when he said, "There is something else going on Gabby and you better tell me before I find out." He said to her, turned around, and walked out of the room. He then left the house and into his car. Gabby watched him out of the window feeling ashamed. She reached for her phone in her purse and made a call.

"Hello," a man on the other side answered.

"I need to meet you after work today," said Gabby.

"Okay," the man replied. "I love you," he said.

Gabby hung up the phone.

At school, it was lunchtime. Emily and Nikki were walking down the hallway. Out of nowhere, Megan and Adriana cut them off.

"Hey, guys. How was the party last night? Did you girls have fun?" Megan asked them.

"Megan, you're really pathetic," said Nikki.

"Oh yeah, I thought I was just being a bitch," Megan responded. The girls laughed and walked away.

"Emily, I'm really sorry. They can be assholes. You just have to learn how to ignore them. They don't even bother me anymore. It's been like three years of their crap in high school. I mean, everyone's over it, you know," Nikki said to Emily.

"Oh yeah, well, I'm just starting," said Emily as she walked away toward the cafeteria.

Nikki watched Emily walk away not really understanding what she meant by that, but she shook her shoulders and followed Emily to lunch.

Down the hall, Mitti, Briana, and the others were in a group talking. Pete grabbed Mitti away from Briana and pulled her into a corner to talk to her.

"Babe, I know what happened at the party was all Briana's planning. I don't want you to be a part of her tricks anymore. This thing is getting old, and she has no life. I don't want you hanging out with her anymore," said Pete.

"Pete, she's my best friend. What are you talking about? Yes, maybe she planned it, but so what? I don't know the new girl, and I have been friends with Briana for a long time. Why should I stop now? Maybe you are getting too attached to the new bitch as well.

Mike wants her, so you want her too now. Is that what this is?" Mitti asked him.

"No!" Pete replied.

"Right, get away from me," she said to him and walked away.

Pete watched her leave.

Emily and Nikki got their food. They were waiting in line to pay. Then, right behind Emily stood Mike.

"Hey, girls, what are you eating today?" he asked them.

"The usual, not much to choose from," Emily replied.

Nikki was trying to get away from them giving them some privacy.

"Harry and Max are at the table. I'll go ahead and sit with them, okay. See you later, Mike," said Nikki as she walked away leaving Mike and Emily alone.

But before Nikki was able to walk away, Emily stopped her and told her she was coming too. Emily took a couple of steps, and Mike grabbed her by her arm.

"Emily, please just stop," he said.

"What do you want, Mike? Why are you so stuck on me? You see your girl over there?" She pointed at Briana. "Go and get her because as far as me, I'm long gone. You want to play games and act like you have no clue with the things that she does and why she does them. You know better than that. Stop walking around pretending like you don't know what these girls out here want from you. Stop playing stupid. I will just tell you this. I'm glad she showed me what type of a man you are. Have a good day," said Emily with pride and strength.

She left him there, alone and speechless. Mike was embarrassed. Everyone was looking at him because they heard everything Emily said, including Briana. Mike stormed out of the lunchroom.

"Wow, Emily, what made you do that?" Nikki asked her.

"I think it was awesome," said Harry who was sitting with them at the table.

Emily laughed.

Briana and her friends stormed out of the lunch room as well. They bumped into Mike in the hallway.

"Why do you do this? Why do you keep fucking around with my life? I will tell you this one last time. Stay the fuck out of my way!" Mike yelled at Briana.

"You act like you're in love with her. You never cared about me that way. I can see the way you look at her. I did everything for you," said Briana.

"No, all you did was turn me into a person that I'm not. Once I stopped living the way you wanted me to, we became enemies; and for the record, you cheated on me. I will not discuss this with you anymore. Stay out of my way and my life, Briana; and just maybe, if I do love her, that's none of your business. I tried being nice to you, but it's not working with you," said Mike and walked passed them.

He hopped in his car and left the school. The girls did not know what to say at first.

"Maybe you just need to cool it off and let him go," said Mitti.

Briana looked at Mitti as evil as possible. Mitti backed away a couple of steps. Megan and Adriana looked at Mitti as well and told her to shut up.

Chapter 5

IN THE FOREST

Back in Arfabele Land, the evil witch has awakened. She was walking around in her castle. Her name was Aza'el. Aza'el was a witch who has been put to sleep by a good witch about two hundred years ago. She has a very dark heart and dealt with evil powers. She's very strong and has great powers to destroy life and keep herself powerful. Her hair was long to the floor. She wore a black gown very uniquely designed, starting from her breast down to the floor. Her nails were very long, and she has a beautiful white skin with red lipstick. She loved being powerful. She wanted darkness to take over. There were good witches and bad ones. The good witches in this world were called "Klexons." She knew where the Klexons lived, and all she wanted to do was to destroy them. She also has a ring on her hand. It was the same ring that Emily has, the one she found in the woods. The dark ring was transferring Emily's energy, youth, feelings, and soul to Aza'el and at the same time making Emily's heart dark. Now that Emily has one of her rings, Aza'el was trying to control Emily's soul and turn it dark and evil. This will help Aza'el become stronger. Aza'el knew someone has her ring and it was a human, but she did not know who. Once Emily placed that ring on her finger, and the portal opened, Aza'el was reborn. Two hundred years ago, the Klexons were not able to destroy Aza'el, instead they placed her under a deep sleep. Unfortunately, they did not find the ring.

Aza'el never had any love from anyone, and her soul has turned evil. Since she never had love, she did not want anyone else to have it either. She wanted to control everything. Aza'el walked around in her castle. She grabbed a knife and cut her finger. Blood was dripping from her finger. She walked over to a bowl as big as a table, and it had water in it. She dripped her blood in it and said a spell, and the water rose up. It splashed out of the bowl onto the ground. Every time it splashed, a body was created. She created more evil witches with her blood to be her followers. She called them "Dark Zals." The Dark Zals stood around Aza'el. They looked scary. Aza'el looked at each and every one of them as she walked around. "You all belong to me now and will do as I say," she said to them. She walked to her mirror, which hung on the wall. It was as tall as her body. She looked in it and said to herself that this time, she will win.

Back at Brent University, there was a football game. The crowd was cheering, the cheerleaders did a great dance, and Emily and Nikki were sitting on the bleachers with Harry and Max.

"Hey, man. Where is Mike?" Pete asked another football player.

"I don't know. The coach was looking for him as well. He's not answering his phone either," replied the player.

They continued to play and ended up winning the game. Mitti ran up to Pete as he picked her up and kissed her, but for some reason, Briana did not like that. Megan and the rest of the cheerleaders celebrated with the football team. Balloons and ribbons were thrown, and the coach got water poured on him for their winning game. The team left to their locker rooms, and Emily and her friends started to walk home. The team celebrated in the locker room by singing, screaming, and hugging each other.

"Man, what a great game," said Roger who was a team player.

"Yes, it sure was," replied Pete.

"Man, this winning tonight we have to celebrate. How about my house guys? Bring some sexy girls, get laid, drinks," said a football player named Sam.

"Now, that's what I'm talking about. You coming tonight, Pete?" Roger asked.

"I don't know yet. I have to see what Mitti is doing," Pete replied.

"You are pussy whipped," said Sam.

All the guys in the locker room laughed.

"Has anyone seen Mike?" asked Pete.

At that moment, the coach walked in.

"That's what I would like to know. Anyone sees him tell him I need to have a word with him. He continues this crap, he will not be playing anymore," said Coach Hank.

Pete was very confused. He was not sure why Mike was acting like that. But then, he was scared if maybe Emily told him what happened in the woods. As the rest of the team left to celebrate, Pete had other plans. He stayed in the men's locker room and took a shower.

Couple of minutes into the shower, as Pete was facing the wall, he felt hands on his shoulders.

He had his eyes closed and said, "Hey, baby. I know you couldn't stay mad at me. I got a surprise for you today." He turned around and saw Briana. She was naked. He grabbed his package and asked her what she was doing. He pushed her out of the showers, but she pushed him back into the wall.

"Don't act like that. I see the way you look at me. Well, here I am. You can have it," she said.

She jumped on him putting her legs around his waist. He took her legs and pushed them back down. He pushed her away again and told her to get out before someone sees them. She got mad.

"Fine. You want me to get out. I will, but you will be sorry for this. You wait until I tell Mitti that you tried fucking me here today. Let's see what happens to your relationship then," said Briana.

Pete told her not to do that. Briana smiled and turned around to walk out when right there stood Mitti.

"Oh, Mitti, thank God you are here. He dragged me here. I did not want to do this, I swear," said Briana.

"You liar! I heard everything. How many times have you lied to me before? I thought we were best friends," said Mitti with anger in her voice.

"Best friends? Please, I only allowed you to stick around because you did everything I wanted you to do," said Briana and left Mitti and Pete alone.

Pete walked over to Mitti and hugged her.

"This is getting too far, baby. I told you that you are a better person than her. Don't let her pull you down too," said Pete.

"I have to go. I don't know what to do now. This is just too much for me," replied Mitti.

She walked out as well leaving Pete thinking. Pete punched a locker, grabbed his clothes, and went to get dressed. A couple of hours later, Megan and Adriana were looking for Briana. They drove to her house and found her on the couch, crying. They asked her what was wrong, and she told them that Pete came on to her and she had to fight him off. Megan and Adriana could not believe what they heard.

"How could he do that? Mitti will be crushed," said Adriana.

"Yeah, but she's our friend and we have to tell her," said Megan.

"Wait. They are going through some things now. I think we should just leave it alone," said Briana. The girls agreed.

Chapter 6

HE CARES

Emily was still walking home from the game. When she arrived at home, she stopped at the front door because she heard different voices. She opened the door, and there was her father and Mike sitting together at the table talking. She got very upset.

"Oh, hey, sweetie. Come on in. Your friend stopped by looking for you," said her dad.

"I see that. Why are you here?" she asked Mike.

"Hey, little lady. Why are you talking like that? He's your guest," asked her dad.

Emily turned around and walked out of the house. Mike followed her. Emily's father started to follow after them but then stopped. He decided to give them some space.

"She better walk back in here in five minutes or he will have a problem with me," her father said to himself.

Mike grabbed her by her arm as she sped down the driveway. She turned around and told him to let her go.

"Look. What happened at the party, I had no idea she was going to do that. I swear. You have to understand we dated. Yes, it was a long time ago. I tried to make things work with her. She started changing me. She started changing who I was. She would make fun of people, bully them, and I allowed it to happen. For a moment, I thought it was fun until she slept with my best friend Marcus who is no longer living with us because he took his own life after feeling guilty for sleeping with her and betraying me. I have not looked back to be with her since. She is cruel. Yes, but I thought people grow up, and maybe she has too but apparently not. I have realized she will do anything to have her way. But I won't allow her to win. I want you to understand I am here, willing to do what it takes to make you understand that I want to be with you and only you," said Mike.

She looked at her house noticing her dad peeping through the window, watching. She knew he was watching to make sure she was okay. She felt better. She turned her attention back to Mike.

"Whatever happened between you guys happened. I do not care about it. However, I care what you have done to me. Also, why did you not play football today?" Emily asked him.

"Because I wanted to be here. I thought you would be home," replied Mike.

"Well, you do not need to keep looking for me," she said. Emily stepped closer to his face. "I do not care about your feelings. I don't care what you are feeling or if you are hurting. Who cared when I was hurting? No one did. You left me not at one party but at two. And I will never forgive you or your fucking friends. I am going to go back in my house now, and you will leave this property," Emily told Mike with seriousness in her voice and her body language.

"What do you mean my friends?" Mike asked her.

Emily was not listening to him anymore. She walked away leaving him standing there. He watched her go still wondering why she mentioned his friends.

The following day at school, everyone was acting normal. Emily and Nikki met by their lockers.

"How are you feeling today?" Nikki asked Emily.

"I am actually feeling very good, like a newborn person," Emily replied.

They both smiled and went to their class. At the end of the school day, Emily was walking home again. She passed the woods where she found the ring. She had a very strange feeling rushing through her body. She felt very weird. She crossed her arms as she stared at the woods and continued to walk. As she was passing the woods, the ring started to glow. It had a dark glow. She saw it on her hand, got scared, and ran home. She stormed into the house, up the stairs, and into her room. Her heart rate sped up, and she did not know what to do. She dropped her book bag on the floor and walked over to her stand-up mirror. She looked into the mirror and saw her eyes were changing colors again. They seemed to be getting darker with a yellow glow around them. She looked back at the ring on her hand, and all of a sudden, she remembered. She remembered seeing a book at the old bookstore that had an image of the same ring she had on her hand. She decided to pay the bookstore a visit.

The old gray-headed man was just closing the bookstore when Emily banged with her fist on the door. The man told her they were closed. She asked for him to please open the door she had something to show him. She told him she really needed his help. The old man told her to come back tomorrow when they open. He turned around and was walking away from the locked door. Emily was outside. She walked over to the window and slammed her hand on the glass. The man turned around and saw her hand. He saw the ring. He looked at her and walked over to the door. He opened it and she walked in.

"I'm Emily. What's your name?" Emily asked him.

The old man replied, "I'm Gary." He closed the door behind her.

"Okay. The other day when I was walking by, I saw a book on your window. It had the same ring on the front cover as this one on my finger. I can't take this off, and it does weird things to me. Where is that book?" Emily asked him.

Gary reached for her hand and asked where she found it. He held her hand in his hand.

"This ring was supposed to be long gone in Arfabele Land," he told her.

"What? What are you saying? What is Arfabele?" Emily asked him.

"Sit down, my child," he told her. He walked very slowly over to a table and grabbed the large book with the legends of the witch and her rings. He started to tell Emily the story about Arfabele.

Many years ago, there were two worlds between us humans and the witches. Now, you know if there is good, there is also evil. A long time ago, there was a husband and wife. The wife was a witch. The wife's sister was very jealous of their love. One day, she created these two rings. She gave one of the rings to the wife as a gift on their wedding day and the other ring for herself. She said it was keeping the sisters together. The wife thought it was a nice thing her sister did. However, the jealous sister was evil. When the wife placed the ring on her hand, she slowly started to change. As time passed by, the evil witch stole her sister's soul and her heart causing the wife to die. She did this throughout time. The evil sister had to wait until the heart turned dark. The evil sister's name was Aza'el. Aza'el used the rings to take away the soul of her sister. The only thing the good witch, "the wife," was able to do before she died was place a spell on Aza'el. She put her to sleep for a long time. She did that to save her village, the Green Village, where all the good witches so called the Klexons are living. Once Aza'el was placed under a deep sleep and the wife died, one of the rings disappeared. Everyone searched for it, but nobody found it. Now that you have found the other ring, she has awakened from the spell. She will come and hunt everyone again. But that's not all. Now, the portal has opened again between humans and witches.

She will come here. You have to keep this a secret.
Humans cannot find out.

Emily did not say anything for a couple of seconds. She then took a deep breath and started to speak.

"You mean there are witches out there?" Emily asked Gary.

"Yes, there is good and evil. The evil ones follow Aza'el's orders," Gary replied.

Emily started to freak out. She tried to take the ring off of her finger again, but she failed. Gary noticed that it was already halfway black.

"Hey, calm down. We will figure this out," said Gary.

"Am I going to die?" Emily asked.

"No, we have to fight back. We have to be prepared for her," Gary replied.

"Are you insane? You want us to fight back a witch. You are crazy like they say," said Emily, and she stormed out of the store.

Gary yelled for her to come back, but she did not listen. Gary knew he had to get her on his side before he loses her to Aza'el.

Emily was finally home. She felt very scared and did not know what to do. She knew if she told her parents about this, they would probably put her in the mental hospital. She called Nikki and asked her to meet her at the park. They met and were sitting on some swings. Emily told Nikki the whole story of what has happened. Nikki looked at Emily like she was crazy.

"No way. Are you serious? So what do you do now? What's going to happen? I mean is this so-called witch going to come here from somewhere or …?" Nikki asked her.

"I have no idea, but I know I'm scared. Do not tell anyone. I was supposed to keep this to myself," said Emily.

Nikki nodded.

Meanwhile, Aza'el was preparing her witches to search for Emily. Aza'el can feel her energy rising. She could feel that this person who had her other ring had a lot of emotional pain and strength at the same time. Aza'el was very convinced that she will win this soul over. Aza'el was able to transform herself into a beautiful woman to fit in with the humans. "I will find that girl who has my ring and I will win her heart and soul over. She will stand by my side and I will rule. Everyone will then love me while others feel the same pain I have felt for a long time," Aza'el said to her witches, and they all laughed agreeing with her. She then ordered them to get ready for the search. She stared into the mirror again, transformed into a beautiful human woman and then right back into her evil witch self. She smiled.

Chapter 7

SO STRANGE

The following day, Emily came to school looking a little different. Her hair was different, her skin was a little paler, and she dressed different. Mike walked up to her and asked her if she was still mad at him. Emily shook her head. She told him she was not mad anymore, but at the same time, she did not care for him. Briana and Adriana walked by. Briana gave Mike and Emily a nasty look. Nikki walked up to Mike and Emily and asked Emily if she had any plans after school. Emily said she was busy. Mike didn't say anything and neither did Nikki.

"I have to go," Emily said and walked away.

Mike and Nikki watched her.

"What's wrong with her?" Mike asked Nikki.

"I don't know," she replied.

Emily sat in her class staring out of the window. She was not paying any attention in class. She was worried about the ring on her finger.

"Now, that old man does not know what he's talking about. Whatever this is must be some type of joke. Witches? There are no such things," she told herself as a boy next to her was staring at her like she was crazy talking to herself. "What?" she asked.

The boy turned around. Emily looked out of the window again noticing how dark the woods were. She felt like she could feel a presence. She placed her hands around herself for comfort.

After the bell rang, Emily was walking down the hallway and bumped into Pete. Pete only stared at her. He was going to speak to her, to apologize; but before he said anything, she told him not to bother and walked away. Nikki caught up to her.

"I will be stopping by at the coffee shop later on after school today. If you want to come, you know," said Nikki.

"No, thank you. I have a lot of unpacking to do. It's been just sitting around in the house," Emily replied.

"All right, I'll see you tomorrow," said Nikki.

"Okay, see you," said Emily.

Emily walked to her locker. She placed her book bag on the floor and opened her locker. A young man walked by and called her a freak. He kicked her book bag and pulled on her hair. She got upset, turned around, and grabbed him by his throat spinning him around and slamming him into the lockers. As she held onto his neck, she saw her nails were longer and sharp. She dropped him to the floor and he ran off. Emily froze and stared at her hands.

"Oh my God, what was that? What is happening to me?" she asked herself and her nails went back into the shape that they were. Emily quickly threw her things into her locker, shut it closed, and walked out of the school.

As Emily was walking home, a couple of minutes later, down the street, Briana, Megan, and Adriana pull up in Briana's car cutting Emily off. They got out of the car smiling. Emily stopped walking and looked at them.

"Well, well, what do we have here?" Megan asked.

"So you think you can just come into my town and do what you please, take away what is mine, and think everything is okay?" Briana asked Emily.

"I didn't come here to do anything. Trust me. If I had a say so, I would have never moved here," Emily replied.

"You know I was actually going to give you a chance. You know maybe let you come in our club, but now that you are after my man, I don't like you," said Briana.

"Why are you doing this?" asked Emily.

Adriana walked behind Emily and pushed her. Emily became scared. The girls walked closer and closer up to Emily blocking her in.

"You will regret you ever met me," said Briana.

They started pushing her and punching her. Emily dropped her books that she was going to take home and fell to the ground as they continued to kick her in her stomach, ribs, back, and more. Emily was trying to fight back but can't. She held her hands up to cover her head, but the pain was unmanageable. The more pain she was having, the more she was getting scared; and the more she was getting scared, the more she was getting angry. Once Emily reached a high level of anger, the ring filled up with black energy. Emily couldn't take the pain anymore. She screamed, "Stop!" and slammed her fists into the ground. A powerful force shot out from Emily when she slammed her fists into the ground. The force threw the three girls off of her, slamming them into the walls and the street. The windows on Briana's car shattered. The girls were slowly getting back up on their feet.

"What the fuck, you crazy bitch? What the hell are you?" asked Briana as she was getting back into her car. Megan and Adriana followed, and the girls drove off.

Emily slowly stood up breathing really heavy. She looked down at the ring on her finger and noticed it was all black and glowing. She stood for a minute holding her stomach. She tried to walk but fell to the floor again. Next thing she knew, the old man Gary from the bookstore helped her get up and walked her to his store.

"Are you okay?" Gary asked her, as he sat her in a chair.

"No, what's happening to me? How did I do that?" Emily replied with a question.

"I believe you are receiving power from Aza'el through that ring. The ring is dark, which means she is trying to control your soul and your actions. You have to be able to control yourself," Gary told her.

"You have to be able to control your anger. Anger is good but not if you use it in an evil way. She will control you," said Gary as Emily was trying to focus on controlling her pain.

"What will happen to me?" Emily asked him.

Gary looked at her with worry in his face. "I don't know," he replied.

Gary gave Emily a green potion for her to drink to make her feel better. She asked him what the potion was. He told her he has some tricks up his sleeves himself, and it would help her get better. Emily trusted him and she drank it. She did feel much better. She told him she had to go home and think about all this. Gary stopped her and told her to be careful. It was just the beginning and it will get worse. Emily told him she will skip school tomorrow and come meet him here at the bookstore. When Emily was walking out of the store, Mike saw her. He pulled over and asked her if she needed a ride. She said no and continued to walk. Mike noticed a bruise on her face by her cheek. He stopped the car and hopped out to speak to her.

"What happed to your face?" Mike asked her.

"Why don't you ask Briana and her little friends?" Emily replied.

"Did they do this to you?" Mike asked her as he grabbed her face.

"Why don't you just get out of my life, leave me alone, and we will pretend like we never met. I am so sick and tired of your shit and your little bitch and her little friends coming after me. If it is so much work to be with someone you care about, then I'm not interested," Emily said to him and snatched away from him.

"You care about me, ha," said Mike.

Emily turned toward him and said, "I'm starting not to," and then turned back around and walked off.

Mike went in his car and drove off. He sped through traffic and pulled in Briana's driveway. He knocked on her door. As she opened the door, he forced himself in. Mike grabbed Brianna by her arms and squeezed very hard.

"You went too far this time. How many times do I have to tell you to stay the fuck out of my life and leave the people around me alone," said Mike with anger.

"Let me go. You're hurting me," said Briana.

"No, that's not hurt. You keep this bullshit up and you will see what hurt is," said Mike.

"You don't know her. You don't know what or who she is," said Briana.

"What the hell are you talking about? It does not matter who she is. I like her and I will do whatever it takes to make her happy," said Mike.

"She destroyed my car. She has some type of powers. She almost killed me today, and you come in here protecting her without even knowing what she did!" Briana yelled at Mike.

Mike moved closer to her face holding her even tighter by her arms.

"I do not care what she did. I saw her face, and I will tell you this one last time. Do not bother her again," he said to her, and she knew he was serious. She has never seen him care about someone like that before.

Briana's mother walked into the living room asking what was going on.

"Nothing," Mike replied and walked out of the house.

Briana watched him walk out, the anger rising inside of her thinking how he would have never done this for her, he would have never showed this much love toward her.

"She's dead," Briana said to herself.

Chapter 8

THE CHASE

Aza'el was in her castle. She could feel Emily's rage and anger, and that made Aza'el feel good. The Dark Zals were ready to taste real flesh and real blood. See, these witches where not ordinary. They wanted flesh. They want blood to become stronger. The more they feed, the stronger they get. Aza'el knew the Klexons, who are the good witches, were living in the Green Village where all the dwarfs; little creatures of the colors blue, yellow, and green; trolls; and the creative flying farriers lived. The Klexons took care of their land and fed-off nature instead of killing. The Klexons were strong. However, they do not have as much power as Aza'el. The last good witch gave her own life to defeat Aza'el. She was not strong enough to defeat Aza'el, and therefore, she placed a spell on Aza'el to put her into a deep sleep.

Aza'el was walking around in her castle giving orders to her witches. "Go to Arfabele Green (the Green Village) and do some damage. Let it be known we are back and for them to fear us," she ordered them.

The witches got very excited. They all wanted to go, but Aza'el only sent three of them. The rest of the witches got upset, and Aza'el told them not to worry they will have their turn.

Meanwhile in Arfabele Green, in the Green Village, the beautiful natural creatures were happy, taking care of their land. They were singing, dancing, and more. The Klexons were beautiful. Most of them were dressed in long white gowns. Their cheeks have little pink on them from the warmth of their care for others. Their ears and fingernails were pointy. One of the Klexons' names was Mayla. She was the leader. She always kept an eye on everyone in the Green Village. She trained daily for the Klexons to prepare themselves for the day when Aza'el would wake up. She knew it would happen, but she was not sure when that day would come. She made sure that her witches' warriors would be prepared.

At the Green Village, there were beautiful creatures playing outside. The flowers were alive and able to nourish themselves from the moist in the ground. The trees were alive as well. The trees provided water and clean air for the creatures and the witches. There were children playing with the flowers and the trees. They swung and jumped from one tree to another. There were huge flying creatures as well. They had strong wings, long backs, and long tails. These creatures were of different colors. Each one had their own unique color. They were special and not many left. The Green Village was a peaceful place.

At the village, Mayla was sitting at her desk. She was staring at a red light with fog around it. She quickly stood up and ran outside and yelled, "Everyone, take shelter now!"

At that moment, the evil witches were flying above setting their cottages on fire, destroying some of the flowers, killing the grass, and damaging the trees. The trees swung their branches to knock them off their brooms. However, they missed. A couple of minutes later, the three Dark Zals landed on the ground, got off of their brooms, and walked slowly toward Mayla.

"Stop. Do not come any closer," Mayla said.

The three witches stopped and looked around. They smiled as one of them said, "Aza'el wants to warn you. All this will belong to her and so will you." She pointed at Mayla. The Dark Zals got back on their brooms and flew away.

Everyone looked at Mayla with fear. She asked them not to worry and not to get scared.

"We have to get ready and be strong. Help everyone who needs care, heal the trees, and water the flowers. We have a lot of work to do," said Mayla.

Mayla and her assistant ran into her cottage. Her assistant asked Mayla if Aza'el was free.

"Yes," Mayla replied, "and I will go find out how this happened. I have to go find the portal, visit the human's world, and find the ring. You stay here and help others."

Her assistant's name is Lin. Lin asked her how she knew the ring was in the human's world. Mayla told her that she saw it. She saw the ring in the human's world when she was mixing a potion earlier.

Chapter 9

CHANGE OF SOUL

Emily got home feeling very tired. Her father pulled in the driveway. As he was slowly running toward the house catching up to Emily by the stairs, he hugged her and asked how her day was. When she looked at him, he saw her face and noticed a scar on her forehead and a bruise. He grabbed her and looked at her face closer.

"What happened to you?" he asked her.

"Nothing, Dad," she replied.

"Tell me. You know what happened to you. This does not look like nothing, Emily," her dad said angrily.

"Dad, I'm fine. I just hit my head on the locker," Emily replied.

"Stop it, Emily. Who did this to you? Was it that guy who was here the other day? Because I have my shotgun in the truck right now. Let's go, I'll take care of it now," her dad said.

"No, Dad. It was just some girls from school. They don't really like me much," Emily responded. She turned around and ran into the house. Her dad ran in after her. She stormed upstairs as he yelled her name, but Emily slammed her door shut. Emily walked up to her mirror and looked at herself. She played back what happened today with the girls, not the part when they were beating on her but the part when she screamed and they flew off of her and shattered the windows. She wondered how that happened. Emily started thinking about how Briana can be such a bitch and how she set her up today.

Emily also started thinking about the night she was raped. Emily started getting mad all over again. Everything ran through her head. Every mean thing anyone said to her, hurt her and played her. She stood in front of her mirror staring at herself with the image of them kicking her over and over again not caring what happened to her. She also pictured the boys raping her and laughing at her. She lowered her head and continued to stare at herself in the mirror. She thought about herself when she was screaming in pain, but nobody helped her. She started to breathe heavily, her hands turning into fists. She screamed, and her mirror broke into pieces. The vase that was sitting on her computer table broke as well. Emily did not move. For another minute, she just stood there, her breathing calmed down, and she snapped out of it. She looked around and saw all the glass and the broken vase.

"Oh no, my mom will kill me. My grandmother bought me this vase for my birthday. And how will I explain this mirror? Oh, I wish this was fixed. Come on now, get back together," she was saying to herself while she was on her knees picking up the glass from the mirror. She said it again, "I wish this mirror was back together now!" She placed her hands on the glass, and the glass started to move. Emily backed off. She sat there on the floor, watching the glass rise up and place itself like a puzzle back into the mirror stand. It looked like it was never broken. Emily was in shock. She stood up and walked slowly toward the mirror, touching it. "Amazing," she said. Emily looked at her hands and asked herself, "I wonder what else I am capable of?" Emily turned around and took the broken vase. She held the pieces in her hands and focused. She said, "Make this vase together again, in one piece like it's meant." The vase started to form itself back together as she held it in her hands. Emily stared at the vase. "It's all back together in one piece," she said and smiled.

The next morning, Emily did not go to the bookstore. She decided to go to school. When she came to school, she walked right passed Nikki and her other friends. They looked at her with surprise when she passed by not saying a word. Emily went on about her business. Briana and her friends saw her in the hallway, and they wondered where all the bruises and scars from her face went. Her face was clean like nothing ever happened. When Emily passed by Briana, Emily exhaled heavily and her breath traveled onto Briana's face. Briana right away started to feel sick and had stomach pain. Briana fell to the floor and started throwing up. Her friends held their mouths and were disgusted by it. Emily smiled and left to class.

After school, as usual, Emily was walking home. Mike ran after her. He caught up to her and asked her where she had been hiding all day. She stopped walking and asked him why he was following her.

"I thought we had something going on here. I would like for you to become my girl, and I want everyone to know that," Mike said to her. He came closer to her and smiled. He tried to hug her. Before he was able to tell her that he loved her, she cut him off.

"No! What made you think there will ever be something between us? Let me make this clear to you. I never want to see you again," she responded to him and pushed him away.

She walked away from him, but he followed. She tried to ignore him, but he kept talking. Then, she waved her hand back quickly, and a force of energy threw Mike backward and dropped him on the concrete floor. He looked her way and asked her to stop walking. Emily did not listen. Mike stood up, ran, and grabbed her by her hand and pulled her toward his chest.

"What is going on with you?" Mike asked her.

Emily did not answer him. She picked him up by his throat and said in a deep evil voice, "Why the fuck do you care? Leave me alone now or I will kill you." She threw him again into the wall of a building, and he slid to the floor. He sat there. He was breathing heavily and did not move a muscle. Emily stared at him for a little while thinking if she should just finish him off, but then, she walked away.

"What the hell was that?" Mike asked himself. He then got up and yelled her name, "Emily!" but she did not pay him any attention. He stood there gasping for air. "I almost shitted on myself," he said to himself.

Emily was about to walk passed the bookstore but decided to stop in. She walked in and saw Gary working on something.

"Where have you been all day? I thought you were going to be here today. You know, things could get out of hand," Gary said to her.

"You don't understand. I feel so alive. You know those girls who jumped me yesterday? I took care of them real quick, and now, I'm unbreakable. I have powers. Nobody can hurt me anymore," Emily said to Gary with excitement

"That is what I'm afraid of. That is what Aza'el wants you to feel. She wants you to like that power so that you join her," Gary responded.

"I do not care what you have to say. I feel alive now, and I am tired of people hurting me. It is time for revenge," said Emily.

"My child, you have to focus. You can't let her control you like that," said Gary.

While Gary and Emily were discussing the situation inside the bookstore, Mike drove by and saw them through the window. He saw the old man and Emily working on magic. He sat there and waited until Emily left home. Before Gary could close the door behind himself, Mike placed his foot in between the door and the doorframe.

"We're closed for the day," said Gary.

Mike forced himself in.

Gary backed off of the door. "I don't have any money if that's what you're looking for," said Gary as he thought he was getting robbed.

"Relax. I'm not here to rob you. Tell me what's going on with the girl who just left here," said Mike.

Gary calmed down and saw the young man was curious. "I don't know what you're talking about. I will have to ask you to leave now," said Gary.

"Come on, don't play stupid. I watched you guys through the window the whole time. I saw everything," said Mike.

Gary looked at the young man and told him if he wanted to know anything, he better talk to her. He will not give any information. However, he told Mike to help her and to try his best to save her.

"What do I need to save her from?" Mike asked him.

"From herself," Gary replied.

Gary turned his back and walked away from Mike. Mike left the store angry but worried at the same time. He drove off toward Emily's house. When he arrived there, Emily's father answered the door. Mike asked to speak with Emily. Her father called her name. She was not coming. They both looked toward the stairs, and Allen called her name again. She still was not coming. When her father walked upstairs to her bedroom to check why she was not coming down, he saw her window was open and she was gone. Allen came back downstairs and told Mike she was not there. Mike ran out of the house to look for her and Allen followed. They both hopped in Mike's car.

"What's going on here," Allen asked.

"I am not sure, but I have to find her," Mike replied.

"Why? I ran because you ran. Now, you need to explain yourself," said Allen.

"I don't know anything yet. I just want to make sure she is safe," said Mike.

"Why would she not be safe? Is there something extra I need to know? Did she get herself in some type of trouble?" Allen questioned Mike.

Mike just drove and shook his head.

Emily was transformed that night. She was a witch. Emily was out walking around. She had some urge to taste real blood and flesh. She was hungry. She walked around town slowly looking for something tasty. Her black hair fell down her back, her cheeks were pale, and she had cracks on her face. Her teeth were sharp and her ears pointy. Her eyes shined in the color yellow. She was feeling strong. She wanted to take her anger out on someone. As she walked around in the darkness, she spotted a young man by a bar. She transformed back into her human self as she was walking closer toward the gentleman. The young man saw her and smiled at her. She led him on and pretended like she wanted him. They exchanged a couple of words, and she asked him if he wanted to go to the back of the bar. He got all excited and took her hand, and they both walked to the back.

"What did you have in mind?" the young man asked her.

She pushed him against the wall and started kissing on his neck. The gentleman liked it. She threw her head back, and he kissed on her chest. When her head came back and he looked at her, she was transformed as a witch. When he saw her, his eyes opened widely and he screamed. He tried to run, but she held on tight.

"I thought you wanted to see what I had planned?" she asked him and smiled. Her voice was so deep. She struck her teeth into his neck and sucked as much as she could. She then ripped off a piece of flesh and ate it. The young man was still trying to fight back but was not able to get away. As he tried to gasp for air, she lifted him up, placed her mouth on top of his, and inhaled his soul out. She dropped his dry, blue looking body onto the ground and left. As she was walking home, she transformed back into her human self.

When Emily sucked every ounce of that man's soul and drank his blood, Aza'el felt it. She was getting excited. She knew the ring was taking control over whoever was wearing it and soon would join her.

When Emily walked up to her house, she saw her father and Mike outside. She asked with an attitude what Mike was doing here. Allen told her they were looking for her and asked where she was. Emily told them both that she's grown and she did not need permission to be outside. She walked passed them and straight to her room. When she passed right by Mike, he felt something different about her.

Chapter 10

THE BEGINNING

Back in Arfabele Land in the Green Village, the Klexons were practicing fighting and preparing potions for the day they will meet face-to-face with Aza'el. They were building weapons, training, and setting up traps for the Dark Zals. They were nervous because they were almost defeated when Aza'el attacked them last time, and they were not sure if they are strong enough to do it again. Mayla knew she had to find the person who found the ring before Aza'el does. She was getting ready to leave her village and join the human's world to find this person. Lin asked Mayla why she had to go. Mayla explained to her that if Aza'el finds this person first, she will have the upper opportunity to destroy the moral world and become stronger and then come after the Green Villagers. Lin understood and helped Mayla get ready. Toward the end of the day, Mayla was leaving and others watched her go. She stopped, turned around, looked at her people, rose her hand, and spoke, "My people, you do not fear. Together we are united. Together we are unbreakable. We will protect what's ours and others that are good. Work together my people, and we will not be defeated."

Everyone nodded and agreed with Mayla. They all wished her good luck. Mayla left the village, found the portal and walked into it for the search of Emily.

The next morning, Emily woke up with a huge headache. "Oh my God, why does my head hurt so badly?" she asked herself.

"Probably from when those bitches jumped me," Emily answered herself. She got up, turned on the TV, and brushed her teeth. The TV was in her room, but the door was open. She was able to hear the news in the bathroom. As she spat into the sink, she heard on the news about someone being murdered. The newsman said the body looked blue like it has been sitting there for weeks. The skin was so dry almost turning into dust.

"There is no explanation on how this happened or who did it. There are bite marks on his neck like from an animal, but they cannot explain from what animal," said the newsman.

Emily dropped her brush to the floor, walked into her room, and stared at the TV. She quickly started getting dressed and ran out the door.

"Open up," said Emily, as she banged with her hand on the bookstore door. Gary opened the door for her. She stormed in. "Did you watch the news?" she asked.

"Yes, and as I see so, did you?" Gary replied.

"Did I do that? Did I? Answer me," she asked him.

"I believe so," said Gary.

Emily fell to the floor crying. She screamed out loud, "What is happening to me!" She continued to cry. Emily looked up at Gary as he sat at his table reading. Emily continued to cry and rock back and forth on the floor as she sat in a sitting position. Emily looked at Gary and saw him reading. Finally she calmed down.

"How do you know so much about this witch stuff? How did you get caught up in all this?" Emily asked Gary.

He waited a couple of seconds before he decided to answer her.

"The bride who gave her life away to save her people was my wife. A long time ago, the witches were able to use a potion and open a portal up into the human's world any time. There were no problems. The witches would hide, and no human has ever seen them. They stayed in the shadows and would protect us from the bad people. One day, I got lost in the woods. I had no idea how I got there, and I was not able to find my way back. I searched for a whole day for a road that led back to the town. It was getting dark and a wolf attacked me. I thought I was going to die. At that moment, she saved me. I did not see her at first. All I saw was a shadow. She killed the wolf and told me which way was home. I saw her leaving and I followed her. She told me to go away and go home, but I asked to see her face. She said no. I told her I was not going to leave until I saw her face. She finally came out into the light, and I saw her. Her skin was so pale. She had long black eyelashes and yellow eyes. There were blue veins on both sides of her face with ruffles. Her ears were pointy. After she showed me who she was, I could not believe what I saw. She went right back into the shadows and told me she did not mean to scare me. I walked closer to her and grabbed her hand. I pulled her back out of the shadows and told her she was the most beautiful thing I have ever seen. Ever since then, we never left each other. I fell in love with her, and she fell in love with me. Her name was Alona. See, Aza'el was her sister, and she was very jealous of our love. Aza'el then tried to find love with a human, and almost revealed our portal. When she realized what she was doing was not working for her, she decided to work against us and destroy both worlds. She has tried many times to destroy the humans. However, before Alona died, she placed a spell on Aza'el to fall into a deep sleep. The only way we are able to destroy Aza'el was by bringing the two rings together. They have to be destroyed at the same time with love and kindness." Gary explained to Emily as she listened to his story.

She felt very bad for him. "I am very sorry you lost your only love," she said to him.

Gary did not respond. He got back to reading his book.

"But if that happened about two hundred years ago and you are human, how are you still alive?" Emily asked him.

"I have been using magic to keep myself at this age. Once I got old, I was not ready to die. I knew that Aza'el was not dead, and I don't want to die until I see her die, so I kept myself alive through magic," said Gary.

Emily stood up on her feet. She walked closer to Gary and said, "I'm not as strong as your wife was. I'm not like her. I'm weak. I am nobody. So please do not depend on me to save the world because that is not who I am. Whatever this is, it's killing me as well. I am turning into someone that I am not, and sometimes, I like it." She then turned around and started walking toward the door.

As she grabbed the doorknob, Gary told her, "It is very easy to just give up and only think about yourself. Sometimes, you have to make decisions and save the ones you love."

Emily paused for a minute. "Love, what a funny word," Emily replied. She walked out of the bookstore and slammed the door. She threw on her hoody and walked away. When she hit a corner down the street from the bookstore, she bumped into a woman. The woman dropped her basket. Emily said she was sorry she did not see her. The woman dropped down to pick up her basket, and Emily watched her. Emily noticed her pale hands, which did not look like human hands. Emily grabbed the woman and pushed her against the building.

"Who are you?" Emily asked her.

The woman did not respond. Emily was not able to see her face because she was facing the ground and was wearing a hoody. The woman slowly lifted her head up and looked at Emily. Emily saw her face and backed away. Mayla then saw the ring.

"It's you," said Mayla.

"What do you mean? What are you?" asked Emily.

"I'm here to help. You have been experiencing some differences since you placed that ring on your hand, haven't you?" asked Mayla.

Emily looked at her hand. The ring was dark. "How did you know?" Emily asked her.

"I come from Arfabele Green. It's a place where good witches live. I am one of them," replied Mayla.

"No way, but how can you help?" asked Emily.

"Come with me. I will show you. We have to make sure we keep your heart and soul good. Once it turns evil, it cannot be turned back to good. Once your heart is evil, Aza'el will have full control over you, which will make her even more powerful," said Mayla.

Emily and Mayla were walking into the woods. Emily stopped and looked. "You live in here?" Emily pointed toward the woods.

"Follow me. You will be surprised," said Mayla.

Emily did not want to go in there at first because it brought back memories of what the boys did to her. Mayla looked at Emily and told her that she knows what happened and should not worry about that anymore. Mayla told Emily that she was safe now. Emily looked at Mayla and asked her how she knew.

"I am a witch remember," Mayla responded.

They walked and walked deep into the woods, into the darkness, until they reached the portal. Emily could not believe what she saw. It was big and blue like a water sinkhole but floating in the air. Mayla grabbed Emily's hand, and they walked into the portal. When they arrived at Arfabele Land, Emily was nervous but had fun at the same time.

"Wow, that is amazing," said Emily pointing at the portal.

They both started walking toward the village.

"The day you placed that ring on your finger, the portal has reopened between us and your world," said Mayla.

Emily asked Mayla if anyone could go through that portal. Mayla then explained to her.

"If you do not know how to walk through the portal, you can end up anywhere in Arfabele Land. You have to focus where you are going to make sure that is where the portal will take you."

Emily understood. They finally arrived at the village. Emily noticed all the creatures and other witches watching her. She noticed all the different colored flowers that actually moved. She noticed giant creatures that looked like birds flying above her. She could not believe what she was seeing. As she walked around the village, she looked up in the sky watching the creatures fly around. She freaked out when one of them landed right in front of her. It looked like a hawk but with six legs. Emily screamed and fell to the floor as one of the flying creatures was getting closer and closer toward her. She was sitting on her butt, and the creature lowered its head trying to sniff on Emily. Emily was scared and started kicking it with her feet telling it to go away. Mayla ran to calm Emily down. The bird did not move. Mayla asked Emily to calm down, informing her that it would not hurt her. The animal backed away and gave Emily some space. Mayla walked in between them and helped Emily get up.

"What are those things?" Emily asked Mayla.

"We call these Visionairs. They have the ability to feel who their new owner will be. It looks like it is you Emily. It chose you. Once they chose an owner, they are able to provide you with short visions. You have to learn how to bond with it and become as one," said Mayla.

"How does it know that it's me?" asked Emily.

"It just knows," replied Mayla.

Emily approached the creature slowly and placed her hand on its side moving slowly toward its face. She placed her hand on the side of its face, and they had an eye to eye contact. Their eyes locked, and Emily had a glimpse of a short future. She had a vision seeing herself working along with Aza'el and Aza'el murdering her mother. The vision ended, and Emily backed away from the creature. She screamed, "No!" She fell to the ground and started screaming again, "No, no, that can't be. I won't let her do that!"

Mayla helped her get back up. "What's wrong? What did you see?" Mayla asked her.

"I saw her killing my mother," Emily replied in tears.

Emily and Mayla looked at each other, and Emily started to cry.

"Those visions are true. They do not lie," said Mayla.

Emily pushed Mayla out of the way and ran off back toward the portal. She wanted to go back home. Mayla was trying to stop her but was too late. Mayla knew if she was able to find Emily so will Aza'el. Mayla told Lin to hurry up and pack her a new bag and gather up three witches to go back into the human's world with her. Lin did just that.

Emily arrived back in the human's world, ran out of the portal, through the woods and into the street. When she ran across the street, Briana saw her. Briana started to follow Emily in her car. Emily ran into the bookstore. Briana parked her car and sneaked around the back of the building. Briana found an old window on the side of the building that was cracked. She overheard Emily's and Gary's conversation. Emily told Gary about Mayla and the trip into the Arfabele world and the vision she had. Emily told him everything. Gary did not know what to say at first. Emily was talking fast and breathing heavily.

"Oh, that is why she was able to do what she did," said Briana to herself as she overheard everything. "She has powers. I have to find out more," said Briana. Briana turned around, walked toward her car, and drove off. When Emily left the bookstore and was walking home, it was already dark. As she was passing by a restaurant, three young men approached her.

"Hey, baby," one of the guys said to her with a laugh.

She pretended like she did not hear them and continued to walk. The faster she walked, the faster they walked. She started to run and so did they. As she ran, she yelled to them to leave her alone, but all they did was laugh. They were catching up to her. One of them grabbed her arm and said, "I said hi, bitch."

"Let me go," said Emily as she tried to get away.

The three young men laughed and surrounded her. One of the guys was touching her face and went lower toward her breast. Emily was getting mad. She started to breathe heavily and spoke in a deep evil voice. "I told you not to touch me." She turned her face to the side and looked at one of the guys. The three men started backing away after they heard her voice.

"What did you say?" one of the men asked her.

Emily turned her head toward him and laughed. Her voice was very different. It was evil.

"This bitch is crazy. Let's get out of here, man," said the second man.

"Why? The fun just started," said Emily.

Within a flash, she was face-to-face with one of the guys. Emily transformed into a witch. She grabbed him by his throat. She lifted him up off the ground with one hand. She turned to the other guy and asked him if he wanted to join. He tried to run away, but she lifted her other arm up and used her power to lift his body off the ground. She looked at the man who she was physically holding and told him to watch his friend. While she was holding his friend in the air, she was slowly turning her hand into a fist forcing the man's head to turn around while his body stood in one place. She snapped his neck and laughed. She dropped her hand back down, and the body fell to the floor. She watched the third guy take off. "Oh, go ahead," she said. She then turned back to the man she was holding. He was very scared and was begging her not to kill him. "Oh, now you're scared, but what happened a minute ago when you were touching me? How come you were not scared then?" she asked him. She took a bite on his neck and started to eat. The young man tried to scream but only air came out of his mouth. She then dropped him to the floor and left him there to die. Blood was gushing out of his neck. Emily transformed back into human and left home.

Aza'el felt it again. She was feeling everything Emily was doing. It felt so good, and she was getting stronger. When Emily's heart reacted in evil, Aza'el was able to sense a direction of where Emily might be. "I can feel you and smell you, and I will find you," Aza'el said to herself. She laughed loudly as she stood in front of her mirror. Aza'el then walked into a different room where her witches were eating on animals they caught. She looked at all of them and saw that most of them were pathetic. But she found three who looked more aggressive. She picked those three and told them to come with her into the human's world to find the girl.

Chapter 11

EVERYONE NEEDS REVENGE

T he next day in school, Mike was looking for Emily, but she was nowhere to be found. Mike asked around, but no one has seen her. He decided he was going to look for her later. He left for football practice. At football practice, the boys were talking among each other.

"Hey, guys, did you hear what happened last night?" Pete asked the team on the field.

"What?" Mike asked.

"On the news, man. They said they found two guys on the street, man, all fucked up, man. One of them, his neck was all twisted and the other one ..." Pete was saying and paused for a minute.

"What, man?" Mike asked him again.

"Looked like someone or something was eating him," replied Pete with disgust.

Mike's eyes opened wide. Pete walked away, and every player went to their positions. Mike was wondering if Emily knew something about it. After practice, he was looking for her again. He was not able to find her. He also checked at her house, but nobody was there. He decided to go home and see if she will show up to school the following day.

It was nighttime, and the football players decided to hang out. Mike was not with them and neither was Pete. It was one of the football player's house parties. They were drinking, dancing, and making out with one another. Brian, the guy who raped Emily first, happened to be in the kitchen. He was pouring himself more alcohol into his cup. He then felt some soft hands from behind touching over his shoulders toward his chest. He was drunk. He thought it was just another drunk girl trying to get laid tonight. He grabbed her hand and kissed it. He said, "I wonder who lucky girl is this tonight?" He laughed and placed the bottle back on the counter. The female did not say anything. She continued to touch him around his neck and lowered her hand toward his stomach. She grabbed his package and he laughed. "Oh, you like that, baby girl. Well, you are lucky tonight," he said. He turned around to face the female, and it was Emily. "What the fuck!" he said and dropped his drink on the floor. Emily stared at his face. She did not blink or move. He looked at her and told her to move. She did not. He asked her what the hell she was doing here. Emily tilted her head to the left and straight up again. She grabbed his package again and asked him if he liked that. Brian smiled and asked her if she wanted more. Emily dropped her hand and turned into a witch right in front of him. The young man screamed and jumped on top of the countertop. Emily watched him trying to run, but she quickly grabbed him from the back around his neck. She slammed him against the refrigerator.

"You took something very special from me, and now, you will pay for it," said Emily.

Her voice was very deep and dark. She struck her long sharp nails through his dick. He screamed and tried to grab it. Emily wanted to torture him, but she heard voices coming in. She quickly placed her lips on top of his and inhaled his soul out. His body dried out, and she dropped him to the floor. She quickly disappeared. Three boys and two girls walked into the kitchen trying to grab more drinks. One of the guys tripped on something and noticed it was Brian's body. They screamed running out of the house. Others walked into the kitchen to see what they were screaming about and saw Brian as well. Everyone was scared and disgusted at the same time. His body laid there in blood all blue and dry. Everyone else started running out of the house and calling the police.

Again Aza'el felt it. She felt more human's blood and evil spirit running through her body. She moaned as she felt the soul rising inside of Emily. Aza'el felt more energy. She laughed out loud in her castle right before she left with her three witches to look for Emily.

The following morning, Brian was on the news. Pete was watching it at home, and he couldn't believe what happened to Brian. On the news, it was announced that there is someone or something out there killing and asking the people in town to be safe. Pete was thinking about what Brian did to Emily in the woods. He knew he had to tell Mike and apologize to Emily but was not sure when the right time was.

Emily woke up with a huge headache again. She was hardly able to walk. She remembered some stuff from the night before but not much. She did not think about it anymore. She really did not care anymore what she did to people even if she did not remember much. Emily was starting to like her new self. But sometimes, she felt confused. She felt like she was not herself and her emotions and actions get out of her control. She got up, got dressed, and left the house. She went straight to the bookstore. She looked tired, beat, like she has not slept in days. Gary asked her how things were going. She opened up to him and told him how much she remembered from last night. The more she talked about it, the more she got emotional. She then started to cry.

"I have killed about four people so far. I can't control it. When I'm out there doing this, I feel good and powerful. Every time it happens, I wake up with a huge headache," Emily said to Gary.

Gary was getting very worried about the whole situation. He knew he had to go pay Mayla a visit. Emily told Gary she wanted revenge on everyone who hurt her but not like this. Gary felt bad for her. He knew she has been through a lot and now this. He also knew Aza'el would be able to control her easily because of her emotional pain. But this was no excuse to kill people. Gary had to stop Emily before things really get out of hand.

"We have to go see Mayla, she will helps us," said Gary.

Emily was quiet.

"You need to be strong!" said Gary.

"What do you want me to do? I'm just a college student who had a normal simple life, who lost her best friend and was living day by day," Emily yelled at Gary.

Gary approached her closely. "You were the one who found that ring, and now, it is your responsibility to think of others as well," said Gary.

Emily slowly started walking out of the store while shaking her head, "You want to know who I am. You want to know what this ring turned me into. Ha, do you? Well, take a good look at me!" Emily screamed, turned into a Dark Zal, and made evil noises. She laughed and started walking toward Gary. She tried to jump on him, but he threw a blue rock that lit up right in front of her and it made her jump back. She was not able to see him anymore. She tried to walk around the blue light but did not succeed. The blue rock hurt her. It burned her every time she got close to it. She backed away from it and left the store. Outside, Emily turned back into herself and left.

Aza'el finally made it into the human's world. She transformed herself into a beautiful young woman. She walked through town. Her witches were watching over her but hidden in the shadows so no humans would see them. As Aza'el continued to walk down the sidewalk looking for Emily, she bumped into Briana and Adriana. Aza'el said, "Excuse me," and continued to walk. Suddenly, she overheard Briana telling Adriana about Emily.

"I'm telling you, she has some type of magic. How was she able to throw us around like that? No way. Plus, I saw her walking to that old man's bookstore and they were talking about some witches and spells," said Briana to Adriana.

"Are you telling me that Emily is a witch?" Adriana was asking.

"Yes, no, maybe. I'm not sure. I am just telling you what I saw and heard her and that old man talk about," said Briana.

"Okay. Well, this is just crazy, but I do have to go now. I have to go pick up my little annoying brother from school. I will call you later, and we will look into this more. Okay," said Adriana.

Briana nodded and waived her friend away. As Adriana was walking away, Aza'el approached Briana.

"Hey there, could you tell me a little more about what you and your friend were talking about?" Aza'el asked her.

"Who are you?" asked Briana.

"Let's just say I can become your best friend or your worst nightmare," said Aza'el.

Briana looked at Aza'el, and she was not sure how to take that comment, but she did not say another word to Aza'el.

"I am looking for this girl you mentioned to your friend. Do you know where I can find her?" Aza'el asked Briana.

"What's in it for me?" Briana asked her as she stepped closer to Aza'el's face.

"Come with me, and I will show you," said Aza'el with a smile on her face.

Chapter 12

UNMANAGEABLE

E mily was walking around in town. The first turn she took, she bumped into Mike. She rolled her eyes and turned away from him. He followed after her. Before he was able to speak, she cut him off.

"Stay away. Stay away from me before I hurt you too," she yelled at him.

Mike ignored her.

"What is going on with you? Why are you acting this way?" he asked her as he was getting closer to her.

"Stay away from me. Go home please. I am warning you. I do not want to hurt you, Mike, so just, GO!" she yelled at him again and raised her hand in the air, and Mike flew backward and onto the ground. As she walked past him, he grabbed her hand.

"Wait, I'm not letting you go. I love you," Mike told her as he held onto her hand not letting her go.

Emily looked down at him. He looked up at her. She turned her head from one side to the other. "NO YOU DON'T!" she screamed and turned into a witch.

That was the first time he saw her like that. He let her go and stayed on the floor. After seeing her face and hearing her deep evil voice, he was not sure who Emily was anymore. Emily then grabbed him and lifted him up by his throat.

"Emily, please, this is not you. I love you. I can help you," Mike said.

Emily just stared at him side to side. Her breathing was heavy. She exhaled and white fog came out of her mouth. Mike looked at her face closely and noticed how dark her eyes were. Her cheeks were hard and shaped to a point. It looked like ruffles, but they were hard. Her face looked scary, but he was not frightened by her anymore. He touched her face softly with his hand, and she slowly put him back down onto his feet. She released her hand from his throat, and he took a couple of deep breaths. She did not move her eyes off of him. Mike looked at her.

"What's going on, Emily?" he asked her.

But before he could say anything else, she felt a presence and started running. Mike followed her. The closer she got to her house, the screams she heard got louder. She was finally down the street from her house and heard her mother scream again. Emily transformed back into herself. She managed to snap out of the darkness and realized her family needed her.

When Emily ran into the house, it was quiet. She walked through the living room looking around, but nothing. She then saw Briana.

"What are you doing here?" Emily asked her.

"I told you this was not over. I have a good friend who is helping me get what I want," Briana replied.

"What friend?" Emily asked.

From behind the wall, Aza'el stepped into the living room. Emily was not sure who that was. All Emily saw was a pretty woman. Aza'el smiled at Emily.

"So this is the girl I have been looking for," said Aza'el.

"Who are you?" Emily asked her.

"Oh, I am sure you heard about me by now," said Aza'el as she slowly walked around the living room.

She then transformed into a witch, and Emily's eyes opened widely.

"Why so surprised? You knew I was looking for you," said Aza'el.

"What do you want?" Emily asked her.

"I want you!" Aza'el said out loud and pointed at Emily.

Emily looked down at the ring. She knew what Aza'el wanted. Emily told her she did not want to be a part of this. It was not her choice. Aza'el waived her hand around as she continued to pace around the living room and told Emily she did not want to hear her cry about it. Aza'el told Emily when she placed that ring on her hand, she became part of Aza'el and has no choice but to follow her. Aza'el's Dark Zals stepped into the living room and attacked Emily. Emily transformed into a witch, and they fought. At that moment, Mike arrived at the door. He could not believe what he saw. He yelled out for Emily, and Aza'el saw him. He tried to come in between them two, but Aza'el placed a holder shield around him so he couldn't come any closer. Meanwhile, Emily's mother and father were tied up. As Emily and the two Dark Zals were fighting, Aza'el came from behind Emily and threw a sparkling potion into Emily's face. Emily started to lose sight and then fell to the floor. Aza'el ordered her Dark Zals to carry Emily back to their world. As Aza'el, Briana, and the two witches who were carrying Emily out of the house were leaving, Gabby was yelling out to leave her daughter alone. When they left the house, the shield that was around Mike broke and he was free. He ran up to Allen and Gabby and untied them.

Gabby was asking Mike what was going on. She was scared, and she have never seen anything like that before. Mike told them he was not sure what was going on, but they had to help Emily. Gabby then asked what was happening to her daughter, but Mike had no answers. Allen ran downstairs to their basement. When he came back up, he gave Mike a shotgun, and he had a shotgun as well and two knives. Mike looked at Allen and asked him if they were really going to use them. Allen looked at Mike and told him he better if he wanted to stay alive.

Meanwhile, Mitti, Adriana, and Megan were looking for Briana, but she was nowhere to be found. They checked on her house as well, but she was not there. As they were leaving Briana's house, Adriana told Mitti what Briana said happened in the locker room with Pete. Mitti was not trying to hear it, but the girls would not let it go. Mitti had enough.

"Oh, you know what, both of you can shut up, okay. I don't even know why I hang out with you guys. You are annoying, Briana is a bitch, and you," she pointed at Megan, "I just don't like you," said Mitti and turned away from them. Mitti started walking away from them, but then, she stopped, turned around to face them, and said, "Oh yeah and I was in the locker room that day and I heard everything. She came onto him, and he rejected her."

Mitti then left and never looked back. Megan and Adriana just looked at each other with nothing to say. Mitti, however, well, she was looking for Pete. She felt terrible of the way she has been treating him and went straight to his house. She knocked on his door and waited. When he opened the door, he right away said to her, "I am glad you came over."

Mitti walked inside and said, "I am sorry for being such a bitch, and you were right the whole time. They are not my friends, and I really don't like them. I do not know why I stuck around so long. But I do want to say that I ..."

Before she was able to finish her sentence, Pete interrupted her by saying, "It's okay, baby. I have not been the best boyfriend myself. But right now, I need you to come with me."

He grabbed her hand, and they left his house.

"Where are we going?" she asked him.

"You will not believe this. There is something I want you to see," he responded to her.

Pete took Mitti to the place where she, Briana, and the other girls attacked Emily. There was a deep dent in the concrete with cracked path lines spreading toward the broken windows of the buildings. Pete and Mitti stood there staring at the ground. Mitti played back in her head the incident when Emily punched the ground and screamed, and something threw them back breaking the windows. Pete was pointing to the concrete showing it to Mitti.

"This is crazy. You see this? I mean, look how perfect it's formed, and this was not here the other day," he said to her.

Mitti started to walk away.

"What's wrong with you?" Pete asked her.

Mitti told him about the incident with the girls and Emily. She told him she did not know how Emily did that, but she did. Pete stared at Mitti and had a confused look on his face. He shook his head.

"I don't know what to believe you anymore, Mitti. You jumped the girl, for what reason? But now, you are telling me that Emily did this with her hand? You are really losing it," Pete said to her.

As they were about to argue, Pete saw something. He saw a group going into the woods. Mitti and Pete decided to follow them. When they ran into the woods, they saw Aza'el, her two witches carrying another person, and Briana. Pete jumped out of the bushes and asked them to stop walking. When they stopped, they all turned to face Pete. That is when Pete saw the Dark Zals up close. Pete and Mitti could not believe their eyes. The two Dark Zals dropped Emily to the floor, and that's when Pete saw it was Emily.

Mitti whispered to Pete, "I told you so."

Briana told Mitti and Pete to stay out of it. Aza'el was not in the mood to mess around with the two humans. She ordered her witches to pick Emily back up and to keep walking toward the portal. Mitti yelled out for Briana, but Briana ignored her.

"Why is Briana with them?" Mitti asked Pete.

"I don't know, but I have to go help Emily," said Pete.

Mitti gave him a confused look.

"I owe her, okay," said Pete because he knew why Mitti was giving him that look.

Before they could discuss the situation more, Mike, Allen, and Gabby showed up.

"Where did they go?" Mike asked Pete.

Pete pointed the way, and everyone followed. Everyone already went through the portal. Right before the Dark Zals and Emily disappeared into the portal, Gabby grabbed onto Emily's clothes. She was pulled into the portal with them. Allen yelled out for Gabby and tried to jump in right after them. At that moment, Gary from the bookstore yelled out "STOP!" He was walking toward Allen slowly with his cane. Gary explained that you had to know how to use the portal. The portal sends you into their world, but if you didn't know what you were doing, the portal will drop you off anywhere.

"What about my wife?" Allen asked.

"She grabbed onto Emily. Wherever Emily ends up, she will be there as well," said Gary.

"So what do we do now, and who are you?" Allen asked Gary.

"I'm Emily's friend. She has been dealing with this for quite a while now," said Gary.

"I'm here to help. Don't worry. We will find her," said Pete to Mike.

"What you mean we? Where are you going?" Mitti asked Pete.

"Don't worry, baby. I will be back. I promise. Mike is my boy. I have to help him," said Pete.

Mitti was upset that he was going to risk his life for Emily.

"I cannot believe you are going to fight some animals over this girl!" Mitti yelled at him, and she turned away and ran out of the woods.

As she was running out of the woods, Gary yelled to her not to say anything to anyone. Mike watched Mitti run, and then, he turned to Pete. He placed his hand on Pete's shoulder and said, "You do not have to come along."

Pete kept his eyes on the path where Mitti ran and then slowly turned his head toward Mike.

"I need to," said Pete.

Gary pulled out a potion to guide the way through the portal to the Green Village.

"Where are we going?" Mike asked Gary.

"We are going to see my old friends," Gary replied.

He threw the powder potion into the portal, and it turned green.

"Well, come on," he said and walked right into the portal.

Allen and Mike looked at each other.

"Well, here we go," said Allen and followed Gary.

Mike followed right behind, and then Pete. When they arrived at the Green Village, the Klexons were already waiting at the gate. They were prepared to attack because they did not know who was coming through that portal. When Mayla recognized Gary, she came out of the bushes and lifted her hand up to notify the others not to attack. Mayla slowly walked up to Gary, and they hugged. Mike, Pete, and Allen looked around. They were amazed at the things they saw. As they all were walking toward the village, there was a witch walking right next to Pete. Pete couldn't take his gaze off of the witch. She was so close to him that he was able to see every detail on her face: her pale skin; her hard, strong facial features; her long fingernails, which were so pointy and crystal clear white. He was examining the ruffles on her face. The witch got aggravated with Pete staring at her. She turned to him and growled at him. He backed off. The witch smiled as she continued to walk.

The Dark Zals and the Klexons looked different. The Klexons have more of a paler skin and ruffles on the side of their cheeks. The inner of their cheeks, moving toward their noses are smooth and crystal looking. They have blue veins going through their necks and into the side of their faces. As for the Dark Zals, which are created by Aza'el, they have dark cracks on their faces. But each Dark Zal had their own unique designed cracks right underneath their eyes.

As they were getting closer to the Green Village, the Visionairs were flying above. One of them landed right next to Allen. Pete screamed and backed away.

"What is that? Will it eat us?" Pete asked.

Mayla stepped in front of the creature. "No they will not eat you. This one is Emily's Visionair," she said.

"Emily's. What you mean? Was Emily here?" Allen asked her.

"Yes, she was here. I tried to help her, but after she saw a vision of her mother dying, she ran off back home and I couldn't stop her," Mayla replied.

"My daughter and my wife are in trouble. A witch came to our house and took her. My wife followed. We have to find them. Can you help us?" Allen asked Mayla.

"Yes, but the only way your daughter can come back as herself is if she finds her true self-love. Meaning she has to find love within herself, love herself, and be happy with who she is. The way the spell works is through the ring that Emily placed on her finger, which is evil. It is changing her soul from good to evil. Aza'el is doing this to become powerful and have another evil strong soul with her to rule the worlds. She is not strong enough to do it on her own. This way if she has someone else doing the dirty work for her, she has a better opportunity to succeed," Mayla explained to everyone. "Aza'el tried this before with one of our witches. Our witch sacrificed her own life to save us and our forest. Before she died, she was able to place a long sleeping spell on Aza'el. Well, the ring that Aza'el created disappeared. We have been looking for it for a very long time until Emily found it." Mayla walked over to Gary and said, "That good witch who saved us all was my sister and Gary's wife. I will do whatever it takes to stop Aza'el."

Mike and Allen gave their sympathy. Mike wanted to find this Aza'el.

"Let's do this then. How do we find Aza'el?" Mike asked.

"Finding her is not hard, destroying her is," Gary replied.

Mayla told the humans to get comfortable at their village and rest. She told them to be ready tomorrow. Mike asked her what was tomorrow. She told them training.

"Training for what?" Mike asked.

Gary walked passed him. "To fight," he said and left toward his cottage.

Lin who was Mayla's assistant showed everyone where their cottages were. Everyone went to bed to get some rest. The following morning, the Klexons woke Mike, Pete, and Allen and told them to get up and follow. The Klexons wanted to teach the humans how to fight against other witches. After all day of training, the Klexons gave the humans the rest of the evening off to relax. Mike, Allen, and Pete decided to take a look around the village. When they arrived at an open field, one of the Klexons that came along with them blew a shofar releasing a deep sound. Everyone stood around and looked at each other. Suddenly, they felt the ground shaking. Then, they saw huge dinosaur-size–looking species running toward them. They were very big, tall, and wide. They had three horns on their noses going from bottom to the top, biggest to smallest. They had tails that were two times longer than their bodies. On their tails were spikes. They have very sharp teeth. There were four teeth in the front of their mouth that stuck out. Two of them came from the top of their mouth pointing downward, and two were coming from the bottom of their mouth pointing upward. The rest of the teeth were smaller and did not stick out.

As the species were running toward the witch, Pete started to panic. He started to run back toward the cottages, but one of the species jumped in front of Pete. Pete fell to the ground and screamed. "No, no way, help me!" he yelled.

The Klexon ran over to the creature by Pete and placed her hand on the side of its body and ordered it to calm down. The animal calmed down and lowered its head in front of Pete.

"It wants to belong to you," said the Klexon.

The animal blew air into Pete's face through its nose. Pete wiped his face. The Klexon jumped and sat on top of one creature.

"These are called Grounders. They help us protect our place. We all live together here," the witch explained.

"I don't know what you're scared of Pete. They seem pretty cool to me," said Mike as he sat on one.

Pete turned his attention back to the Grounder that was standing in front of him. He walked closer to it and touched it. The Grounder lowered its body to the ground and Pete finally sat on it.

Then, the Grounder lifted its body up, and Pete realized how high off the ground he really was.

"Okay, okay, I can do this," he said to himself as he held on tightly. Once Pete, Mike, and Allen all sat on a Grounder, the Klexon was showing them how to ride the animal and how to use it as a weapon.

"I thought we were done with practice for today," said Pete.

"Come on, we are almost done," said Mike as he passed by Pete with his Grounder.

Mike tapped the animal twice with his feet, and the animal took off running into the open field. The Klexon and Allen followed. Pete was left behind. He was still unsure about trusting those animals.

Chapter 13

SEARCHING

B ack home, Mitti was looking for Nikki. Mitti knew that she and Emily were good friends and she had to break the news to her and also ask for her help. She knew Nikki would be at the coffee shop hanging out with Jack. Nikki ran into the coffee shop and grabbed Nikki by her arm. Jack stepped in between them and told Mitti to let her go.

"I really need to talk to you," said Mitti.

Nikki saw the fear in Mitti's face. Nikki told Jack it was okay and she will just go talk to her outside. They both walked outside, and Mitti told Nikki everything that happened.

"They all disappeared into this portal over there in the woods. Emily, your friend, she's not Emily anymore. Briana also left with them. I have been waiting for a while now to see them or hear from them, but nothing. I need you to come with me through that portal and look for them," said Mitti as she was trying to take a breath.

"Oh really," said Nikki. Nikki seemed to be interested in the portal.

"I know you don't believe me, but if you come with me, I can show you," said Mitti.

"I believe you. Emily told me something about some witches before, but I did not think it was this serious. I will come with you," said Nikki.

They started walking toward the woods but then bumped into Megan and Adriana.

"Watch where you're going," said Adriana.

Nikki and Mitti did not say anything. They continued to walk toward the woods.

"Since when does Mitti hang out with her?" Megan asked Adriana.

"I don't give a shit," said Adriana.

Nikki and Mitti walked through the woods deep into the darkness.

"I cannot believe how dark it is here even in bright daylight," said Mitti.

The girls finally found the portal. They grabbed each other's hands and jumped in. They came out in an empty place, with a long road in front of them. There was nothing else around. No village, no houses, nothing, just an empty dirt road.

"Great, now what? Which way do we go?" Nikki asked.

"This way," replied Mitti.

They started walking down the long empty road.

Chapter 14

THINGS DONE FOR LOVE

When Emily woke up, she was tied down to a table. Her vision slowly came through. She saw Aza'el walking around the table. Emily started yanking her arms trying to untie herself, but nothing happened. She was screaming and yelling for them to let her go. Aza'el placed her palm on Emily's forehead and told her to calm down. Aza'el took a bowl filled of her evil blood and told Emily that she will become one of them permanently tonight. Aza'el lifted Emily's head, placed the bowl onto her mouth and poured the blood down her throat. The other Dark Zals were dancing and singing around the table. The blood was running down Emily's chin and neck as Aza'el forced it down her throat. After Emily forcefully drank it, she started to shake and then became still. Her eyes turned dark. Emily looked around while lying on the table. Aza'el leaned over her head and stared into Emily's eyes. She saw nothing but darkness. Aza'el smiled and told her Zals to untie Emily. They untied her, and Emily stood up. She walked over to Aza'el and gave her hands. Aza'el took Emily's hands into hers and smiled. One of the Dark Zals started to smell something. She followed that smell and found Emily's mother hiding behind a stone. The witch grabbed Gabby by her shirt and pulled her.

"Look what I found," said the witch.

Aza'el turned her attention to the witch and so did Emily.

"Well, well, what do we have here?" Aza'el asked as she walked over to Gabby.

"Do not hurt her. Take me instead," said Gabby.

"Sorry. I need her, but I will save you for later. Lock her up!" Aza'el yelled, and two of her witches locked Gabby up in a cage that was hanging from the ceiling. As Gabby sat in the cage, she was able to see the witches and Emily. Gabby yelled out for Emily, but one of the witches punched the cage and Gabby got quiet.

"Bring the boy out!" Aza'el yelled out.

The Zals brought in the boy who was from Emily's school, the boy who was the second guy who raped Emily on that awful night. When Emily saw him, she remembered everything. Rage started building up in Emily's chest. When Gabby saw the young man, she remembered that he went to Emily's school. She was wondering why he was here. Gabby continued to watch them from the cage. Aza'el faced Emily. The Dark Zals dropped the boy on the floor right in front of Emily's feet. Emily looked down at him. He looked up at her. He knew it was her. He begged her to let him go. He kept saying that he was sorry. Emily was transformed into a Zal, and the young man was scared.

"Sorry? Let me remind you what you did," said Aza'el to the boy as she walked around him. She then walked over to her mirror. She raised her hand over it, and a clip started to play. It showed what the boys did to Emily that night in the woods. Gabby saw the whole thing and started to cry. She had no idea her daughter was hiding that. She wished she was there for Emily. Gabby looked at her daughter and yelled.

"Emily, Emily, I am so sorry you had to go through that; but please, my child, think what you are doing," said Gabby.

"Shut up!" Aza'el yelled at Gabby. Aza'el turned her attention back to the boy. "It is because of people like you why I exist!" Aza'el said as she pointed at the boy. Aza'el walked up to Emily, placed her hand on Emily's shoulder, and said, "He is all yours."

Emily lowered herself down to his level. She was face-to-face with him. He said he was sorry again. Before he was able to say another word, Emily grabbed him by his face and dug her nails into his cheeks. He was screaming as blood was coming from both sides of his face. Emily pulled her nails back out and dropped him. He tried to back away from Emily. Gabby was yelling out to Emily asking her to stop. She tried to convince Emily that she was not like Aza'el. Emily did not listen. Emily told the boy to get on his feet. He did. Emily punched him with both of her fists into his ribs and broke them. He fell right back to the floor. He was still alive. She then turned him around onto his stomach and stabbed her nails into his back pulling out a piece of his spine. The boy was screaming as loud as he could. Emily then picked him up, threw him in a corner, and left him there to bleed to death. Aza'el laughed. The Zals were hungry and Aza'el okayed for them to go ahead and eat him. The witches piled on top of him and started eating him while he was still alive. Gabby turned around. She was not able to watch it anymore.

"How did that feel?" Aza'el asked Emily.

Emily turned to Aza'el, smiled, and said, "It felt good. Nobody will ever hurt me again."

Aza'el smiled, touched Emily's face, and said, "Welcome to my team." Aza'el then walked over to a window and looked out into the sky. She knew the Green Villagers would come looking for Emily. She had to make sure she was ready for them. Aza'el had guard dogs watching over her castle. They are very big and have six legs. When they bark, the ground shakes causing everyone to lose their balance. These dogs are very fast because of their six legs. Aza'el has four of them. Aza'el also had her own goblin. When it was not flying, it turns into a shadow and you cannot see it. As Aza'el was looking out of the window, she heard her goblin howl. "Here they come," she said. She looked straight ahead and saw six Grounders running toward her castle with humans riding on them. Right behind the Grounders were the Green Villager's witches flying on their brooms and running along with them. Aza'el quickly turned around and called out. "Now, now is the time!"

All her Dark Zals quickly grabbed their brooms and flew out of the windows, and some jumped out. Both sides attacked. The witches fought. Mike, Allen, and Pete fought as well. The Grounders jumped and smashed Aza'el's witches, as did Aza'el's large six-legged dogs. One of the dogs barked, and Mike's Grounder tipped over. Mike fell off. Mike got up quickly onto his feet and fought with the weapons he brought from the village. The dog marched toward the Grounder that was tipped over. The Grounder got up onto his feet before the dark dog had the chance to bite it. The Grounder waived its long sharp tail around the dog's neck, lifted the dog up with its tail, and slammed it onto the ground. They tossed and turned fighting each other. The dog managed to back away from the Grounder and jumped toward its neck. The dog bit the Grounder, and the Grounder growled in pain. The Grounder then stabbed the dog in its back with its tail. The dog pulled its teeth out of the Grounder's neck and it fell to the ground. The Grounder's tail was still inside the dog's body. The Grounder threw the dog to the side with its tail, and the dog died. The Grounder stood up straight and growled. The Grounder then saw Mike fighting alone, and the creature ran to help him.

"Good boy," Mike said while they both were running next to each other toward the castle. Mike knew Emily was in there, and he wanted to get her. The Grounder was helping Mike make it to the castle as it protected him from the Dark Zals.

Mayla noticed there were more Dark Zals on their brooms than on the ground. It became a problem for the Klexons. Mayla used her magic to knock down the Dark Zals off of their brooms, and the Klexons attacked. Mike was still running toward the castle with his Grounder right next to him protecting him. One of the witches ran up to Mike's Grounder and stabbed him on the side of its body. The creature stopped running and turned toward her. He let out a small growl and a breath and swung his tail around the witch's neck.

He lifted her up with his tail and threw her away. The Grounder got right back on track and guarded Mike again. Pete and Allen had each other's backs. One of Aza'el's dogs attacked Pete's Grounder, and Pete fell off as the two animals went head on. They pushed each other around with their heads. The dog took a couple of steps back and barked, and the ground shuck. Pete was thrown around on the ground. Right before the dog was going to step on Pete, the Grounder slammed into the dog with his front horn stabbing it. The Grounder carried the dog away on its horn. A Dark Zal saw the opportunity to kill Pete. She ran toward him and got her teeth ready to bite him from the back. She stood right behind him, but before she was able to bite him, a knife went right through her forehead. She dropped to the ground. Pete turned to see what happened and saw the Dark Zal on the ground, and Mitti standing over her.

"I told you not to go without me. In what type of shit did you get us into?" Mitti asked Pete.

He walked over to her and hugged her. "How did you find us?" Pete asked her.

"Don't worry about that now," replied Mitti.

"It was a long ass walk and for what, for this?" asked Nikki as she was looking around trying not to get killed.

"Mike went inside the castle to find Emily. Hurry, I will take you somewhere safe," Pete said to Mitti and grabbed her by her arm.

"No, I am not leaving you," said Mitti and pulled away.

Pete's Grounder returned to be with Pete, but then, a huge sword went straight through its neck. Mitti screamed and Pete yelled, "No!"

The animal slowly dropped to the floor. Pete walked over to the animal and touched it. He placed his hands on the wound and whispered to it, "Thank you for everything."

The animal took its last breath, and Pete got pissed. He looked up and saw the Dark Zal who killed his Grounder.

"A head for a head," the Dark Zal said. She was talking about her sister that Mitti killed.

Pete slowly stood up with his hands rolled up in fists. The Dark Zal ran away. Pete told Mitti and Nikki to hide somewhere in the castle and he will find them later. Mitti agreed, and they both left. Pete wanted to find that witch. He grabbed his bow and arrows and followed her.

Mike finally made it into the castle. As he was running up the stairs, he was calling out for Emily. Aza'el heard Mike and told Briana to go and take care of him. Briana left the main room and met Mike on the stairs on the second floor. She slowly walked up to him and tried to talk him into joining her. Mike did not want to hear it. She pushed him against the wall. He grabbed her by her arms and told her to back off. He told her to go home that she did not know what she got herself into. Briana told him that she was doing everything for them. She still loves him. Mike made it clear to her that it was too late. Mike pushed her, and she fell down the stairs. She looked up and saw him running up to help Emily. It made her angry. She saw a sharp sword hanging on the wall, picked it up, and ran after him. He turned around because he heard her. She tried to stab him with it. "I love you, but you don't care!" She screamed at him as she struck with the sword. He dodged it, but she struck again and again. She cut him on his chest, and the blood was visible through his shirt. "What do you have to say for yourself now, Mike?" she asked him as she walked closer and closer toward him. "If I can't have you, nobody will," she said and swung the sword again. Briana was getting closer and closer toward Mike. She ran at him with the sword toward his chest, but Mike moved to the side and she ran into his knife. She stood for a minute looking into Mike's eyes. She dropped her sword and grabbed the knife that was in her chest. "You killed me. How could you kill me?" she asked Mike as she was slowly backing away from him.

"I'm not ready to die," Mike replied to her.

Briana fell to her knees and then flat on the floor. Mike heard voices upstairs and grabbed his knife back out of her chest. He also took the sword. "Sorry," he said to Briana as she laid there dead. He started running up the stairs again.

Meanwhile, outside of the castle, the Dark Zals were starting to back away and surrender. Two of the dogs were dead and two were left. The dogs were backing away as well. Two of the Grounders were dead, but the other two were still alive. The Klexons surrounded the Dark Zals, and they had nowhere to go. The Dark Zals dropped down to their knees as the Klexons held their weapons aiming it at them. Now, they all were just waiting for Emily and Aza'el. Mayla told the lead warrior Eliot to keep the situation under control while she goes inside the castle. Eliot agreed and told Mayla to be careful.

Mike got to the top and ran into the room. Emily screamed, and her powers threw Mike back again out of the room. He ran back in. At that moment, the cage, where Gabby was held, shook and fell. It cracked, and Gabby was able to kick the door off. She was free. Emily jumped creating a dent into the floor and landed right in front of Mike. She grabbed him by his throat and said, "I am sick and tired of you following me around. I think it's time that ends." She slammed him to the floor. She placed her hands over his chest and applied pressure. He was not able to breathe. At that moment, Pete and Allen ran in through the door.

"Baby girl, what are you doing?" her father asked her and ran up to her.

But instead of her listening, she stopped what she was doing, turned around, and grabbed her father with one hand. She took a knife off the ground with another hand and held it against his throat. At that moment, Mike pulled out the blue antidote rock, which she can't resist but to stay away from. He threw it on the ground right by her feet. She dropped her father and grabbed her stomach as she was backing away from Mike and the rock. Mike got up onto his feet, and Pete asked him if he was all right. Mike and Pete saw their friend lying there dead, broken in pieces, and half eaten. Pete was disgusted. Mike turned his focus back to Emily.

"Listen to me, Emily. This is not who you are. We came here to save you because we love you. I love you, Emily. Please come back to me. Let me have that chance to show you how love is and let me show you who you really are," said Mike.

Aza'el knew what Mike was trying to do, and she had to stop him. She used her power and destroyed the blue rock. The pain Emily was feeling faded. She stood up straight and attacked Mike. She kept throwing him around the room as Aza'el continued to watch and smile. Allen and Pete tried to attack Aza'el, but they had no chance. She lifted her hand up, and her powers threw them both against a wall and held them there, choking them. Meanwhile, Mayla was on her way up.

Mike was thrown around so much by Emily. His shirt was ripped apart. The last time Emily threw Mike against the wall; he stood up onto his feed and locked eyes with her. He felt tired and beaten.

"Why do you keep standing up? Give up already," Emily said in her dark voice.

Mike stood there without his shirt on. He had dirt on his face and was breathing heavily. The sweat was falling off his chest and his back. He had the cut on his chest that was bleeding. Allen and Pete were still not able to move. Mayla finally jumped through the door and saw Aza'el. Aza'el turned her focus to Mayla.

"Well, look who joined our party," said Aza'el.

Mayla attacked Aza'el and Pete, and Allen were free. Mayla and Aza'el locked their eyes at each other as they pushed each other around.

"I will finish you the same way I finished your sister," said Aza'el.

They were throwing punches and kicks at each other. Mayla has gotten hit too many times in the face that she started to bleed. Aza'el was quick and strong. Allen saw Mayla needed help and started walking toward them two, but then, he heard Gabby. Instead, he ran over to Gabby to help her.

Aza'el and Mayla dropped to the floor. Aza'el was on top of Mayla. Aza'el was throwing her fists at Mayla, but Mayla moved her face from side to side and Aza'el missed. When she missed, the prints of her fists showed on the concrete floor right next to Mayla's head. Aza'el got frustrated because she missed, so she grabbed Mayla, picked her up, and started throwing her into the walls. Mayla was getting weak. She did not have any more strength to fight. Allen saw that Mayla needed him so he told Gabby to get up and get moving to a safer spot. He had to help Mayla. The last time Mayla was thrown, she went right through the wall, and the bricks collapsed on top of her. Allen yelled out, "No!" as he watched Mayla get covered by the bricks. Allen looked at Aza'el as she smiled.

Meanwhile, Emily was beating Mike up very bad. He kept on getting back up. Every time he fell, he told her how much he missed her and loved her. He did not even try to hit her back. Emily started to slow down with her punches. She actually started to listen to what he was saying.

"Why do you keep saying all that to me?" she asked him.

"Because I love you," he said to her.

Emily stood in front of him, tired. She lowered her hands down.

Mike closed his eyes for a second and said, "Thank God." He slowly walked closer to her and grabbed her by her arms. He looked into her eyes, and she looked into his. He saw they were still dark. He was not sure what she was going to do next, but he knew he had to try. He continued telling her that she was the love of his life and he would never hurt her. No matter how many times she beat him down, he will not hurt her. She did listen.

"Come back to me, Emily," he said and kissed her.

Emily allowed him to kiss her. She was still breathing heavily from being tired of fighting. She slowly started to relax, and her anger calmed down. Emily's eyes slowly started turning back to her own, but she was still transformed as a Dark Zal.

Aza'el saw it, and she screamed, "No! This cannot be happening. It is not possible. You are a Dark Zal, and no Dark Zal is good." Aza'el was going crazy.

When Mike kissed Emily, her memories came back. Her life flashed inside of her head. She remembered all the good she did for people and all the happiness she had in her life. She remembered who she was. She started apologizing to Mike and telling him she had no idea what she has done to him or anyone else. At that moment, Aza'el tried to run toward Emily to stab her in the back, but Emily's mother jumped in between. Aza'el struck and the knife went right through Gabby's chest.

"Noooooo!" Allen screamed and ran toward his wife. He caught her as she was falling down. Aza'el backed away. He was screaming no over and over again as he held her in his arms. Emily turned around to see what happened and saw her mother lying in her father's arms with a knife in her chest. The same knife she knew belonged to Aza'el. Emily dropped to her knees and looked at her mother. Emily transformed back to human.

"Mom, why did you do that? Mom, please don't go. I need you," she said to her mother.

"Baby, you are my life and my love. I would die for you. Emily, please find a way to find your heart. It is not dark, my child. Fight it. This is not who you are. Find yourself," Gabby said to Emily as she took her last breath. Gabby tilted her head to the side and died right there.

Emily started to breathe heavily again, and she transformed back into a witch, a Dark Zal. Her eyes looked up at her father as she screamed very loud. "Nnnnooooooo!" When Emily screamed, a very strong wind passed through the room. Even the others who waited outside felt the wind push them around.

"What is going on in there?" Eliot asked herself as she continued holding her guard up against the Dark Zals.

The wind was so strong it pushed everyone in the room around including Aza'el. Pete was unconscious the entire time from getting hit in the head with a brick. Emily stood up and faced Aza'el. Aza'el looked at her ring, and she could see that the darkness of it was fading.

"Not possible," said Aza'el.

Mayla was coming back up from under the bricks. She pushed the bricks off of herself. As she was getting back onto her feet, she saw Emily. She couldn't believe what she saw either. Nobody had defeated the power of Aza'el's ring.

"How did you do that?" asked Aza'el as she was slowly backing away from Emily. She was scared now. She did not know what to do. She does not understand how she could lose power from that ring that she herself created. Emily opened her mouth and screamed. Her scream threw Aza'el against the wall. Emily lifted up her hand, and her powers started choking Aza'el. Aza'el waived her hand using her powers to lift up a brick and throw it at Emily. Emily got hit and lost her concentration. Aza'el fell to the floor onto her feet. Emily ran toward Aza'el, and Aza'el waited for her. Emily jumped, but Aza'el stood on the ground waiting. Emily was trying to land on top of Aza'el, but Aza'el caught Emily in air and punched her to the ground. Emily quickly got up, and they fought. They punched and kicked. Both got hit many times, and both were bleeding, but neither of them was giving up. Mayla and the rest of the crew were watching.

Allen was still holding his wife. Pete was coming back to himself. When Pete saw Gabby was dead, he walked over to Allen for support. It was loud in the room because the wind that Emily brought on was still in the room like a tornado. But it did not stop Emily and Aza'el from fighting. Aza'el hit Emily in the back of her head with a brick and Emily fell. When Emily was on the floor, Aza'el was getting closer toward her body. Aza'el kneeled next to Emily's body and grabbed a knife out of her boot.

"You are no use to me now," she said and swung the knife at Emily.

Mike jumped on Aza'el, and he grabbed the knife that was in her hand. They tasseled for it as Emily was getting back onto her feet. Mike used his own knife to try to stab Aza'el, but he missed. However, Mike got her one time right on the side of her face. They both froze for a second. Aza'el touched her face, licked the blood off of her hand, and said, "You mother fucker, you got my pretty face."

Mike exhaled. "Someone lied to you," he responded to her.

Aza'el was about to finish him off, but then, Emily jumped in between them, grabbed Aza'el and jumped out of the third floor window. The wind inside the room went away, and everyone ran toward the window to see if Emily was all right. Emily and Aza'el both landed on their backs. All the Dark Zals and Klexons saw them both lying there. Neither of them moved. Eliot was walking closer to their bodies until Aza'el started to move. Eliot then backed away.

"Help her!" Allen yelled after Mike.

Aza'el was getting up, and Emily was not moving. Aza'el slowly turned to her side and saw Emily still on the ground not moving. She slowly stood up, grabbed the knife that was on the ground, and walked closer to Emily's body. Aza'el sat on top of Emily below her stomach and held the knife with both of her hands above her head. She struck and Emily opened her eyes. Emily grabbed Aza'el's hands and pushed back. They struggled back and forth, and finally, Emily was able to manage to lift her leg up and kneed Aza'el off of herself. Emily quickly got onto her feet. Emily attacked Aza'el by throwing punches, but Aza'el gave them right back. Emily ran and jumped against the castle's wall and did a backflip kicking Aza'el in the face.

"Okay, enough!" said Aza'el and used her power of force to throw Emily against the wall.

As Emily slid to the floor after hitting the wall, Aza'el walked over, and picked Emily up by her shirt. Emily grabbed Aza'el's arms and held on. Emily jumped over Aza'el's head doing a front flip pulling Aza'el along lifting her off the ground and slamming her right back onto the dirt. Emily was in a lot of pain, and she was feeling weak. As Emily stood over her, Aza'el threw some sort of black powder into Emily's eyes, causing Emily to lose sight. Aza'el took that advantage to continuously punch Emily in her stomach. Emily fell on one knee. She had her hands out looking for Aza'el. Aza'el was walking around Emily in a circle.

"Look at you. You look pathetic. With me, you could have ruled two worlds. But no, you had to create more work for me," said Aza'el as she kicked Emily in her chest.

Emily fell backward all the way to the ground. She was not moving. Aza'el jumped up high with the knife in her hand. She planned to land on top of Emily stabbing her right through her heart. Right before Aza'el landed on her, Emily rolled to her side and Aza'el missed. Emily got quickly back on her feet and screamed. She was not able to see anything yet, but the scream threw Aza'el away from her giving Emily time to hear her. Aza'el ran up on Emily again, but Emily listened closely to her footsteps. Before Aza'el struck, Emily pulled out the knife she took from Aza'el while they were fighting, and stabbed Aza'el in her stomach. Aza'el stumbled and fell to her knees. Everyone watched as Emily gave her a push on the shoulder and her body dropped to the ground. Aza'el was laying there, not one movement. Mike and Mayla ran out of the castle and saw Aza'el lying on the ground not moving. She really looked dead. They ran to Emily and hugged her. Emily was weak. They had to hurry up and get her back to the village to give her proper care. She was hardly walking, but Mike was helping her. Eliot approached Emily and gave her a hand. Emily shook her hand, and they smiled at each other. Next thing they knew, they heard Mayla calling out for Emily. Emily and Mike walked over to see what was going on. There was nothing on the ground but the outline where Aza'el's body was lying. She was gone.

"Where is she?" Mike asked.

Emily did not move. She stood next to Mayla.

"It's not over," said Mayla in a low sound voice.

"I know," Emily replied.

One of the Dark Zals was laughing. "You guys thought she was done, ha," said the evil witch.

Emily looked at the evil witch who laughed and told her that she will find Aza'el again and destroy her. At that moment, Allen and Pete walked out of the castle as well. Allen was carrying his wife.

Emily walked as fast as she could to her dad. He placed his wife slowly on the ground and hugged Emily.

"She gave up her life for you," said Allen.

Emily kneeled down by her mother's body and started to cry. Everyone around her was sad.

"That is what people do out of love, my child. She never wanted you to think she didn't love you," said Allen.

"I was a fool. I treated her wrong, and now, I will never be able to tell her how I feel," said Emily.

"She is always listening. She would want you to move on and be happy," said Allen.

Emily held her mother's hand. Mike placed his hand on Emily's shoulder and told her it was time to go. They picked up Gabby and carried her back to the Green Village. Emily walked along, and then, she actually realized that Pete was there. She walked right in front of him and said, "Why are you here? Who gave you any rights to be here?"

Pete was not sure how to respond to that. Mitti got upset because of the way she spoke to him, and she said to Emily, "He helped you. He came here to help you and the others. What is your problem?"

Emily turned her head toward Mitti and said, "He's not here to help me." Emily looked at Pete and asked him, "Is that really why you were here?"

Pete lowered his head down. He did not say anything to Emily, and he did not answer her question. Emily then walked away. Mike and the others were not sure what that was about, but they continued on their walk back to the village. Mike on the other hand did not take his eyes off of Pete. He wondered why Emily was so upset with him. Pete looked back at Mike, and they locked eyes. Mitti asked Pete what that was about, but he told her it was not the right time to talk about it.

Chapter 15

THE NEW BEGINNING

As Mayla and the others returned to the village, they were being greeted kindly and with respect by the others who stayed. Some Klexons and children ran up to them and helped. However, when they noticed Allen carrying his wife, they stood in two lines and bowed their heads down, and everyone got quiet. Emily asked Mayla what they were doing.

Mayla told her, "That's how they show respect toward someone that's not with us anymore."

Emily turned around and saw her dad carrying her mother. That night, Gabby was buried in the Green Village. Emily sat by her mother's grave late into the night. She started to cry thinking about all the bad things she has said to her mother. Mike saw her there from a distance and walked up to her from behind.

"She loves you. No matter what happened between you guys, she still loves you," said Mike.

Emily's tears dropped on the grave. She looked up at the cross they placed for her, and she broke down.

"It is so easy for you to say. I will never be normal again. I will never see my mother again. Everything has been destroyed since I placed this ring on my finger," said Emily and she stood up. She was angry and sad. "If you did not do what you did at that party, I would have never ran into those woods and find this," she said as she lifted the ring in front of his face. She slapped him. When she tried to slap him again, he grabbed her hand and pulled her against his chest. She cried, and he held her closer.

"I am sorry. Nothing was intentionally done. But have you ever for one second thought about that this has happened for a reason? What if someone else found that ring, someone who is not as strong as you are? Aza'el would destroy our world and all these creatures that live here," Mike said to her as he held her.

Emily did not want to hear anything. She backed away from Mike.

"Well, you guys can go home tomorrow. I will stay here," said Emily.

"I'm not going anywhere," he replied and hugged her, lifted her chin up with his hand, and kissed her.

At that moment, a Visionair flew right above them. The big wings spread open, and it flew far into the night. Mike picked Emily up and carried her to their cottage. He laid her down onto the bed and covered her with his body. He took her clothes off and kissed her neck and her chest. She asked him to stop. He looked at her and asked her if that was what she wanted. She did not respond. He slowly moved his way downward spreading her legs open pleasuring her with his mouth. Her head pushed backward as she felt warmth and ready to release. She let out a moan, Mike's hair sliding between her fingers. She releases as she held on tightly around Mike's head. Mike came back up and faced her. He told her he loved her. She stared at him for a second. She knew she loved him too, but she was not sure if this was enough. She always second-guessed their love. She did not respond, and they stared into each other's eyes. He slowly slides himself inside of her. He struck her over and over again slowly holding her body tightly against his. Emily's hands were all over his back holding on tight, her nails digging into his skin. His mouth was by her ear, and they both could feel each other's breath. Emily was feeling pain as she took all of his large manhood. They felt hot and passionate. They both released at the same time. Both laid down next to each other and didn't say a word. Mike turned to hug her, and she turned the other way. Emily was thinking about them and their relationship. She loved him but was unsure. Being with Mike felt amazing, but was it just a fantasy? Emily wondered. Mike asked her if she wanted to talk about what was on her mind. She told him no. Mike still leaned over and placed his arm around her. They both fell asleep.

That next morning, Allen and the rest of the crew were getting ready to go back home. When Emily met up with her father and Mayla, she looked at both of them.

"What will you do, Emily?" her father asked her. Emily was not sure if she wanted to stay with the Klexons or go back with the humans. Emily looked deeply into the ring on her hand. Now that she has control over her powers, her soul, and her heart, she can choose to return back home and have nothing to do with the witches' world; however, she will always remain half human half witch. Or she can let the ring go and worry if someone else will find it again the way she did. She did not know what to do. So much was running through her mind.

"You are able to keep the portal open between the humans and us as long as you have that ring on," said Mayla

"I will never be human again," said Emily.

"Unfortunately, no. Her blood is mixed up with yours," said Mayla.

"Sweetheart, come home with me. I can't lose you and your mother at the same time," said Allen.

Emily looked up at her dad and said, "Dad, I will never be your little girl anymore. I will never have a normal life again."

Allen walked closer to her, grabbed her face with both of his hands, and said, "I accept you the way you are."

Mayla then interrupted and said, "I will be by your side whatever you choose to do."

Emily looked around at everyone. Pete, Mitti, and Nikki were ready to go.

"You all should go now. I will stay here and help Mayla look for Aza'el," said Emily. Emily turned to her dad and said, "I will find her, and she will pay for what she did to Mom."

Allen hugged her and held on real tight. Pete tried to walk up to Emily to say goodbye, but she turned around and walked the other way. Mitti saw that but did not say anything. The humans walked back into the portal and went home, besides Mike. He stayed with Emily. Allen held Emily's hand. She could see tears in his eyes. He hugged her and told her he loved her.

Emily replied, "I love you too, Dad."

Allen was the last one to go home. He walked backward into the portal as he watched his daughter slowly disappear. Emily dropped to her knees and her head down. Gary came from behind and placed his hand on her shoulder.

"It will be okay, my child," he said.

She looked up at him. "You're not going?" she asked him.

Gary turned toward Mayla and said, "I think it's better if I stay here and keep an eye on things."

Emily stood up, faced Gary, and said to him, "I saw her. She said she still loves you and don't ever forget about her and that she keeps watching over you."

His eyes opened wide, and he smiled. "I feel her with me all the time," he said.

Emily smiled and said, "I see her in my dreams, Alona, your wife. She is very pretty. She gives me strength when I can't hold it together."

Gary nodded and thanked her.

Mike walked up to Emily and grabbed her hand. "Everything will be all right," he said.

"I have to find Aza'el and make her pay," said Emily.

"I understand, and I will help you, but you have to be careful. Tell me something. I noticed you acting very strange toward Pete. Is there something I should know?" Mike asked her.

"No!" Emily yelled and started walking away.

"Why are you being so defensive?" Mike asked her as he followed after her.

"I don't want to talk about it, okay," she replied to him.

Mike grabbed Emily by her arm right before they walked into their cottage. "You need to stop playing around. I am here because I love you, and if there is something I should know, you need to tell me," said Mike.

"What do you want from me? To open up all the way to you just because you fucked me?" she asked him.

"Oh is that what I did? Just fuck you. I call it something else," he said to her.

Emily turned away from him, opened the door, and went inside their cottage. Mike followed. The Klexons were watching them argue. Mike closed the door behind himself and yelled at Emily, "You are so blinded, you don't see what you have standing right here in front of you. But you know what? If you do not want to talk, that's fine. I tried and I know I fought hard for you." Mike turned around, grabbed the doorknob, and was about to leave and that is when she said, "He watched them do it."

Mike stopped at the door. "Who watched who doing what?" Mike asked her. He turned back around away from the door to look at her. But she had her back turned to him and crossed her arms like she was hugging herself. "What is going on, Emily?" Mike asked her again.

"That night, at the school party, when you disappeared, those football players and Pete chased me all the way to the woods across the street from the school. They were being all touchy and stuff, so I ran outside looking for you. But I did not see you. They came after me, and I ran away into the woods. It did not take long before they found me," said Emily. She turned around and looked at Mike. "They raped me, Mike. They raped me, both, one after another while I laid there on the ground asking Pete to help me as he stood there and watched. It felt like it lasted for years how terrible it was," said Emily as tears fell down her face.

100

Mike stood there, he did not know what to say to her. He balled up his fists, punched the cabinet that was next to him, and stormed out the door. Emily yelled after him, but he did not return. Mike stormed out of the cottage, down the path, and into the woods. The Klexons who were working outside watched him leave. He was going toward the portal. Mayla saw him leave as well, and she ran into Emily's cottage. Mayla asked Emily if everything was all right. Emily looked at Mayla with tears in her eyes.

"He had to know the truth," she said.

Mayla nodded and walked over to hug Emily.

When Mike got out of the portal in the human's world, he walked straight to Pete's house. He had to make sure nobody saw him coming out of the woods. Mike was so mad he banged on Pete's door with his fists. When Pete opened the door, he welcomed Mike with a smile. Before Pete was able to say anything, Mike started punching him in his face. The boys were inside the house fighting. More like Mike was beating him up. Pete was being thrown around in his house. Pete's parents and Mitti who were there tried to stop Mike, but they did not succeed. Mike pushed them off of him. Pete's mouth was bleeding badly. Mike held Pete with one hand by his shirt and continued to punch him over and over again. Mitti started screaming at Mike telling him to let Pete go. Finally, Mike was done and he yelled, "That is for Emily, for allowing those basters to do that to her."

When Mitti heard those words, she dropped to the floor right next to Pete. She held Pete as she looked up at Mike. "What the fuck are you talking about?" Mitti asked Mike as he was walking out of the house.

Mike stopped at the doorframe, turned to Mitti, and said, "He let them rape her."

Mitti was shocked with what she heard. She remembered when Pete disappeared with the football players that night and she questioned him where he was but he couldn't give her a good answer. Mike left the house and slammed the door behind himself. Mitti got up from the floor and slowly grabbed her things and her purse. She started walking out of the house as Pete called after her. Pete's parents walked over to help him get up onto his feet.

"Where is Mitti?" Pete asked his parents.

"She left son," replied his dad.

Mike returned back to the Green Village. He stormed into his cottage and slammed the door shut behind him. Emily was sitting on the bed waiting for him. She asked him where he was. He did not respond. She saw his bloody hands.

"What did you do?" she asked him.

"I gave him what he deserved," Mike responded. He then went into the bathroom to clean up.

Chapter 16

THE TWIST

A driana and Megan were still looking for Briana. The girls finally went to her house and asked her mother if she knew where Briana was. Her mother said no that she thought Briana was with them.

"She is probably with Mitti. We will go find her," said Adriana and the girls left.

Briana's mother told the girls to inform Briana to check in.

Meanwhile, Aza'el was back at her castle, alive and well. She had a hidden underground passage that led to a cave. No one knew of this underground area. She was healing herself with healing water and leaves. She was naked sitting on a rock and pouring healing water over her wounds. She was healing quickly.

"Damn that girl. How did this happen? I have to find a way to gain control over her again, or get my ring back, but how?" Aza'el asked herself.

She slowly got up on her feet and wrapped herself around with a gown. She walked over to one of her water pons and asked the water to show her where her Dark Zals were being captured. An image showed up in the water, and Aza'el saw her Dark Zals being held as hostages in the Green Village inside a cottage, passed the forest. The cottage was fenced in. Aza'el made a decision that she will get them out. She waived her hand over the water, and the image disappeared. She turned quickly and walked away from it.

Back at the village, Emily was sitting on her bed. She was worried about Mike. She knocked on the bathroom door, but he did not say anything. She knocked again, and he opened the door. He stood there looking down at her. She looked up at him and hugged him. Mike did not do anything but stand there. He then walked toward the bed and sat on it.

"What is wrong?" Emily asked him but he didn't respond.

"Why are you giving me the silence treatment?" she asked him. Mike was quiet for about a minute and then asked her why she did not tell him sooner.

Emily did not say anything.

"All these days passed by and you never mention anything to me. I just want to know why. Do you not trust me or not believe in me? I just left my life behind and my education and my family for you. So I would like to know why you can't talk to me about things that happened to you," Mike asked her angrily.

"Do you really think you are the only one who left something behind? That is why I don't talk to anyone about my problems. Everyone acts like they are perfect. When they hear my problems, they just look at me like I'm such a fuck up. I have learned to deal with life on my own. If you feel like you have left something behind for me, you know where the portal is. I don't have a choice but to be here, but you do," Emily responded.

Emily stepped outside for some fresh air. It was getting dark. She walked down onto the open field and whistled for her Visionair. Maxi flew over the forest and onto the field landing in front of her, and she hopped on him. They flew away. Mike stepped outside and watched them fly away into the deep moonlight. Mayla's assistant (Lin) stood outside of Mayla's cottage and watched Mike. Mike felt a presence, and he looked her way. She quickly turned around and walked across the village into her own cottage.

"What was she doing out here at this time of the night?" he asked himself.

Emily was flying around with Maxi, between the trees and mountains. They flew high into the sky and then low. Maxi flew fast high up passed the clouds and stood in one place. His wings opened and closed. Emily laid her head on the creature's back and said, "I just feel so free up here with you. No worries, no thoughts, no evil. I wish I could stay up here forever." She held on tight as he spread his wings wide and sped through the clouds and into the forest. Emily enjoyed the ride. She was dropped back off at her cottage, and Maxi flew away.

When she entered the cottage, Mike was up waiting on her.

"I am going to bed," Emily said quickly.

"Wait, I did not mean what I said in a wrong way. I am here because I want to be here. I just ask for you to allow me to be there. As long as you allow me to be by your side, you will never be alone," he said to her.

Emily looked at him and said, "That is good to know." She laid down and Mike followed.

The following morning, Megan arrived at Adriana's house. As Adriana opened the door, Megan right away asked her if she heard from Briana. Adriana said no.

"I am really starting to worry," said Megan.

"It is too early for this, Megan," said Adriana as she stood in the door with her pajamas on rubbing her eyes.

"Come in. Let me get dressed. We will go and look for her. Maybe her mother found her," said Adriana.

The girls and Briana's mother were starting to question Briana's disappearance. They finally went to the police station and filed a missing person report. Later on in the day, Adriana and Megan left to knock on Emily's door and her father answered.

"What are you two doing here?" Allen asked them.

"Hey, sir, we just stopped by to see if Emily was home," asked Megan.

"Why? What do you need her for?" Allen asked them.

"We have been looking for our friend Briana and we cannot find her anywhere, so we wanted to see if Emily maybe saw her somewhere," said Adriana.

"No, Emily has left to see her grandmother for a couple of days. She will be back soon," said Allen and quickly closed the door. The two girls thought he was a little weird, and they walked off his porch. Allen watched them leave through the window. Allen knew they already reported it to the police and he hoped the police would not stick their noses too far into the woods once they start looking for Briana. He knew he had to warn the Klexons.

Chapter 17

ACCEPTANCE

Back at the Green Village, Emily and Mike were outside helping the Klexons build more weapons. Emily was sitting on a rock heating up the metal part of her knife. She turned her head and watched Mike. He had his shirt off and was sweating. His chest was dirty. She was checking out his arms the way he struck the hammer at the swords making them sharper. Mike dropped the hammer, swiped his hand over his forehead, and looked up catching Emily looking at him. She quickly put her head down and got back to work. Mike smiled and got back to work as well.

Suddenly, Mayla interrupted Emily. She wanted to show her something. She took Emily on a walk.

"I want to show you why it is very important for us to take care of our land and our nature. It has life, which gives us life. You see, Alona was the one who created all this for us. She taught us that we do not need to be evil. She taught us that we do not need to kill to survive," said Mayla.

Emily listened closely. As they walked down a path through a couple of trees and passed the forest, they ended up in another different type of forest. It was very colorful. Many different creatures were flying around, walking, swimming, and working. Emily asked Mayla what they were doing.

"They are taking care and nourishing the tree-flower," Mayla responded.

Emily looked closer. She noticed a big tree in front of her. She moved her head upward and saw how big and tall it was. It had big, long, green branches with white leaves. It opened up just like a flower. It grew out as a tree, but on top, it blossomed into a flower. The flower was transporting energy into the land, and when the creatures would eat and drink from that land, it gave them life, energy, and powers. This is how they survived. Emily walked slowly toward the tree-flower. When she got close, she heard something. Emily touched the tree-flower with her hand. She placed her ear onto the body of the tree-flower and was able to hear a beat, a beat that sounded just like a heartbeat. Emily looked at Mayla.

"Yes, it's alive," said Mayla.

"This is incredible," said Emily.

"Aza'el would love to take this away from us. She wants us to kill others and humans to survive just how she does. She feeds off from killing, blood and flesh. We have an opportunity to live differently. Not all witches have to be evil," said Mayla.

Emily understood, and then, they both left the forest allowing the creatures to continue working on nourishing the tree-flower.

Toward the end of the day, Mayla told everyone to go ahead and relax for the night. She reminded them how hard they worked and that she was proud of them. Emily sat down on a rock, tired and feeling dirty and sore. Mike walked up to her and asked her if she was okay.

"Yes, just very tired. All this is a lot of work," she said.

Mike laughed and picked her up. He carried her away, behind some bushes. She asked him where he was taking her. He said he found this beautiful waterfall he wanted to show her. As they arrived, he put her down on her feet. She looked around. The water was nice and clean. The waterfall was glistening from the moonlight above.

"This is beautiful," she said. Mike slowly approached her from the back. He placed his hands on her shoulders taking her shirt off. He started kissing her neck as she closed her eyes and placed her head backward on his shoulder. She then turned around and kissed him.

He was unbuckling her pants and pulled them down. He picked her up and carried her into the water. That's when she noticed he was naked. She smiled at him. He carried her into the water dropping her onto her feet. He continued to kiss her, his fingers grabbing her long dark hair. He unbuckled her bra and took it off including her panties. He picked her up in the water, and she curled her legs around his waist. Now, she was able to look down at him as his face was by her breast. He placed her on top of his manhood, and it slid right in. She held on around his neck. Her head fell backward as he struck himself deeper and deeper inside of her. She let out a moan. He kissed her breast and sucked on her nipple. He then looked up at her and watched her face as he continuously lifted her up and down on his manhood. He thought to himself how beautiful she looked in the moonlight. Water slowly splashed around them from the movement. She released first and he right after. They held on tightly to each other's bodies. Mike lifted her up and off of his manhood and dropped her down onto her feet. Her hair a little wet. The water surrounded her around her breast. He told her how beautiful she was. He told her how happy he was that she was back in his life. She placed her finger on his lips telling him to be quiet.

"Everything is fine now. I know what you did for me. I should have told you sooner, but I was ashamed. You made me realize that I should not stop living my life because of other people and what they did to me. As far as me being a half Dark Zal, I can control and deal with that now. I'm not going anywhere," she said to him.

They both continued to kiss in the moonlight.

That following morning, Emily and Mike decided to go back to their world. Emily told Mayla that she had to go visit her father, to make sure he was all right and to make sure none of the humans found the portal. Mayla agreed. Mayla told Emily to return by the following day because she knew Aza'el would be looking for her.

"Aza'el knows that together, we are strong. Return quickly because she will try to find you when you are alone," said Mayla.

"I will," Emily replied.

"I will look after her," said Mike.

They both left into the portal.

When they arrived home, she told Mike she was going to see her father alone. Mike understood and told her he would check on her later. Mike left to see his family. When Emily arrived at the house nobody was there. One of Emily's neighbors told Emily that her father moved. Emily asked her neighbor where, and the neighbor told her. Emily walked around looking for the new house. When she found it, she saw her dad working on his car in the backyard. Emily walked to the backyard and called out to her father. Allen looked up and saw his daughter. He was so happy to see her. He dropped his tools, walked up to her and hugged her. He then quickly went back to work on his car. Emily noticed he was acting strange. They were both quiet until Emily finally spoke.

"Why the move, Dad?" Emily asked him.

"I had to. I couldn't stay another day in that house. We have to start fresh, Emily," Allen replied.

"What do you mean? Because Mom is gone?" she asked him.

Allen stopped working on his car and dropped his tool to the ground. He looked at Emily and said, "I heard a voice mail on your mother's cell phone. You know, when I got home, I went through her things, cried all day and all night, smelling her clothes. Well, I saw her phone had a voice mail. I listened to it. She was having an affair, Emily."

Emily couldn't believe what she just heard. She thought her parents loved each other. Emily got frustrated and upset.

"Why did you guys get married? It seems like our entire life has been fucked up and filled with lies. Was anything real here? Now, Mom is gone and she did not even have a chance to explain herself," Emily yelled at her father with anger.

She was so tired of lies and betrayal. Emily didn't even care anymore. She started walking toward the front of the house, and then, her dad said, "Hey, hey, now calm down. She is till your mother. We both love you very much. Your mother had a hard time showing you love, but that does not mean that she didn't."

Emily stopped walking. "But she gave her time and love to another man. How did she have time for this other man but not us?" Emily asked her father.

She turned to face her dad. Allen got mad. He did not want to hear that.

"I said enough, Emily!" he yelled at her and walked up to her face.

Emily looked up at her dad.

"Your mother is dead, and I will always love her and miss her," he said to her.

Emily did not say anything. She stood there, helpless. Her dad saw in her eyes she was hurting and he hugged her.

"I love her too," said Emily.

Allen held his daughter.

"I know you are going through a lot. Everything will be okay. I got us a new house, and we will start fresh. Your mother will always be in our hearts," said Allen.

Emily nodded and told her dad she will go see her new room. He let her go. As she walked away, before she entered inside the house, she turned to her father and said, "I think it's time for me to move out on my own, Dad."

Her father stared at her with nothing to say. She entered the house and disappeared. Her father watched the door shut behind her. He did not want to hear that. She was all he had left. But he also understood she was growing up.

A couple of hours later, Allen went upstairs to check on Emily. She was going through some of her mother's things. Allen asked if he could join her. Emily nodded. Both of them were looking at pictures. They laughed and had a good time. When they were done, Allen told Emily that the two girls from her school were looking for her.

"I don't know why they would be looking for me. We are not friends," said Emily.

"They were looking for Briana. The cops cannot snoop around in the woods looking for her because they might find the portal," said Allen.

Emily agreed with her dad and said that she will bring it to Mayla's attention. Allen stood up off of the floor and told her he was going to the store to get them some food. Before he left her room, he asked her if anything was going on at the village. Emily told him the Klexons were preparing themselves for another of Aza'el's attacks. Allen told his daughter that maybe she should leave that stuff alone and let them handle it. Emily kept her head down as she flipped through more pictures of her mother.

"I don't really have a choice, Dad," she said.

Meanwhile, in the middle of the night, Aza'el made it into the Green Village. She did not want to attack, but she wanted to free her Zals. She found them and slowly crept through the woods, over the gate, and into the cottage where they were kept as hostages. She used her powers to break the lock and entered. Her Dark Zals saw her and got excited. Aza'el told them to be very quiet and to follow her. She showed them the way out, and they followed. They took the passage through the back of the forest. Once they were out of the village, Aza'el had their brooms waiting on them. Each Dark Zal grabbed a broom and followed Aza'el back to their underground cave. Once they arrived back at the underground castle, the Dark Zals were laughing and celebrating because they were free. Aza'el yelled at them to be quiet.

"I am very disappointed in each and every one of you. You failed me. There are enough of you altogether to destroy the Klexons, but you failed. You will fight again and don't you even think about losing, because if you do, I will kill you myself. Do I make myself clear?" she yelled at them, and they all nodded their heads. Aza'el then ordered two of her female Dark Zals to go into the human's world and kill some humans and bring them to her because she was thirsty for their blood. The two Dark Zals bowed their heads and left the castle. When the two Dark Zals arrived into the human's world, they were hiding between the trees. They were very careful not to be seen by any humans. The two Dark Zals locked their eyes on two human males. They looked young and healthy. One of the Zals licked her top lip and smiled. The two males were walking back to their car from a bar. They were drunk, talking and laughing. One pulled out his car keys and tried to open his door. Before he opened his door, there was a crash sound on top of his car.

"What the hell?" the driver said, and both males backed away from the vehicle. They looked up and saw one of the Dark Zals standing on top of the car. The driver dropped his car keys. Both of the men saw her ugly scary face. They started running. However, the other Dark Zal came down from above and landed right in front of them. The witch that was on top of the car hopped down and laughed. One of the young men asked them what they wanted. One of the witches told them they wanted their flesh. The witch that was in front of them ran quickly like the wind and grabbed one of the guys along. She kept on running until they disappeared into the woods. The other young man who was still standing heard his friend's scream slowly fade away as he was being dragged into the dark woods. The man that was left behind tried to run, but the Dark Zal caught him.

"Please don't kill me. Please don't kill me," he said.

The Dark Zal ripped his shirt open, and she saw his smooth, tasty chest. She knew she was supposed to bring the flesh and blood back to Aza'el, but she really wanted to taste him herself, so she did. Her teeth so sharp went right through his neck. She was not able to stop drinking his blood. She left his neck and went for his chest and the wrists. His body slowly dropped to the ground, and the Dark Zal continued to eat his flesh. When she was done, she left the body in the parking lot and ran into the forest and back to Arfabele. When she arrived, Aza'el asked her why she was late. The Dark Zal said she was trying to find a human to bring to her but had no luck. The other witch who was with her earlier knew she was lying, but did not say anything. Aza'el walked around her, looked closer at her face, and saw a drop of blood on the side of her mouth.

"You liar. I sent you out there, and you come back empty handed and lie about it? I will show you what happens when my kind betrays me," said Aza'el.

Aza'el raised her hand, and the witch started screaming. Other witches (Dark Zals) who stood around backed away. The lying witch continued to scream in pain as Aza'el used her powers to rip her skin right on her chest, and then, Aza'el struck her nails into her and pulled out her heart. Once Aza'el pulled the lying witch's heart, she turned into ashes. Aza'el held the witch's heart in her hand, and faced her other followers.

"I will destroy you if you betray me," she said to the rest of her Dark Zals and then slammed the heart onto the floor.

The other witches were terrified.

Allen was home alone. He was cooking dinner and felt very lonely. He sat down and turned on the TV. The news was on. On the news, it showed a young man missing and the other murdered, but nobody had any answers. Allen placed his food down on the table.

"No, this can't be. This would mean that the Dark Zals are here," he said to himself.

At that moment, there was a knock on the door. He opened it, and it was Nikki.

"Hi, I was wondering if Emily was home," Nikki asked Allen.

"Sure, she should be upstairs," Allen replied.

Allen went upstairs to get her, but she was not in her room. He came back down and looked at Nikki.

"What is it?" she asked Allen.

"She's not here," he responded in a confused way.

"I will come back later then," said Nikki.

Allen nodded and Nikki left.

Mike was at his parents' house packing. He knew he was going back to Arfabele to help Emily. As he was putting his belongings into his car, Pete was walking up his driveway.

"What are you doing here?" Mike asked him.

"I came to talk to you," Pete replied. He had a bruise on his face and a fat lip. "Look, man, you have been my boy for a very long time. I never meant for any of that to happen. I made a huge mistake. I did not hurt her or touch her, man, but I know that is not an excuse. I should have helped her," said Pete.

Before he was able to speak further, Mike cut him off. "You should have fucked both of those guys up. That's what you should have done! What they did was some sick shit, and in a way, I don't feel bad for what they got," said Mike aggressively.

"You are right. But what was I supposed to do? She was new to the school, and they were my boys. We are a team, and we stick together," said Pete.

Mike looked at Pete with his angry face and said, "Fuck you and your team." Mike hopped in his car and left. He stopped at a coffee shop to grab a few things for Emily. That was when Megan and Adriana walked in.

"Hey, Mike, what are you up to? Where is Emily?" Adriana asked him.

"Around, why?" Mike replied.

"Well, we have been looking for Briana, and we cannot find her anywhere. So we thought maybe Emily knows where she is," said Megan.

"Why would Emily know where she is? They are not even friends," said Mike.

"Last time I spoke with Briana, she said something about Emily being weird, something about witch craft. Do you know anything about that? I mean, I find it strange that all of a sudden Briana just disappears," said Adriana.

Mike looked at both of the girls, and he did not know what to say at first.

He inhaled and said, "Good luck finding her." He walked passed them, out of the coffee shop, and into his car.

"He did not answer my question," said Adriana to Megan.

Meanwhile, Emily was at Gary's old bookstore. She had the keys and let herself in. She walked around the store looking for more books about witches. She searched for solutions on how to defeat Aza'el and how she could become a human again. However, she did not have any luck. She left the store late at night and walked back to her dad's house. Mike was outside Allen's house waiting on her. As Emily walked up the driveway, she asked, "Are we ready to go?"

"Yes, but your dad was looking for you. Also, Megan and Adriana bumped into me today, and they questioned me about Briana. It seems Briana said something to Adriana about you having powers," said Mike.

"Okay, that is bad. I forgot about Briana. I will take care of it. Don't worry. Let me say goodbye to my dad. I will be right back," said Emily.

Emily walked into the house, and her dad was sitting at the dining room table.

"Where were you? Nikki was looking for you," said Allen.

"Why is everyone looking for me? What did she want?" asked Emily.

"I'm not sure. She didn't say," said Allen.

Emily was holding some books in her hands. Allen watched her gather her things.

"Are you leaving now?" he asked her.

"Yes, Dad," she responded and walked up to him.

They hugged, and he held his daughter for a while. He kissed the top of her head as he always did when she was little. She remembered those kisses. A tear fell down her face.

"I love you, Dad," she said.

"I love you too. If there's anything you need, you come to me," said Allen.

She nodded and left the house with Mike. Her father stayed at the front door watching the car leave. Emily looked back at her dad as they drove off. She hated leaving him.

"Are you okay?" Mike asked her.

"Yes. Let's finish this, so everyone can get back to their lives. I need to find Aza'el," said Emily.

Emily and Mike arrived that night at the Green Village. They went to their cottages and relaxed for the night. Mike left his car in the woods covered with leaves and bushes. The following morning, Mayla knocked on Emily's door. Emily yelled out to come in, as she was reading a book.

"We have a problem," said Mayla.

"What is it?" asked Emily.

"The Dark Zals escaped. Aza'el must have helped them. I don't understand how nobody saw anything," said Mayla.

Emily quickly got onto her feet and ran toward the door. She looked outside and saw how everyone was freaking out.

"What are we going to do now?" asked Emily.

"That's not all. She murdered two humans last night. I have to send a couple of Klexons into the human's world for protection," said Mayla.

"That is risky," said Emily.

"Yes, I know, but what choice do we have?" asked Mayla.

"I will go back and forth to check up on things. Nobody will suspect anything," said Emily.

Mayla shook her head.

"That is too risky. Aza'el will attack you when you are alone. You have her ring. She will want it back," said Mayla.

"Well then, send some protection with me. Tell them to be careful so they don't get seen by any humans. All I need is two of your good warriors, no more than that. I do not want them to create any attention. They just need to stay hidden," said Emily.

Mayla nodded and told Emily to be careful.

"I will go back home later today to check up on things. I am sure they come at night," said Emily.

Later on that evening, Emily made her way back to the human's world. On her way back to her father's house, she knew she had to have a couple of words with Adriana and Megan. She had to find out how much they knew. Two of Mayla's good warriors went along with Emily. When Mayla returned back to her cottage after she walked Emily to the portal, everything inside her cottage was gone and what was left behind was destroyed. Mayla ran outside and screamed at everyone.

"Who was here? Who came into this cottage? Answer me!" she yelled, but nobody answered.

"We did not see anyone," one of the Klexons replied.

Mayla looked at everyone. Lin walked up to her and asked her what was wrong. Mayla did not respond to Lin. She knew she couldn't trust anyone until she found out who destroyed her potions. Mayla turned her back to Lin, walked into her cottage and closed the door.

When Mike returned from working in the forest and practicing with the Grounders, he was tired and dirty. Before he went into his own cottage, he heard some banging noises in Mayla's cottage, so he decided to stop there first. He knocked on her door. She told him to come in. She was cleaning up. Mike saw how everything was destroyed. He asked her what happened.

"I don't know who did this, but all my potions are destroyed. Whoever did this did it to help Aza'el," said Mayla. Mike could hear the worry in her voice.

"Hey, we will defeat her. We can do it without magic. We have to believe in one another," said Mike.

Mayla listened to his words. She looked up at him.

"You are right. Everyone here is worth fighting for," said Mayla.

"Where is Emily?" Mike asked her.

"Something happened in town so she left to check on things," said Mayla.

"What? She left alone?" asked Mike.

"Yes, but I did send a couple of my warriors to look after her," said Mayla.

Mike nodded his head. He said he will check up on her if she does not return soon.

Meanwhile, Emily was home with Allen. As they both sat on the couch, her father asked her if everything was all right. She told him that all of Aza'el's witches escaped. He asked her what will happen now. Emily said she did not know but she had to talk to Megan and Adriana to find out how much they know.

"I hear they have been questioning too many people about me and Briana," said Emily.

"Yes, what can we do about that? I mean the girl is dead," said Allen.

"I will take care of it. It will look like she ran away," said Emily.

Emily then stood up and went to her room and changed into different clothes. She came back downstairs and straight out the door. It was nighttime outside, and her dad watched her leave.

"I wonder what she meant by she will take care of it?" her dad asked himself.

Emily was looking for Adriana around town and then realized she might be at the boxing facility. As Emily walked into the gym, she right away saw Adriana. She was boxing. Adriana also saw Emily at the door and stopped training. Adriana told her trainer to give her a second, and she walked off of the ring. Emily walked inside and toward Adriana. Emily asked her if she had a minute to talk. Adriana told her no that she was training, but they could meet up tonight at the restaurant around the corner. Emily agreed to meet her there tonight and left. Adriana went back to her training. Later on in the evening, Adriana was still in her workout clothes carrying her backpack. She waited in front of the restaurant for Emily. She finally saw Emily walking down the street toward the restaurant. Adriana started to walk toward Emily's way.

"You are late," said Adriana.

"I had something to do real quickly," said Emily.

"Well, anyways, I wanted to ask you if you have seen Briana anywhere. She has been gone for a couple of days now, and we can't find her. Her mother is getting worried as well," said Adriana.

"Why would I know where she is at? We are not even friends," Emily told her as she stared into Adriana's eyes.

"Listen, Briana saw you talking to that old bookstore guy. She said something about you doing magic and having some sort of powers. Did you do something to her because she found out? I am not sure what she was talking about, but ever since she found that out, she has disappeared," said Adriana.

"So she runs away from home and goes who knows where, and you blame me for it? How many times did you guys treat me like shit and all I did was stay away from all of you? Briana was a bitch. But that does not mean that I have anything to do with her disappearance. You need to stop looking for me and leave me alone," said Emily, and she started to walk away.

"I don't believe you. I think you got mad at her for treating you like crap, and now, you did something to her. I think you know where she is and I will go straight to the cops," said Adriana.

Emily stopped walking away, but then, Adriana turned around and was leaving.

"Wait, you are making a mistake. You can't walk around accusing people of something stupid like that when you don't even know what happened to her or where she could be at. Why do you choose to mess with me? We don't even know each other," said Emily.

Adriana stopped walking and turned around to face Emily. They were a couple of feet away from one another. They started to argue in the parking lot. Emily got tired of going back and forth, but she knew she had to get rid of Adriana. Adriana told Emily she had nothing else to say, and she was going to the cops. Adriana turned away with her back toward Emily and was walking away across the parking lot. Emily turned her focus onto a parked car. Emily used her mental powers to turn the car on and move it. She made the car drive right into Adriana killing her. Emily then parked the car back where it was and walked over to Adriana's body.

"I told you to leave me alone. You made me do this to you," said Emily.

She then looked around to see if anyone saw her, but nobody was around and it was dark. Emily left the scene and walked home.

Aza'el felt Emily's rage and she laughed. She was sitting in her thrown chair, laughing. She held up the ring and watched it swirl in the color of black.

Aza'el said to herself, "She is coming back to me. I can feel her." Aza'el laughed loudly. She quickly got on her feet and ordered her Dark Zals to get ready.

"We will go destroy the villagers and find Emily. Go get ready. Do not make me tell you twice!" she yelled at them, and they all ran to grab any weapon they could find inside the castle.

"How will we do this? Emily is very powerful," said one of the Dark Zals.

"If I can feel her evil actions, this means we still have a chance. We will destroy the Klexons first and then capture Emily while she is alone," said Aza'el and smiled.

The following morning, Adriana was on the news. Allen was watching it as Emily was in the kitchen making herself some food.

Allen turned to her and said, "The girl that was looking for you, Adriana. The police said she was hit by a car last night," said Allen.

"Oh, damn, that sucks," said Emily.

"Emily, you left last night looking for her. Did you have anything to do with this?" He asked her.

Emily stopped preparing her breakfast and turned to her father.

"I did not see her last night. I looked everywhere for her, but I did not find her."

She turned back around and continued on preparing her food. Allen nodded and turned back to the TV. Emily grabbed her food and sat next to her dad and started to eat. She looked at her dad one more time and then at the news. She was saddened by the news; however, she also felt like Adriana deserved it.

Back at the Green Village, Mike and Mayla were still inside the cottage when they heard loud noises. They ran out to see what was going on. They saw Dark Zals flying on their brooms attacking their village.

"It's Aza'el!" Mayla yelled out loud and ran to help others.

The Dark Zals were setting their cottages on fire and their trees. The Klexons were fighting back. However, they were not prepared and did not make it in time to their weapons. The ones that did make it quickly geared up and fought back. Mike ran into Eliot's cottage, grabbed the horn, and blew into it to call out to the Grounders. It took a couple of minutes for them to show up, but Mike saw them coming. He ran toward his Grounder and hopped on top of it. The Grounder used its long tail to wrap it around the flying Dark Zals and smash them against the ground. At that moment, Aza'el flew in with her goblin. She was sitting on its back. They were up in the air. The goblin's wings opened and closed. The wind from the wings blew at Mayla and her Klexons. Mayla and the others watched Aza'el from the ground, as nobody moved.

"Hi, Mayla, we meet again," said Aza'el as she was looking down at Mayla. "Well, you have made it very comfortable here I see," she said.

"What do you want?" Mayla asked her.

"Where is she?" Aza'el yelled.

Mayla did not respond. Mike and three Klexons that were sitting on top of the Grounders had enough of Aza'el, and they started to attack. One of the Klexons aimed an arrow right at Aza'el and shot it out. Aza'el caught it with her own hand and then threw it back at the Klexon hitting her right in the chest.

"You guys still don't know who you are fucking with!" Aza'el said as she flew to the ground with the goblin and landed right in front of Mayla. Aza'el stepped off of the goblin and walked around Mayla. Everyone else was still. Nobody knew what was going to happen next.

"Well, well, sister, we meet again. What a shame if our parents saw us like this right now. What do you think they would say? Oh no, let me guess. That you are their favorite, their good one, their no problem one. Well, guess what. Right now, I don't give a damn what anybody thinks, because I am so fed up with everyone's bullshit, including you. I could just rip your throat out right now," Aza'el said as she gripped her hand around Mayla's throat.

Eliot ran to attack Aza'el, but Aza'el raised her other hand at Eliot and yelled to stop. Eliot did.

"You know what? This is too easy. I need you to put up a fight, okay," Aza'el said to Mayla and quickly turned around and jumped onto her goblin, and they flew up in the air.

As the goblin was flying passed the village, Mayla ran after her sister and grabbed onto the goblin's leg. The goblin's body turned left and right almost knocking Aza'el off. Aza'el grabbed a hold of the creature and told it to stay steady. Aza'el looked down and saw Mayla holding on to the goblin. Aza'el took the creature for a rough ride, but Mayla did not let go. The goblin smashed Mayla against trees, branches, and rocks, but Mayla still held on. Aza'el finally jumped off of the goblin and pulled Mayla with her. Aza'el slammed Mayla against the ground and continued to kick her in her stomach. At this point, they were in the Green Village forest. Mayla got back up onto her feet and returned the favor by kicking and punching Aza'el. Aza'el grabbed Mayla by her throat and started choking her. Mayla tried her best to get away, to take Aza'el's hands off of her throat, but Aza'el was too strong. Mayla tried to kick her, but Aza'el moved. Mayla started losing her conscience.

"Finally, die already," said Aza'el as she squeezed around Mayla's throat.

Aza'el slowly lowered Mayla's body to the ground and cracked her neck to make sure she was dead. Aza'el looked up, and there it was. She found the living tree-flower. Aza'el walked toward it and around the living thing. She was amazed how she could hear its heartbeat when she placed her ear on it. She remembered when she was a kid, she used to help take care of it.

"Well, it is time for this thing to go," she said to herself.

The small creatures that lived there tried to jump on top of Aza'el to stop her, but Aza'el waived her hands and her powers blew the creatures away. Aza'el approached the tree-flower closer and pulled out a potion. As she opened the top of the bottle, she heard Mike yell.

"No! Don't!"

Aza'el exhaled and got very annoyed with him.

"Okay, like I will listen to you," she responded to him.

"Where is Mayla? She is your sister. What did you do to her?" Mike asked her.

"She is not my sister anymore and has not been for a very long time! We are very different," said Aza'el.

Mike was walking closer and closer toward Aza'el, and that is when he saw Mayla's dead body. He felt crushed but had to focus on Aza'el right now. Mike was trying to get closer to Aza'el, but she was already ahead of him. When he took one more step toward her, she blew him away with her force. He flew backward and landed in a pond. Aza'el turned her focus back to the tree-flower and poured the potion all over it. As the sprinkles flew around, Aza'el puffed at the potion so it could spread all over the place. The tree-flower slowly started to rust. Aza'el was laughing.

"All this will be dead, and all of you will belong to me!" she said as she pointed at the little creatures, fairies, and trolls that lived there.

The creatures lowered their heads. The tree-flower was dying, and that meant that the rest of the forest will die too. There will be no life there anymore. Aza'el whistled for her goblin. It came to her and picked her up, and they flew away. Mike was coming out of the pond and saw what she did. He slowly walked closer to the tree-flower. He asked the creatures if there was anything he could do. One of the fairies answered him, but he was not able to understand their language.

"Oh, man, I can't understand a damn thing you are saying," he replied to the fairies.

He realized there was nothing he could do and decided to grab Mayla and carry her back to the village. When he arrived at the village, Aza'el and the Dark Zals were gone. There was a lot of damage done. The Klexons saw Mike carrying Mayla's body. They knew she was dead. Everyone lowered their heads for respect.

"They are going to the portal toward the humans," one of the Klexons said as she ran to help Mike with Mayla's body.

They carried Mayla into her own cottage and laid her in her bed. At that moment, Lin showed up and asked what happened. Mike took a long look at Lin and realized he has not seen her at all while Aza'el was here, but now, she popped up out of nowhere. He didn't say anything to her. Instead, he stepped outside and Gary followed.

"They are on their way to the humans. I need you to help me. Gather up all the warriors and Grounders. We have to go and help them," said Mike to Gary as Gary stood behind him.

"Make sure the humans do not see Emily transform," said Gary.

"Got it," said Mike.

Mike stood frozen there in the dirt staring out into the field.

Gary started to walk away to get things ready for the fight as Mike spoke again.

"Keep an eye on Lin," he said.

"Why?" asked Gary.

"There is something I don't like about her," said Mike.

Gary nodded and left. Mike ran into his cottage and packed up a couple of things he would need. When he came back outside, the Grounders and the warriors were ready and waiting for him. Mike hopped on top of his Grounder and looked at Lin who was standing at a further distance watching them leave, and then, he turned his focus toward Gary. Gary knew why Mike looked at him that way, and Gary nodded as he was acknowledging the message.

Chapter 18

OTHERS MATTER

Emily was walking toward the school to see if she could find Megan. She stood by a tree across the parking lot from the school. At the end of the day, the school bell rang and Emily watched all the students leave. Finally, she saw Megan. Emily walked across the parking lot and tapped on Megan's shoulder before she sat in her car.

"Hey, what the hell? You scared me," said Megan.

"I am sorry. I did not mean to," said Emily.

"What do you want?" Megan asked her.

"I heard you been looking for me," said Emily.

Megan looked at Emily funny.

"Actually, we have been looking for you. We want to know if you know what happened to Briana," said Megan.

"No. I don't know," said Emily.

"Ok. I will let Adriana know," said Megan.

"Oh, you did not hear, did you?" said Emily.

"Hear what? What are you talking about?" asked Megan.

"Adriana was hit by a car yesterday," said Emily.

Megan's eyes opened up widely.

"What! How did that happen? I was just with her yesterday," said Megan.

"It was on the news. It looked like someone was going too fast and did not see her walking in the parking lot. Well, I have to go now. I will talk to you soon, maybe," said Emily.

Megan watched Emily leave. "I think you know a lot more," said Megan to herself as she sat in her car and drove off.

Emily felt a small relief as she walked to the coffee shop down the street. Emily decided to leave it as it is and not open anymore doors to questioning people about Briana. Emily got herself a cup of coffee and sat right by the window facing the forest. Emily looked down at her coffee and saw an image of herself. She looked closer and closer. For a moment, she felt like she was not able to recognize herself.

"What is happening to me? Am I changing again? This can't be happening," said Emily to herself as she thought about what she did to Adriana.

She lifted her head up and stared out the window. Emily had her focus at the woods. For a second, she thought she saw something. As she looked deeper, she saw bodies jumping from one tree to another. They were moving very fast. Emily quickly got up and left her coffee on the table. Emily ran outside, across the street, and over the open field. When she got closer to the woods, the big goblin flew out from the trees along with all the Dark Zals behind it. Emily fell to the floor. The goblin with Aza'el on it flew right above her, and the Dark Zals were on their brooms. Emily watched them fly right above her head.

The Dark Zals were everywhere, and they were heading to town. It did not take too long before the people in town started panicking and running for their lives. Emily ran back into the town, looked around, and saw what a disaster it was. Emily was about to transform into a witch, but she heard Mike yelling from a distance.

"No, not here. Be careful," he said to her, and she knew what he meant.

Emily nodded. So she ran around town trying her best to help the people, and since she was not able to transform, she fought the best way she could. Mike and the Klexons were fighting against the Dark Zals. People were trying to hide inside of their homes, cars, and other places. Some of them even tried fighting back but instead got killed. One particular man was fighting a Dark Zal trying to protect his wife. The evil witch knocked him out of the way, and she went straight for his wife. The Dark Zal grabbed the wife and choked her to death. She then started eating on her. When she was done, she dropped the wife's body back down. The husband who was on the ground, watched the whole thing and cried. The Dark Zal walked toward him.

"Come on, get me. It does not matter anymore," said the man.

She lifted her hand up and played around with her claws. She licked one of her claws where his wife's blood was on. She was about to kill him, but then, Emily jumped in between them and screamed, "NO!"

As Emily transformed into a witch, Emily caught the Zal from behind and twisted her neck killing her. Emily turned and looked at the human who saw the whole thing. In a deep dark voice, she told him to go and hide.

Even though Emily was not evil, the fact that the ring that changed her into a witch was from Aza'el and Aza'el was evil, Emily's transformation is a Dark Zal.

When Emily told the man to go and hide, he ignored her. He sat there staring at Emily.

"How did you do that?" the man asked her.

Emily told him there was no time for that and to go hide. When Emily turned her back to him and started to walk away, he tried to kill her with a sharp wooden stick. Emily quickly turned to face him and caught it. She told him that not all witches were here to kill humans. She threw the stick far away and ran from the man. He watched her leave.

Mike was fighting while riding on a Grounder. Emily stumbled across him. He used his sword to cut a Dark Zals' head off. Her head rolled all the way to Emily's feet. Emily looked up at Mike.

"Sorry," he said.

Emily told Mike she was going to look for her father. Mike nodded and told her to be careful. One part of the town was attacked and the other half was not; however, the Dark Zals were not stopping until the whole town was destroyed.

Meanwhile, Allen came home from a store and saw his front door wide open. He knew something was wrong. He dropped his groceries on the ground and slowly walked into his house. The house was destroyed. He saw something or someone looking for something around his stuff, throwing things around the house. Allen came up on it from behind. He held a riffle toward its head and asked what it was looking for. It stopped fishing around, stood up straight, and turned around to face Allen. It was a Dark Zal. She tilted her head side to side not saying anything but walking closer toward Allen. She screamed and jumped at him. Allen pulled the trigger and shot her right in the forehead. She stood up one more time, and he shot her again. The witch was finally dead on his floor.

"Now, I have to clean this shit up," he said to himself.

At that moment, Emily ran inside. Her dad quickly turned around and held the riffle up. She quickly transformed back into herself.

"It's me, Dad," said Emily.

"Damn it. What are you thinking running up on me like that? I could have shot you. What is going on?" asked Allen.

"Hurry, Dad. We need your help. They attacked us," said Emily.

"I thought the whole plan of you staying in Green Village was to avoid this shit," said Allen.

"Yes, well, not everything goes as planned," replied Emily.

Allen packed up some of his weapons and followed Emily. Emily and Allen were fighting their way back to where Mike and the others were. As Allen got closer to Mike, one of the Grounders ran to Allen and lowered its tail to the ground. Allen ran up the tail and right on its back. The Grounder was running around town as Allen was shooting at the Dark Zals.

Emily whistled and waited for a couple of seconds. Then, Maxi flew in from the portal. The humans were scared of Maxi. He landed right in front of Emily, and she hopped on his back. She ordered him to look for Aza'el. It took a while for Emily to find her. However, she finally saw the goblin. It was hanging around her friend's house, Nikki. When Emily landed in front of her house, she slowly entered in. Emily walked around inside the house, and Nikki was nowhere to be found. Emily continued to walk through the living room toward the guest room. Before she walked into the guest room, Nikki stepped out from behind the corner. Emily saw she was crying.

"What's wrong, Nikki? Where is she?" asked Emily.

"My family," replied Nikki in her crying voice.

Emily did not say anything. When Emily tried to come closer toward Nikki, she passed the couch. That is when she saw Nikki's parents, dead on the floor. Emily placed her hand over her mouth and looked at Nikki.

"What happened here? Where is she?" Emily asked her again.

Nikki just stood there and looked at Emily. She did not move. Then, Megan and Aza'el came out from another corner. Emily looked at both of them. She asked Aza'el to stop doing what she was doing. Emily told Aza'el to stop hurting the humans. Emily then turned her focus on Megan and asked her what she was doing here.

"Aza'el offered me something I couldn't resist. I knew you were up to no good, so I followed you one time through that portal and bumped into Aza'el. She offered me power if I helped her destroy you," said Megan.

"You will not get any power. She wants all the power to herself," replied Emily.

Megan laughed.

"Enough with the chitchat. This is your last chance Emily to come and join me; otherwise, I have to destroy you," said Aza'el.

Aza'el grabbed Nikki and told Emily to drink her blood and kill her.

"Take her soul. It is very easy. Only I and you have the powers to do that. You just place your mouth over hers and inhale. Her soul comes right out," said Aza'el.

Emily said no. Aza'el then told Emily if she did not want to follow her orders and her way, then she did not deserve her powers and told her to take the ring off. Emily said no again. Aza'el was a little startled.

"You like to have those powers, don't you?" asked Aza'el.

"No, I do not, but I will not give it to someone else who will follow your footsteps," replied Emily.

Aza'el grabbed Nikki and told Emily if she does not take the ring off and give it to Megan that she would kill Nikki. Emily did not want her friend to die, so she agreed she would give the ring to Megan.

"How can I take it off? It does not work. I tried before," said Emily.

"I will raise my hand, and the ring will recognize my blood. It will allow you to take it off," said Aza'el. Aza'el raised her hand as she held Nikki with her other hand. Emily started taking the ring off. As Emily was taking the ring off, she looked out of the living room window and saw so many humans dying. She could not believe what her world has become. While Emily was slowly pulling the ring off, Megan was walking closer toward Emily trying to grab the ring. Before Emily took it off all the way, she pushed Megan to the side and used her powers to throw Nikki across the room away from Aza'el. She yelled to Nikki to run and Nikki did.

"No!" Aza'el yelled and waived her hand in the air. The powers of her force threw Megan right out of the second floor window and smashed her against the light pole outside.

"I knew she couldn't do anything right," said Aza'el about Megan.

"Well, well, it is just me and you. You know, I actually like you. You don't give up. You are strong. I mean you keep fighting and you keep fighting against my dark magic. You try to control my ring instead of allowing it to control you. But look here. No matter how many times you fight to be a Klexon, at the end of the day, you are always alone. My blood will always run through your veins, and you can't change that. So even if you do become a Klexon, it won't change a thing. My blood inside of you won't disappear, and you will always have evil in you," said Aza'el.

"Save your speech," said Emily.

"If that's what you want," said Aza'el.

Aza'el jumped and aimed toward Emily. Emily blocked her punches and punched back. They both fought in the guest room upstairs. Aza'el managed to grab a hold of Emily by her back and slammed her face down into the floor. She then lifted her up and slammed her the same way again and again until Emily started bleeding out of her nose. As Aza'el picked Emily up again, Emily screamed and hurt Aza'el's ears. Aza'el dropped Emily to cover her ears with her hands.

"You bitch, that hurts," said Aza'el.

Emily got onto her feet and turned to face Aza'el as she lay on the floor. She used her force to throw Aza'el backward. Aza'el was slammed through the wall and ended up in the next room. Aza'el slowly got back onto her feet. Emily walked through the hole in the wall coming after Aza'el.

"I got some tricks up my sleeve as well," said Aza'el.

Aza'el raised her arm and opened her palm. A long silver cane formed in her hand. As Emily was walking faster toward Aza'el, Aza'el hit the floor with the silver cane and Emily felt like she was being kicked in her stomach. Every time Aza'el would slam the cane against the floor, Emily was getting hit with some sort of force in her stomach and chest. It was painful. Emily felt pain all through her body. Emily was losing strength and fell to the floor.

At that moment, Mike ran into the room. He was holding the blue rock. He threw it at Aza'el. It landed right by her feet. Aza'el lost her focus, and the silver cane disappeared. Aza'el screamed in pain from the blue rock and was backing away from it. Aza'el jumped out of the window to get away from the blue potion rock. When she jumped out of the second floor window, her goblin flew right underneath her and caught her. Mike helped Emily up, and she thanked him. Emily right away got to her feet and jumped out the window as well to follow Aza'el.

"Damn it. Now, I have to find her again," said Mike. He picked up the blue rock, "can't lose you," he said and placed it in his pocket.

Aza'el was flying around on her goblin, and Emily was running on ground right behind her. Emily was starting to lose her, so she whistled. Maxi came and swiped her up. She had to catch up to Aza'el.

Aza'el did not see Emily following her. Instead, she saw an opportunity. She saw a family of humans hiding behind a building. She jumped off of her goblin and landed right in front of them. The man stood in front of his wife and two children to protect them. Aza'el looked at him.

"Oh, well, isn't this cute? You love them, ha?" she asked the man. Then, Aza'el looked past him at his wife. "He must really love you," she said as she laughed. "Nobody has ever loved me or cared for me. Therefore, nobody else will feel love either," she said and raised her arm.

The woman was being lifted from the ground. The man tried to hit Aza'el with a bat, but Aza'el grabbed it with her other hand and broke it in half. The man grabbed his wife trying to hold onto her, but Aza'el pushed him away with her force. The children were screaming and crying. Aza'el turned her hand around and cracked the woman's neck. Her husband screamed for his wife's name, but it was over. Aza'el lowered her hand and the woman's body hit the ground. The husband walked over to his wife's body and held her. The children ran to their mother as well, but the father did not allow them to see their mother dead. He told the children to stay back. Aza'el laughed. At that moment, Emily jumped off of Maxi and stood right behind Aza'el.

"There, the bitch is dead and you, well, you live with it," Aza'el told the man.

"Enough Aza'el!" Emily yelled.

Aza'el turned around to face Emily. The man took his children to safety.

"Oh, I cannot wait to get rid of you," said Aza'el to Emily.

Aza'el started running away, and Emily followed. Right behind them was Mike. The man who hid his children came back and saw Mike running after the two witches. He decided to help Mike and followed them. Aza'el ran into the woods, deep into the forest, and past the darkness. Emily followed. Aza'el stopped at the end of a cliff. There was nowhere else to go.

"Stop and face me!" Emily yelled.

"Oh, I am not running. I have you where I want you," said Aza'el. Aza'el lowered both of her arms and slowly started raising them upward saying, "Thorns of the evil, rise from the ground. Surround this place and don't let us out!"

When she said those words, big thorns were rising from underneath the ground and grew tall. They surrounded Emily and Aza'el. The only opening was behind Aza'el at the end, off the cliff. As the thorns grew taller, the ground shook. Emily looked around, and she could see Mike. He tried to run in through the thorns, but Emily raised her hand and her powers threw him backward. She knew if he tried to jump over the thorns, he would have gotten himself killed. Emily turned back around to face Aza'el, but Aza'el was already in her face. Aza'el grabbed her by her chest, lifted her, and slammed her into the thorns. Emily's back got cut by the thorns, and she dropped to the ground onto one knee. Aza'el then picked Emily up with both of her arms and held onto her. Aza'el jumped up carrying Emily along and then slammed her onto the ground with her elbow into Emily's ribs. Aza'el stood up, but Emily did not. Emily rolled to her side in pain with her back toward Aza'el. Aza'el kicked Emily in her back over and over again until she got tired. Aza'el then walked around Emily's body and said,

"I have asked you many times to join me. I have given you many opportunities, and now, you brought me here to do this stupid shit. I should be ruling the worlds by now, but no, you just had to waste my damn time." Then, she kicked Emily one more time. Emily was not moving.

Mike was able to see through a small opening of the thorns that Emily was in trouble, but there was nothing he could do. He screamed for her name. He yelled for her to get up. Emily closed her eyes as she felt the pain rushing through her body. She remembered how she felt the same pain when she was raped, when Briana and her friends jumped on her, and when she lost her best friend back home. She also remembered her mother. She remembered the last words her mother said to her when Aza'el killed her. Remembering those words made Emily feel stronger. Aza'el tried kicking Emily again, but Emily grabbed her leg. Emily held onto her leg and, with her own left leg, kicked Aza'el. Aza'el dropped to the floor. Emily stood up as she held the side of her stomach. Aza'el quickly got up on one knee. Emily screamed over and over again trying to have the sound of her voice throw Aza'el into the thorns, but Aza'el held her feet tight into the ground and used her fingernails like claws to dig them into the ground to hold her place. Emily stopped screaming and the sound waves disappeared. Aza'el stood up on both of her feet, and they both ran toward each other with full force.

Chapter 19

WHAT IS RIGHT

Both of them jumped high in the air, grabbed each other by their shoulders, spun around in air in a circle, and dropped back to the floor. Emily tried to flip Aza'el, but she did not succeed. Aza'el was too strong. Aza'el then jumped high up holding on to Emily. In midair, Aza'el flipped Emily onto her back and slammed her against the ground. Emily was lying on her back, and Aza'el was sitting on top of her. Aza'el grabbed with one hand around Emily's throat, and with her other hand, she pulled out her knife. It was the same knife she stabbed Gabby with. Emily saw the knife as Aza'el lifted it up in the air ready to strike.

"Here is your chance to join your mother," said Aza'el.

She swung her hand to stab Emily, and right before the knife went through Emily's chest, a gun went off. The bullet knocked the knife right out of Aza'el's hand. Aza'el looked upward and saw Allen standing there shooting between the thorns. Aza'el raised her arm and used her force to make the thorns thicker. Allen lost sight. At that moment, Emily kicked both of her legs upward kicking Aza'el off of her. Emily quickly got on her feet, and Aza'el attacked again. They fist fought, punched each other, kicked, and more. Aza'el pulled out her other knife and started swinging it at Emily. Emily got sliced on her face and her arm. As Aza'el swung the knife again, Emily did a backflip knocking the knife out of her hand; and with her other foot that was coming upward, she kicked Aza'el on the

137

bottom of her chin. Aza'el fell backward and Emily quickly went on top of her. Emily placed both of her hands around Aza'el's neck and started choking her.

"Die already!" Emily said as she squeezed around her throat.

Aza'el grabbed some dirt from the ground and wrapped a long whip made of thorns around her wrist. Aza'el pulled it out of the ground and swung it. The thorn swung around Emily, and it hit her on her back. Emily screamed in pain. Aza'el swung it again, but Emily took her hand off of Aza'el's throat and caught it. It wrapped around Emily's hand, and Emily yanked it out of Aza'el's hand. Emily threw the whip made of thorns to the side as her hand bled. Aza'el then pushed Emily off of her and got up, and so did Emily.

"Haven't you had enough?" asked Aza'el. "I will get rid of you just the way I got rid of your mother," said Aza'el.

Aza'el was talking a lot of shit to Emily, but Emily muted her out. The image of her mother stuck in her head, and Emily screamed out of rage. She then ran as fast as she could toward Aza'el. Aza'el, however, smiled and waited. When Aza'el noticed that Emily was not slowing down, her smile faded away. Aza'el raised her arms to try to stop Emily with her powers, but it did not work. Emily was now stronger. The love for her mother made her unstoppable. Emily slammed into Aza'el and jumped off the cliff, dragging Aza'el along. When they both went off the cliff, the thorns that surrounded them as a gate collapsed and dried out. Allen and Mike ran toward them. They ran as fast as they could to try to save Emily, but they were too late.

There, right off the cliff, in midair, Emily held onto Aza'el. They floated in the air. It almost looked like time stopped. All of a sudden, a bright light shot out from Aza'el and Emily. Allen and Mike turned their heads away from the light because it was blinding. It only lasted for about one second, and it went away. Emily pulled her knife out of Aza'el's heart, and her body turned into ashes and disappeared. Emily took the other ring from Aza'el and placed it on her own finger along with the one she already had.

The two rings melted into one. Emily then fell unconscious and her body started falling. Allen tried to reach over the cliff to catch her by her arm, but she was too far away. Emily's body fell right passed his hands, down the cliff and into the fog. Allen laid on his stomach looking over the cliff down into the fog. He watched her body disappear. He screamed over and over for her name, but no sound from Emily came back. Mike ran up to Allen and dropped to his knees. Tears started overflowing his eyes. Allen cried as well.

"Why? Why my family?" asked Allen.

He asked, but nobody answered. Allen was punching the ground over and over again screaming for Emily. Mike did not do or say anything. He was in disbelief. He lost the love of his life. Allen slowly got onto his feet and grabbed Mike by his shoulder. Both men started walking back to town. As their backs were turned to the cliff, they heard a sound. Both stopped walking. They slowly turned their attention back toward the cliff as they heard a sound again, but then, it got quiet.

"What was that?" asked Mike.

"I don't know," replied Allen.

Next thing they knew, they saw Maxi. He flew high up into the sky carrying Emily on his back. She was transformed into herself, a human. Allen was screaming in joy. Maxi landed in front of Allen and Mike and lowered himself to the ground allowing them to help Emily. Allen picked his daughter up and held her in his arms.

"Oh thank God. Please come back to me. Wake up, Emily," said Allen as he laid her onto the ground.

Mike touched Emily's forehead.

"My love, I thought I lost you," said Mike.

He kissed her forehead. Allen told Mike to take Emily to the Green Village. He was sure the Klexons had something that could help Emily heal fast. Meanwhile, he will go back into town. Mike nodded. Mike placed Emily back onto Maxi's back, and he sat on him as well. They flew out of the forest, and Allen ran back toward the town.

However, the man who had his wife murdered earlier with his children watching, who followed Mike into the woods, well, he saw the whole thing. Now, he knows about Emily.

"So it was that girl's fault. Everything was that girl's fault," the man said to himself and ran back to town.

When Allen arrived back in town, he saw a lot of things he wished he never had to see. So many humans were dead and suffered from major injuries. However, all the Dark Zals were dead as well. Allen made an announcement to the people in town that the war was over and now they all had to be strong for each other.

"Who are you? And where did those witches come from?" asked a man off the street.

"This was a war that should have never happened, but it did. An evil force tried to destroy us humans, and a different form of witches came to help us. Without them, we all would have been dead. They are gone now. We do not know where they live or where they come from. We do not have to fear them. The evil force has been defeated, and we have to be strong now and move forward with our lives," Allen explained to the people in town and left the scene before more questions arise.

When the warriors finally arrived home, the other Klexons who were not fighters cheered them on. The warriors were happy that everything was finally over. About five minutes later, Mike arrived with Emily. He carried her to their cottage and laid her on their bed. Gary followed him. Mike covered her up and asked Gary if he had anything for her to heal faster. Gary pulled out a potion and forced it down Emily's throat.

"Let her rest now," said Gary.

They both left Emily alone asleep in her bed. Gary and Mike sat outside and watched the warriors putting their weapons away and cleaning up.

"So, is Mayla really gone?" asked Mike.

Gary lowered his head, and Mike knew what that meant.

"I am so sorry for the loss," said Mike.

Gary nodded.

Mike asked about Lin.

Gary told him they found her dead. She hung herself with an apology note. Mike asked him what the note said.

"Let's just say she was helping Aza'el," said Gary.

Mike got up and left to clean himself up. He then laid down next to Emily and fell asleep.

The following morning, he placed his arms around her and said, "Emily, baby, do you hear me? Emily, say something." He did not feel her move one bit.

"Am I alive?" Emily asked in a very low sounded voice.

Mike let out a laugh. "Yes, you are," he said.

He was so happy to finally hear her voice. Mike got up and made them breakfast. She got herself dressed and ate. Emily went outside and saw her father talking to Gary. She was not able to walk fast because she was still in a lot of pain. When Allen saw her, he ran up to her and hugged her. Allen asked her if she was feeling any better. She told him yes.

"Is everything over?" asked Emily.

"Yes," replied Allen.

"Why is everyone so sad then?" asked Emily.

"Emily, you need to know that Mayla did not make it that day. She is in her cottage in the bed waiting to be buried," said Gary.

"Also, the tree-flower is drying, which is killing the life in the forest leaving us with no food," said Mike as he walked into their conversation.

"I would like to see Mayla," said Emily.

As she entered her cottage, she saw Mayla, lying in bed, all pale. She sat on a chair next to Mayla.

"I see you left me here. You know I can't do this without you. I want you back. I will miss you so much," said Emily.

She then looked down at her hand and saw the rings melted together into one. "I will never be normal again. I wish you were here to guide me," said Emily.

She then leaned over and kissed Mayla on her forehead. "Be in peace," she said and walked out of the cottage.

Allen and Mike were ready to go back home. Emily told them she was staying longer to figure out a way to save the tree-flower.

"You can't save it. There is nothing else for us to do here," said Mike.

"One thing out of this entire experience I learned is that no matter what happens to you, you do not forget who you are or where you came from. It pays off to put someone else before yourself," said Emily.

Emily turned into a Dark Zal and ran fast into the forest. Mike quickly followed. A couple of seconds later, one by one, the Klexons followed as well. They also wanted to help whatever Emily had planned. Gary watched them leave and he smiled. He was proud of Emily.

"I see she has been studying," he said to himself.

He walked back into his cottage. Allen stayed outside with Maxi. They both sat on the ground with Allen's back leaned onto a rock.

"I am not going anywhere unless it's going home," Allen said to Maxi.

Once Emily arrived at the tree-flower, she turned back into her human self. She watched the fairies and other little creatures including the trolls trying to nourish the tree-flower, but nothing was working. Emily came closer and saw how bad the damage was. She then closed her eyes, and a tear fell down her face. Emily placed her palm on the side of the tree-flower and and held her eyes shut. She remembered letting the evil power take control over her. Then, she remembered what saved her. The love of her mother, the love of her father, and the love of Mike saved her. The old memories saved her. Emily then opened her eyes, and when she did, all the Klexons from the village were there. They were waiting, ready to do what they needed to do to help the tree-flower.

"Care, love, and kindness will heal everything and everyone. Let's show it our love," she said to everyone as she pointed at the free-flower.

Everyone looked at one another, a little confused about what Emily was saying.

"Look at the person standing next to you. That is your friend, your partner, your neighbor, and your blood. Show each other love," she said to them.

They nodded and smiled. They grabbed each other's hands and closed their eyes. They focused on their friendship and the love they give to their forest. The tree-flower was surrounded by the Klexons and all the animals that lived there. It was surrounded with love. Then the ground around the tree-flower lit up. A yellow light formed, and it shot from the ground into the free-flower. Everyone opened their eyes to see what was going on. The tree-flower lit up bright, and its leaves awakened. The light shot away from the tree-flower covering the rest of the forest and the rot started to heal. Emily placed her ear on the tree-flower and she heard the beat. She smiled.

"You all as one created the light of love. When you care for one another, anything is possible," said Emily.

Everyone laughed and cheered. One of the warrior witches walked up to Emily and thanked her. Emily looked at the tree-flower and said, "Mayla, I wish you could see this. I wish you could see that everything is okay. I am so sorry for everything I have done, and I wish I could say my goodbyes."

At that moment, Emily felt a hand on her back. She turned around, and she could see Mayla's spirit. Emily wiped her tears away. She was the only one seeing this.

"Is that really you?" Emily asked her.

"Yes, my child. I am the one that has to thank you for everything you have done. I am in peace now, and I will always watch over you. I am very proud of you. You take good care of yourself," said Mayla as her presence disappeared.

Mike approached Emily and said, "I told you. You don't have to worry anymore. You did great."

Emily nodded, and they walked back to the village along with the rest of the crew. When they arrived, Allen was ready to go. They said their goodbyes with the Klexons. Emily ran to Maxi, and he lowered his body allowing her to hug him around his neck. The creature was sobbing. It did not want Emily to leave.

"I will miss you so much. You have become my best friend. Take good care of yourself out here, okay," said Emily as tears filled her eyes.

She looked into his eyes, and they placed their foreheads together. Maxi had a long neck therefore he was able to lower his head down to her level. Emily kissed his forehead and let him go. As she was walking away from him, Maxi spread his big gold wings open and flew into the sky releasing a painful cry. Emily did not look back, but tears continued to come down her cheeks. She did not want to leave him. Mike and Allen went ahead and walked into the portal. Emily stopped before she entered. She turned around and looked at everyone one last time.

"I will never forget you guys. You are a part of me now, and I am a part of you. I understand you have to close this portal down to keep the humans away. But I will never forget this," said Emily.

She looked at Gary and asked him if he was staying. Gary nodded and told her that he was where he belonged. He wanted to stay closer to his wife. Emily understood. She was walking into the portal backward and watched everyone slowly disappear.

When Emily was pushed out of the portal and into the human's world, Allen and Mike were waiting on her. All three of them watched the portal get smaller and smaller into a ball and disappear. Emily stood there, wondering if she made the right decision by staying with the humans. But it was too late now.

It took a couple of months for everyone in town to get back to their regular lives. Emily has not seen Nikki since the war. She decided to pay her a visit at Jack's coffee shop. As Emily entered the shop, she saw Nikki sitting at the same table she always sat at, studying.

"Hey there, it has been a while," said Emily.

"Yes, it has been," Nikki replied but did not lift her head up from reading her book.

"I am very sorry for everything, and I am sorry for your loss," Emily whispered.

"Are you? Because I honestly don't know if I can forgive you. You know, people here might not know about you, but I do and I cannot forget about it. You are the reason why everything happened the way it did," said Nikki.

Emily wanted to keep the conversation going and make Nikki understand that she was very sorry for what happened to her family, but she could see that Nikki has already made her decision about their friendship. Emily turned around and walked out of the coffee shop. Jack came up to Nikki and sat next to her.

"What's wrong with Emily?" asked Jack.

"Nothing," said Nikki as she continued to read.

Chapter 20

HE WON'T LET GO

As Emily was about to walk passed Brent University, she stopped for a second and looked at the school. She thought about going back to school one day and completing her degree, but for now she was busy with remodeling the bookstore that Gary passed on to her. However, Mike landed a good job as a business analysis, and he and Emily moved in together. Emily turned away from the school and left. She was remodeling and cleaning the bookstore all day long. She finally sat down in Gary's old chair to rest. She looked down at her ring and thought about Maxi and the Klexons. That is when she realized she made a mistake leaving Arfabele.

Emily was on her way home from the bookstore when she noticed a man following her. She thought she knew him from somewhere but couldn't remember from where. Emily tried to ignore him, but he continued to follow her. Emily rushed into a store and waited for about ten minutes. When she came back out, he was standing right in front of her.

"Who are you?" Emily asked him.

"You don't remember me? It has not been that long," the man replied.

He grabbed her by her shoulders and slammed her against the wall. Emily dropped her books that she was carrying. He placed his face right against hers and asked her where the portal was. She looked at him and told him she did not know what he was talking about. He told her that he will find it with her or without her and punched her in her stomach. Nobody was around to help her, and she did not want to transform into a witch right in front of him. He grabbed her by her chest and lifted her up. He told her to go ahead and turn into the ugly thing. Emily did not say anything. He threw her around and kicked her more. She couldn't bear the pain anymore and was about to change into a witch, but then, she remembered promising Mayla that she would not allow a human see her transform. If she did, she would then have to kill him. The man continued to beat on her. He screamed at her over and over again telling her to change into a witch, but Emily ignored him. Emily told him that she did not know what he was talking about. He decided to take her with him. He wanted revenge for the death of his wife. He injected some sort of liquid into her shoulder, and she fell asleep. The man carried her over his shoulders, into his car, and to his house. He took her to his basement and tied her down to a table. Emily slowly started to open her eyes. She could see a person dressed in black working on something down by her feet, but it was a blurry sight. She opened her eyes more and let out a sound. The figure came closer to her head, and she saw it was the same man again.

"Why are you doing this?" Emily asked him.

"You are one of them. Show yourself. I saw everything in those woods by that cliff. I know who you are, and you will take me to them. Each and every one of you has to pay for what you have done to the people in this town including my wife!" said the man.

"No, you need to stop. Let me go. There is no way getting to them. They are gone," said Emily.

"Okay, even if that was true, you are still here and you are one of them," said the man.

He punched Emily in her stomach as she lay on the table, tied up. He hit her at least three to four times. When he swung again to hit her, she transformed into a witch and used her scream to throw the man backward against his basement wall. Emily then freed her arms that were tied up. The man hurried up onto his feet and ran toward Emily trying to strike her again. Emily saw him coming with an ax. Her feet were still tied up. Emily rose her arm up and used her power of force to stop the ax from swinging at her head. Emily turned her hand, and the ax turned as well. Now, the sharp end of the ax faced the top of his head. Emily held it that way as she quickly untied her legs with her other arm. She stood up on the table and then jumped in front of him.

"I have told you not all witches are the same! Why do you still want to hurt me?" Emily asked him angrily.

The man looked at her while the ax was still above his head. He held it, but he was not in control of it.

"If I let you go, will you promise to leave me alone?" Emily asked him.

"You all have to pay for what you have done," the man replied.

"Wrong answer," said Emily.

Emily then slammed her hand on the table. The ax dropped down right in the middle of his head, and he died. Emily walked right passed his body and up the stairs. When she walked out of his house, she turned back into a human and walked home.

When Mike came home from work and saw Emily sitting on the couch. She looked like a mess. He did not ask any questions, but she started talking.

"There was this man who seen it all," she said.

Mike walked over to the couch and sat next to her.

"What do you mean he saw everything and who?" Mike asked her.

"Passed the woods by the cliff, he saw me, okay. He said his wife was killed when the Dark Zals came across and attacked the humans. Well, one of the humans that was killed was his wife. He tried to kill me, Mike. I remember him and his wife. I remember trying to help him," said Emily.

Mike stood up and asked her where this man was and he will take care of it. Emily told him to sit down that she had something else to say. Mike slowly sat back down. She told him everything that happened. Emily told Mike she killed the man in his basement. She also told him that she did not feel bad or sorry for killing him.

"What if it's happening again? What if I can't control its powers?" she asked.

Mike told her it had nothing to do with that and she did what anyone else would do to protect themselves. He reminded her of all the good she did and how she put her life on the line to save others, the humans, the witches, the creatures. She took responsibility for her actions and dealt with them. Emily looked down at the ring on her hand. Mike looked at it as well. He asked her why she was still wearing it. She told him it did not matter if she wore it or not. She was stuck being a Dark Zal. The ring reminded her of what she went through, and it brought back memories of her friends from the Green Village. She told him she missed them and she missed her mother and Maxi. Mike touched her face and looked into her eyes. He felt sorry for the pain she went through. He loved her very much. He hugged her, and she hugged him back. He lifted her head up and started to kiss her. He picked her up and carried her into their room. He laid her down and placed his body on top of hers and kissed her again. He took his shirt off and slowly placed his hand under her shirt. He looked at her and told her how beautiful she was.

"You just need some pleasure and you will be all right," he said to her.

He continued to kiss her and slowly started taking off her shirt. He kissed down her neck. Her emotions rose, and she was feeling warm. She did not want to do it right now, but her body couldn't resist. Mike slowly moved downward and was on his knees while she lay on the bed. He then lifted her legs up and started to please her with his tongue. He focused on her and her body language. He held her legs open and continued pleasing her. Emily rubbed his head with her nails, and her head moved backward. She enjoyed every minute of feeling his tongue between her legs. She could feel the heat from his breath, and she started to release. Her legs were wrapped around his neck tightly as she moaned loudly, digging her nails into his neck. Mike rose up slowly looking at her breathing heavily. He kissed her on her lips. He told her that he loved her and then laid down next to her. She turned to face him, looked at him, and smiled. She did put her shirt back on but no bra and then sat on top of him. He placed his hands around her waist and asked her what she was doing. She started taking his pants off and asked him if he really thought he was not getting anything in return. Mike smiled and told her he was not expecting anything, but if she would like to, to feel free to do so. They both laughed. His pants were off. Emily sat back on top of him as he lay down. Emily leaned down and kissed him. She slowly placed herself on top of his manhood and started to ride it with her hands on his chest. Her head leaned back, and her long hair fell down her back. Her nipples were showing through her shirt. Mike held her by her waist and bit his bottom lip. His veins in his arms popped up, and the outline of his muscles more visible. He held her tightly onto his manhood as she continued to ride him. As Emily tilted her head back and moaned, Mike was watching her. Blue lines traveled through her chest, to the side of her neck, and into the side of her face. She looked back down at him and exhaled hot breath, with the blue lines contracting on the side of her face all because she was feeling energetic and horny and was getting ready to release. As Emily released, the blue lines on her cheeks got brighter. Mike watched her moan and squeezed her by her waist. Emily let out a scream, and Mike lifted himself up in a sitting position and locked his arms around her. He held her tight. Mike's head was resting on her breast. Mike used his arms to pull her tighter against his manhood making sure every inch of him was inside of her. As Mike released, he bit his bottom lip and got stiff. He made sure he filled her up with his sperm. Mike still held her tight against his body, and his manhood stayed inside of her. They were both breathing heavily. He then looked up at her and saw the blue lines on her face slowly disappear. They kissed and Mike lifted her up slowly off of him. Mike turned to her and told her he loved her. She told him she loved him too.

The blue lines on the witch's bodies represented emotions. Whether it was anger, happiness, hurt, or anything else.

A year has passed by and the town slowly forgot about the witches. Nobody talked about it anymore. However, Emily always thought about Mayla and their village. Pete and Mitti were still having their moments where they want to be together but did not get along. Mitti did not trust Pete anymore. Mike and Emily didn't have much contact with them.

It was a Saturday morning and Emily left the house to take care of some things in town. She also decided to have a chat with Nikki. Emily knew she would be at the coffee shop. When Emily arrived, she right away approached Nikki as she was putting away some tea cups.

"Hey there, I know you are still upset with me, but I am having a little house get-together tonight at about seven o'clock. I would really like it if you and Jack would stop by. It's just me, Mike, and my dad," said Emily.

Nikki did not say anything. Emily saw she did not want to be bothered, and therefore, Emily turned around and walked out. After Emily left the coffee shop, Nikki turned her way and watched her go. Later that evening, at about seven o'clock, Emily, Mike, and Allen were getting some food together and cooking out by the fire at Mike's and Emily's house. As Emily was putting the plates on the table, she looked up and saw Jack and Nikki walk in from the side of the house. Emily walked up to both of them and thanked them for coming. Mike and Allen were quiet because they knew the two girls have not been good of friends lately. Nikki looked at Emily and hugged her.

"I am not mad at you anymore. I did not have anyone else to blame, so I blamed you. What happened was not all your fault. You saved most of us. You saved the ones you could. I really miss my friend," said Nikki.

"I miss you too, and I am so sorry. But you are not alone and never will be. You got us and Jack," Emily replied.

"I know," said Nikki, smiled, and turned to Jack.

"We have an announcement to make," Jack and Nikki said.

They both laughed because they said it at the same time. Emily, Allen, and Mike gave them their attention.

"I am pregnant," said Nikki.

Emily's eyes opened up with surprise.

"Oh my God, congratulations, guys," said Emily.

Mike and Allen also congratulated them two on their unborn child. The group of friends ended up having a great cookout and a good time. After Nikki and Jack left, Emily was in the kitchen washing the dishes and Mike was cleaning up.

Allen walked into the kitchen with a beer in his hand. He stood next to Emily and said, "You know I am very happy for your friends on their unborn child. However, don't you even think about doing that."

Emily turned her attention to her dad.

"Dad, stop. Just because I moved in with Mike does not mean we are going to start a family. I have so much more to accomplish for myself," said Emily.

"I'm just saying," said Allen and walked back outside telling her he was leaving.

Emily looked after her dad and smiled.

"He is so crazy," she said.

Mike walked in with the rest of the dishes.

"Your dad left?" Mike asked.

"Yes, he just left," replied Emily.

"Well, leave those dishes there. We will finish them tomorrow," said Mike and picked Emily up and placed her on the kitchen counter. He took her shirt off and they kissed as he touched her breast. He then grabbed her by her throat while his other hand was moving up her skirt. He moved her panties to the side and slid his fingers inside of her. Emily's eyes closed and she had no control over her body. He played just enough with her until he had her where he wanted her. Mike took his fingers out, flipped her over onto her stomach with her legs hanging off the kitchen counter. He lifted her skirt over her buttocks, held on to her waist and from behind he slid his manhood inside of her.

Meanwhile, Mitti was shopping, and she happened to bump into Alex who was an old friend of Mike.

"Hey, is that you Alex? It's been a couple of years since I seen you. Where have you been?" Mitti asked him.

"Oh hey, Mitti. Yeah, it's me. I've been busy. Ever since that one incident I lost my sister, I decided to move out of town. I just moved back here a couple of weeks ago. How have you been?" Alex asked her.

"Well, you know, a little lonely since all of my friends were killed that night. You know Briana, Megan, and Adriana, all three of them are gone," replied Mitti.

"Oh yeah, I remember. Well, I am glad that is over. I mean I don't know how that happened or where those witches came from, but I am glad they disappeared," said Alex.

"Well, you know not all of them have disappeared," Mitti slipped out.

"What do you mean?" Alex asked her.

Mitti tried walking away, but Alex came after her. He grabbed her hand and made her face him.

"What do you mean, Mitti?" he asked her again.

"You did not know?" Mitti asked.

"Know what?" Alex replied.

"Have you talked to Mike lately?" she asked him.

"No, not since he left college," Alex replied.

"Well, if I tell you, will you promise to keep it a secret?" Mitti asked him.

"Sure," he replied.

Mitti told Alex everything she knew. Alex could not believe what he heard. He told her they had to get rid of Emily before something else happens, before more people die because of her. Mitti told him not to do anything. He promised her he was going to keep that a secret. Alex agreed and told her she does not have to worry. Mitti thanked him and left. Alex watched her go.

"I will do something about it anyway," he said to himself.

Emily was in the school library studying. She only had to take a couple more classes to graduate. As she sat there, reading, she felt that she had to use the bathroom. She left her book sitting on the chair she was sitting on. She walked down the hall and into the bathroom, used the stall, and flushed the toilet. Nobody else was in the bathroom but her. She walked up to the sink to wash her hands. She turned the water on. She thought she heard a voice, a woman's voice. She quickly turned the water back off but then nothing, no sound. Emily turned the water on again and continued washing her hands. She turned the water off and used the paper towel to dry her hands. As she threw the towel into the garbage, she looked into the mirror and saw a woman. The woman was Aza'el. Emily screamed and ran out of the bathroom. Everyone in the library was looking at her. Emily stumbled over a chair and ran outside. She stopped running once she got outside in front of the library. She was gasping for air and breathing heavily. She grabbed her hair with her hands and asked herself what was happening to her. At that moment, a woman passed by and asked Emily if she needed help. Emily shook her head, and the woman left. Emily looked down at her ring to see if there were any changes, but nothing. The ring looked the same as it did for the past couple of years. Emily decided to go home, take a long bath, and relax. She thought she was probably overreacting.

Chapter 21

REALITY OR NOT

When Emily got home, she took her clothes off and dropped it one by one as she walked into the bathroom. She turned on the water and let the tub fill up. She then sat in it and laid back. She closed her eyes and relaxed. She drifted away in thought. A couple of minutes later, she felt her water got colder, quickly. She slowly opened her eyes. She was looking at the water how dark it was. She screamed and jumped out of the tub grabbing a towel and wiping away all the black stuff off her body. She looked at the tub. The water was black. It was thick blood. "What the fuck is going on?" she asked herself. She was too scared to let the water go down the drain. She left the water there and left the bathroom. She cleaned up with wet wipes and got dressed. She was pacing around the living room until Mike came home.

"Mike, you have to come see this," said Emily.

"What? What is it?" he asked her.

Emily pulled him toward the bathroom. When they walked in, the water was gone and the tub was clean.

"It was right here, I swear," said Emily.

"What was?" Mike asked her. He was confused.

"Look, I know I am not going crazy. Today, I saw Aza'el in the mirror, at the library, in the bathroom. When I got home, I took a bath and the water got very cold quickly and black. It was blood. I jumped out of it. I did not clean the tub," said Emily.

"Maybe you are just stressed out," said Mike.

"I do not know," Emily replied feeling frustrated because he did not believe her.

"Okay, maybe you have been dreaming about it. All that stuff is done. You can move on now, okay," said Mike.

Emily looked at him. "Right," she said.

Emily stood there in the bathroom staring at the tub. Mike left back to the living room and asked her loudly if she was hungry. She whispered, "No." Emily knew something was wrong. She knew it had nothing to do with trauma or the bullshit stress she has been told. Emily looked down at her ring.

"You will not win. I will not give you away or take you off, but you will not win," she said as she stared at Aza'el's ring on her hand.

The following day, Mike was bringing in some office boxes from his truck into his house while Emily was in school. As he lifted one of the boxes and started carrying it into his house, he saw Alex approaching him.

"Hey there, you came right on time. Why don't you grab a box?" Mike said to Alex.

Alex ignored him and watched Mike struggle with the box.

"So how is your living situation going?" Alex asked him.

"It is going well," Mike replied.

Mike carried a box into the house as Alex just watched. Mike came back outside and wondered why Alex was not helping. Mike stopped picking up boxes and faced Alex.

"Is there a reason you are here?" Mike asked him.

"Yeah, there actually is. Do you know what happened to all of those witches that were here?" asked Alex.

Mike got frustrated and turned back around and started lifting more boxes.

"Who cares? They are gone, and that's what matters," said Mike.

"Are they all gone?" Alex asked.

Mike dropped a box onto the ground and faced Alex again.

"What are you asking, man? Is there something specific you are implying?" Mike asked.

"I think you know what I'm asking," Alex replied.

"No, I really don't," said Mike.

"Should I wait here for Emily to come back, and then, we all find out what I'm talking about?" Alex asked.

Mike grabbed Alex by his shirt and slammed him against his truck.

"Spit it out. What do you know?" Mike asked him.

"It's Emily, isn't it? She is one of them!" Alex yelled.

"Who ran their mouth? Was it Pete or Mitti?" Mike asked aggressively.

Alex did not answer.

Mike let Alex go and backed away a couple of steps. Alex was fixing his shirt.

"What the hell do you think you are doing with her?" Alex asked him.

"What do you mean, man? I love her," said Mike.

"Mike, she is a fucking witch!" yelled Alex.

Mike turned to Alex again. He acted like he was about to punch Alex but held back.

"Do not talk about her like that," said Mike.

"What makes you so certain that she won't hurt any of us?" Alex asked him.

"Because it's Emily. You don't know what she's been through. She is strong, and she has saved your ass and everyone else if you ask me. You do not know the whole story, so stop listening to Mitti or whoever is telling you this shit. Leave Emily alone," said Mike.

Mike got back to what he was doing and left Alex alone. Alex watched Mike carry in some more boxes and then slowly walked away.

As Alex was walking away from Mike's house down the street, he saw Emily walking his way. She was coming from school. As she passed him, she said hi to him, but he did not respond. He walked right past her like she was not even there. Emily watched him walk away and wondered why he was acting like that. When Emily arrived home, Mike was building shelves inside the house. He had a shirt on, jeans, and a pair of shoes. He was sweating. Emily walked in and dropped her book bag on the floor.

"Did you see Alex?" Emily asked him.

"Yeah, he was here," Mike responded.

He lowered his equipment to the floor and walked up to her. He placed his hands on her shoulders and exhaled.

"He knows about you," said Mike.

Emily felt her heart drop to the ground.

"What do you mean he knows about me? How did he find out?" Emily asked him.

"Someone ran their mouth. I think it was Mitti," said Mike.

"You know if more people find out, who knows what they will do to me? I should have stayed in Arfabele Land," said Emily.

"Just go talk to her. Remind her that she needs to keep her mouth shut," said Mike.

"What about Alex?" Emily asked.

"I would not worry about him much," said Mike.

Emily nodded and picked her book bag up. She then left upstairs. Mike watched her go. He continued to work on the shelves. Emily went to the bedroom and closed the door. She stood in front of their mirror that was hanging on their wall.

"How could she? How could she do that to me? She is still after me just like how she was when Briana was here. She still wants to try to ruin my life. Well, we will see about that," said Emily in an angry voice.

She did not want Mike to know, but Emily decided to pay Mitti a visit and not a friendly one.

It was in the middle of the night when Emily got quietly up from the bed, turned into a witch, and jumped out of the window. Mike did not hear a thing. She was on her way to Mitti's house.

Mitti was at home sleeping as she felt a chill breeze and covered herself better. However, she felt colder.

"Why is it so cold in here?" Mitti asked herself.

She opened her eyes, turned, and looked toward the window and saw a shadow standing. Mitti got scared. She screamed and jumped out of the bed.

"Who are you?" she asked.

The figure came closer toward her. Mitti ran to turn the light on. When she did, she saw Emily.

"You scared me. What are you doing in my house?" Mitti asked her.

"Why did you do it? Why did you open your mouth to Alex?" Emily asked her.

"Damn it, he was supposed to shut his mouth," said Mitti.

"Yeah, well, you were supposed to keep your mouth shut. You think I want to be this? You want everyone to look at me differently and be scared of me? Is that what you want, Mitti? Well, let me tell you something. I will never be mistreated again and people will not find out about me because I am just like you and everyone else here. You are nothing better than me. Do I make myself clear?" Emily yelled at Mitti.

"I understand that was not my intention," said Mitti.

Emily then transformed into a Dark Zal, and within a flash, she was very close to Mitti's face. Her nose almost touched Mitti's nose. Mitti was very scared, and did not move a muscle.

"Let me find out you run your mouth again and see what happens," said Emily.

Mitti nodded. Emily turned around and disappeared out of the window. Mitti stood there, scared. She was afraid of Emily and wondered what Emily was capable of. Mitti did not know what to do anymore.

The following morning, Mike woke up next to Emily. She was still sleeping. She woke up about an hour after him. He was downstairs getting ready to go to work to handle some leftover paperwork. As she was coming into the living room, Mike said, "Well, you sure overslept. Did you not sleep well?"

"I'm fine. I slept fine. Was just tired I guess," Emily replied.

Mike gave her a kiss, said he had to go, and left the house. Emily sat in the kitchen and looked around for food.

Later on that day when Mike was on his way back home, he stopped at a gas station. He bumped into a man who was close friends with his parents. They both asked each other how they were doing. Mike told him good, and that is when the man said, "What is going on with that girlfriend of yours? I hear she knows something about the attack."

Mike was surprised to hear that.

"She does not know anything. Do not listen to anyone. Who told you that though?" Mike asked him.

"Nobody. Just heard it around. Well, take care," the man said and Mike waived him off.

Mike walked into the gas station, paid for his gas, came back out, and started pumping it. Then, Mitti pulled up in her car. Mike watched her park her car at the pump next to his. When she got out of her car, she saw Mike.

"Hi, Mike," she said as she continued to walk toward the station.

Mike grabbed her by her arm and pulled her closer and whispered to her.

"Why are you spreading rumors about Emily?" Mike asked her.

"Look, I only told Alex. What he does with that information, I cannot control. And also, please make sure that Emily does not come to my house anymore in the middle of the night threatening me," said Mitti.

"What are you talking about?" Mike asked her.

"You didn't know? She came last night around like two or three in the morning as I was sleeping. She got in through my second floor window. She threatened me, and I don't like it," said Mitti as she snatched her arm away from him.

Mike let her go and did not say anything else to her. Mitti slowly backed away and went on with her day.

"So that is why she slept in," he said to himself.

When Mike came home, Emily was studying on the floor in the living room. He walked in mad. He passed right past her and straight into the kitchen. She watched him walk by as she lay on the floor. She stood up and went after him.

"What is your problem?" Emily asked him.

"Where were you last night around two o'clock in the morning while I was sleeping?" Mike asked her.

She did not answer him. She turned around and was walking away back to her studying. Mike followed her.

"Don't walk away, Emily. Answer me. Where were you and what did you do?" Mike asked her, but now, he was yelling.

"It seems to me like you already know what I did and where I was so why are you asking?" Emily replied. She raised her voice as well.

"Yeah, I know. Why would you do that? Why did you go to her house?" Mike asked.

"Because she was spilling information about me to Alex, and who knows who else she would tell!" Emily yelled.

Mike paused for a minute. "So what? Who cares? It is her word against yours," he said. Mike was getting closer to her. He raised his voice at her. "You need to stop doing that to people!" he yelled.

"You told me to pay her a visit, so why are you mad?" she asked.

"I meant talk to her not threaten her," he replied.

"Well, I'm done talking!" she yelled.

Emily transformed into a Dark Zal, raised her arm and her force threw Mike against the kitchen cabinets. She lowered her arms and stood there, breathing heavily and looking at him. She realized what she did. She transformed back into herself, said "sorry" and ran out of the house. He did not go after her. He decided to give her some space.

Emily ran all the way to her father's house. When she entered, she knew he had a room for her upstairs. She ran right up the stairs and into that room closing the door after herself. Allen was sitting in the living room watching TV. He watched her run up the stairs and yelled after her. She did not respond. She was so angry at Mike that she did not want to see him for the rest of the day. She felt as he should be on her side since he was her boyfriend and not stick up for Mitti.

"I cannot believe he had the nerve to question me why I did what I did to Mitti. He is supposed to be on my side no matter what I did," she said to herself as she walked back and forth in her room.

She stopped and sat down on her bed facing the floor. Emily felt a presence, and she looked up. There, in the mirror on the dresser, she was, Aza'el. Emily got onto her feet, screamed, and ran toward the other side of the room. The image went away.

Her father came knocking on her door.

"Is everything okay in there? I heard you scream," said Allen.

"Yes, Dad, I just need some time to collect my thoughts please," said Emily.

"Oh you kids, you get on each other's nerve so quick," Allen said to her and went back downstairs.

Emily walked slowly toward the mirror. She touched it and nothing.

"Is there really something wrong with me? Am I just imagining this?" she asked herself.

She continued to stare at the mirror, and there, it showed up again for a quick second, Aza'el's face. Again, Emily backed away toward the wall and the image went away.

"What is happening to me?" she asked herself. Emily looked at the ring she wore. Then she remembered when Mayla told her that the ring will react to her feelings and emotions. Since Aza'el's blood runs through her veins, there will always be a connection.

Mike was at home waiting for Emily to return. Hours passed by and there was no sign of Emily. Mike called Allen and asked if she was over there. Allen told him that she was. Mike left his house to go and get her. When Mike pulled up to Allen's house, he knocked on the door. As soon as the door opened, Mike took a punch right to his face.

"Aw, what was that?" Mike asked.

Allen stood in the doorframe. "That is for making my daughter run back home," said Allen. Allen moved away from the door and allowed him to come in.

"That hurt, man. I don't know what's wrong with her. She has been acting strange. It's like when she gets mad, she's a totally different person. I really hope it's not happening again. I don't know what to do," said Mike.

Allen gave Mike a cold bag to put on his face.

"I am not sure, but you took her out of my house and she moved in with you. It is your responsibility now to keep an eye on her and keep her safe," said Allen.

Emily heard Mike in the house and decided to calm down and go downstairs. When she walked into the living room, she kindly looked at Mike and apologized for what she did. Mike got up from the sofa and walked over to her.

"Come home," he said and grabbed her hand.

She nodded and followed him out the door. Emily was walking behind Mike, and Allen grabbed her by her arm. She stopped walking, and Mike turned back to see what was going on.

"I need a minute with her, Mike," said Allen.

Mike left her, and he walked to his car.

"Emily, what is going on? You seem to distance yourself, and Mike is worried," said Allen.

"Nothing. I am fine. Just have a lot on my mind," said Emily.

Allen let her go, but he could see Emily was holding back on the truth. She left the house and hopped in the car. Allen watched them drive away as he stood at the door.

"She needs to get rid of that ring," said Allen to himself.

When they arrived home, Emily did not say a word. Mike asked her if she was all right. She told him yes and went to bed. Mike sat on the edge of the bed and stared at his girlfriend. He could see something about her was different again, but he was afraid to find out what it was. He decided not to worry for the night and went to sleep.

The following morning, Emily went to school to finish off her class for the semester. She sat in the classroom, completed her test, and turned it in. She looked out into the hallways through the open door and saw Mitti pass by. Emily followed her. Mitti met up with Pete in the back of the school, and they talked about their relationship. Emily was hiding behind the brick wall and listened.

"I honestly do not know what to do about us. I love you, but I can't be with you. I just don't see this working out," said Mitti.

Pete grabbed her hand and told her that nothing has changed. He still felt the same way about her. He loved her.

"I understand, but the fact that you watched her getting raped and did nothing about it bothered me," said Mitti.

"I understand. It bothers me as well. There is not one day that passes by that I don't think about it. I should have done something about it," said Pete.

"Honestly, I don't feel bad for her anymore. I am just mad she got you dragged into this mess. You know, everything was fine in this town until she moved here. She fucked everything up," said Mitti.

"Do not talk like that. Nobody deserves what happened to her. She has been through a lot. You used to be a nice girl. What happened to you?" Pete asked her.

"See, I don't know. I am just upset that our lives turned around so quick because of her," said Mitti.

"But it does not have to be like that. Just give us a chance," said Pete.

"You know, people in this town do not know that she is one of them. What do you think would happen if I told her to the authorities? Do you think they would kill her?" Mitti asked Pete.

Pete grabbed Mitti by her shoulders.

"Do not even think about doing something like that. They might lock her up and experiment on her. You know the government. She is not doing anything to anyone, so just let it go, Mitti," said Pete.

She exhaled and said, "Whatever," and then hugged Pete.

Emily placed her back against the school wall. She heard everything that was being said. "That bitch just won't stop," said Emily to herself. Her eyes turned fully black, and she ran across the grass away from the school.

Emily went to visit her dad again after school. When she walked into his house, he was in the living room.

"Hey, how was your day today?" he asked her.

She stepped in front of him, looked him in his eyes, and said in a very calm voice, "It was fine."

Her dad did not say anything else. The eyes he just saw were not his daughter's eyes. Emily walked upstairs and into her spare room.

"What is going on?" Allen asked himself.

Emily was in her room pacing back and forth. She was having bad headaches and chest pain. The tone of her voice was changing from deep to normal over and over again. She grabbed herself by her hair as her body had the urge to transform into a Dark Zal, but she tried her best to fight it off. She sat down on her bed and placed her head into her palms. She rocked back and forth saying, "No, no." She stopped rocking and got quiet. She quickly lifted her head up and looked into the mirror that was right across from the bed. She was a Dark Zal. She was feeling good, calm, and in peace. She did not have to fight the urge anymore. She smiled at herself. She slowly got up from the bed, walked over to the window, opened it, and jumped out. Emily was on her way to find Mitti.

Emily sat at Mitti's house and waited. It was about eleven at night, and here comes Mitti with a man she met at a bar. She was drunk and so was he. "I thought she was trying to make things work with Pete?" Emily asked herself. Emily was standing in the dark in a corner, watching them. Mitti and the man laughed, said jokes, hugged, and kissed. Mitti then opened the door to her home, and they walked in. Emily walked around and jumped in through a window. She walked quietly down the hallway and into the living room. She watched them from a corner, behind a wall. The man picked Mitti up and carried her to the couch. The man took her shirt off and was kissing on her breast. Mitti was moaning. The man asked her if she liked how he was kissing her, and she said yes. He then took her skirt off and her panties. She laid there naked on the couch. He took his shirt off and started kissing her again.

"I should not be doing this," said Mitti.

"It's fine. Trust me. You will enjoy it," the man said to her.

He placed his manhood inside of her and struck her over and over again, harder and harder. She moaned in pain and pleasure at the same time. Mitti tilted her head to the back and moaned. Her body was moving up and down. She told him to keep fucking her and not to stop. Her head was hanging off the couch and rocking back and forth as he was stroking her. Right before she was about to release he stopped. Mitti opened her eyes and looked at him. Her legs were still around his waist and his penis inside of her.

"What is wrong with you asshole? Keep going. Why did you stop?" asked Mitti.

The man did not move. He just looked down at Mitti.

"What the hell are you doing?" she asked him again.

Then, blood came out of his mouth, and his body was dropping on top of her. Mitti moved to the side and off the couch. His body fell faced down. She saw a knife in the back of his head. Mitti screamed and tried to get up to her feet. She quickly put on a long shirt with nothing underneath. She tried to run out of the door, but she heard a voice.

"You better not touch that doorknob."

She recognized that voice. Mitti turned around, and in the corner, she sees Emily.

"What are you doing here? Look what you have done, you crazy witch!" Mitti yelled at Emily as she pointed at the man.

Emily let out a short laugh and then her smile quickly disappeared as she yelled, "I am not crazy!" And at the same time, she transformed into a Dark Zal. Mitti was scared. She did not know if she should stay or run. She looked at the door, then at Emily, then at the door again and ran. Emily raised her hand, and the force of

Emily's power grabbed Mitti throwing her backward back into the living room. As Mitti's body flew away from the door, everything in the way was being knocked down, including lamps, and she hit the floor. When Mitti got back onto her feet, Emily was standing right in front of her face. Mitti begged Emily not to hurt her. Mitti saw Emily was not responding, so she pushed her out of the way and ran back toward the door. Emily grabbed her by her arm.

"Why didn't you leave me alone? I have done nothing but be nice to all of you, but all you do is keep fucking with me. Well, guess what. I think everyone should pay for what they have done to me, don't you think so?" Emily asked her as she held Mitti's hand aggressively. Mitti did not respond.

She picked Mitti up and threw her against the living room wall. She then picked up a scarf that was sitting on the couch and wrapped it around Mitti's neck. As she was strangling Mitti she said, "You had the nerve to tell Pete you were going to tell authorities about me. You want them to experiment on me? Is that what you planned to do? When I told you to keep your mouth shut, I meant it."

Mitti was struggling for her life as she was listening to Emily's words. She started shaking her head trying to tell Emily she was not going to do that, but it was too late. Mitti slowly stopped moving. She was dead.

Emily slowly laid her on the floor, looked at her body, and said, "It had to be done." Emily walked out the door, transformed back into herself, and walked home.

The following day, Mike pulled up at his company. Before he walked into the building, he saw Alex sitting on the side of the building. Mike stopped walking toward the building and instead walked toward Alex.

"What the hell are you doing here?" Mike asked him.

"Hey, man, I just want to know if you heard or seen Mitti. Pete and I have been calling her on her phone, but she's not answering. She's not answering her doorbell either," said Alex.

"No, why would I see her?" Mike asked him.

Alex did not answer his question. He thanked Mike for his time and walked away. Mike watched him leave and then left to work. As Mike was in his office doing some work, he overheard the newsman on the TV saying that the police found a dead body and it was identified to be Mitti. Mike could not believe what he saw. The police said they had no leads because no prints were left or clues, but they thought it was personal because there are no signs of robbery or forced entry. Mike sat at his desk with his elbows on the table and his head in his hands.

Emily was finishing up some paperwork at school and then started walking to Allen's house, when a classmate interrupted her.

"Hi, I'm Gia. I remember you from a couple of years ago. You have been gone for a while. What made you decide to come back to school?" Gia asked her.

"I don't know. I don't have anything else going for myself, so I thought I might as well finish the degree. Why you ask?" Emily asked her.

"Well, aren't you embarrassed to come to school after everything that has happened between you and Briana? Don't you think you should stay home or even better move back where you came from? Everyone thinks you did something to Briana," said Gia.

"Well, since everyone thinks that, don't you think you should be scared of me? How dare you walk up on me like this and question me?" Emily asked Gia as she stepped closer and closer toward Gia and Gia had to take a couple steps back.

Emily grabbed Gia by her throat and started squeezing. Gia got scared. Emily was going to choke her to death, but then, she heard more students walking their way.

"Today is your lucky day," said Emily to her, and she let Gia go.

Gia ran as fast as she could and called Emily crazy.

"I am not crazy. Just tired of your shit," Emily yelled back at Gia.

When Emily arrived at her father's house, he was already making dinner.

"Hey there, how was your day so far?" Allen asked her.

"It was fine, Dad, and yours?" Emily asked him.

"It was okay. Come sit down. We have to talk," said Allen.

"Do we really, Dad," Emily replied.

Her dad placed some food on the table, and they both sat down to eat.

"I'm not sure if you heard yet or not, but Mitti is dead," said Allen.

"Oh, wonder what happened to her," said Emily.

Allen was surprised by that statement but decided not to make a big deal about it. They continued to eat. They finished their dinner, and Emily was about to go home when Allen asked her to go to the backyard. She did, and he followed after her. Emily turned to her dad and asked what was going on. He then pulled out a pair of car keys and gave them to her. She was so excited. She took the keys and hugged him. She said, "Thank you," over and over again. She ran to the car that was in the driveway, sat in it, turned it on, and started to drive off. She stopped where her dad was standing. She rolled down the window and said, "Thank you, Dad. I love you," and she drove off.

When Emily got home, Mike was already there. He right away started questioning her if she had anything to do with Mitti's death. Emily told him she was not sure what he was talking about. The more Mike spoke of what he saw and heard on the news, she started to lose the sound of his voice. Her memories of being in Mitti's house replayed in her head. Tears overfilled her eyes. Emily looked up at him and the sound of his voice returned.

"What did you do, Emily?" Mike asked her in a more serious voice.

"I remember being there. I remember holding a scarf around her neck," said Emily.

After she said that, Mike was backing away from her. Emily saw how he was trying to get away from her.

"What is happening to you? I thought you said you are able to control your transformation? You can't walk around killing people," said Mike.

As Mike continued to talk down on her, she was sitting on the couch, rocking back and forth with her hands covering her ears. "Enough!" she yelled.

Mike stopped talking. She stood up with her head downward. Her arms were on the side of her body. Her hair fell over her face.

"You have no idea what it feels like to be in my shoes. You have never had to struggle, with your perfect parents, your perfect friends, your stupid perfect life," she said to him. She then lifted her head up and said, "You always had it easy. From high school straight to college, everything paid in full, had all the girls you wanted. Popular football player who never had to feel pain, and now you stand here and judge me? How dare you?"

Before Mike had the chance to say anything, she transformed into a Dark Zal and Mike backed away.

"Years have passed by, but the pain of being mistreated, hurt, bullied, and raped just can't go away. Do you know how bad that shit hurts?" she asked him. She did not let him respond. She raised her arm and used her powers of force to throw him around the house. Mike was hurt lying on the floor close to the kitchen. She turned her head toward the knives that were sitting on the kitchen counter and used her force to lift the knives up and they flew across the room.

"Emily, don't! Please!" Mike screamed.

At that moment, one knife stabbed Mike in his stomach. He moaned in pain as he held his wound.

"Shut up," said Emily as Mike held tightly to his wound trying to stop it from bleeding so much. She looked at him one last time, turned around, and left the house. Emily ran away from the house, and she did not want anything to do with Mike or anyone else. She was tired of hiding her real emotions to make others happy. As she was running she thought about how hard and overwhelming it was to fight her emotions every day. How hard she tries to overcome the anger she had built up over time. No matter how hard she tries, the emotional pain is still there. "I might as well let go and be a Dark Zal. It would be much easier," she said to herself.

Emily stopped running and leaned against a tree nearby the town. She saw the girl from school, Gia, walking down the street. It looked like she just got done reading at the library. Gia hopped into her car and drove home. When she pulled up at her house and got out her car, there she was, Emily, standing there in front of the garage.

"What the hell are you doing here?" Gia asked her.

Emily transformed into a Dark Zal, and Gia's eyes opened up widely. She could not believe what she saw.

"You are one of them?" Gia asked her.

Emily did not respond. She only stared at Gia. Gia started running away from her house. Emily used her force and dragged Gia backward back to her car. Gia dropped her purse to the floor. Emily slammed Gia against her car, and Gia screamed, "Help me! Someone please help me!"

Emily's force held Gia against her car not allowing her to move. Emily got closer to her face. Gia was crying and asked Emily why she was doing this.

"I will make sure you never mistreat anyone again. People will have to respect me from now on if they like it or not," said Emily.

"You are crazy just the way they said you were," said Gia.

"You know if I was in your situation right now, I would not be talking shit," said Emily.

Emily did not want to hear another word out of her mouth. She placed her sharp fingernails against Gia's forehead and started to dig, slowly, allowing her to feel the pain before she bled to death. Emily watched her die and then pulled her fingers back out of Gia's head dropping her body to the floor. Emily transformed back into a human and left.

Meanwhile, Allen was calling Emily all day on her phone but was not able to reach her. He also called Mike but no response. Allen drove to Mike's house at about one o'clock in the morning and saw the door was open. He right away new something was wrong. He grabbed his gun out of his truck and walked into the house. He quietly walked around and into the kitchen. He then saw Mike lying there with a knife in his stomach. He quickly ran up to him and placed a rag on his wound. He tried waking Mike up but nothing. He quickly hopped on the phone and called the ambulance. A couple of minutes later, the ambulance came and took Mike to the hospital, but Allen stayed at the house to wait for Emily. The police asked Allen if he knew what happened. Allen told them no, but it looked like a break in. The police asked Allen if anyone else lived there, and Allen told them no. Once the police left, Allen was looking around the house hoping he would find a clue.

"What have you done, Emily?" Allen asked himself.

Emily had nowhere to go and decided to spend the night at the bookstore. She walked to the bookstore because she left her car back at Mike's house. She unlocked the door, stepped in, and kept the lights off. Even if she wanted the lights on, she could not have it because the electricity was off. She did not pay the bill. Emily was looking around the bookstore looking for that book with Aza'el's ring on it. She knew she still had so many questions and was not sure which side to choose. She needed more answers. She finally found it. She sat in Gary's seat and opened the book. It was thick and dusty. She read so much, but she did not find any new information about the ring. She wanted to know why she was feeling the way she was even after Aza'el's death. She read more and more but nothing. She slammed the book shut and curled up in a corner. She started thinking about everything that has happened. "I don't know who I am anymore. I am scared of myself. I don't know what else I am capable of doing," she said to herself. She laid down on the ground against some books and closed her eyes. Then, she heard a sound. She slowly stood up and followed the sound. The sound sounded like someone or something was fishing for something. Emily transformed into a Dark Zal and continued to follow the sound. She walked between bookshelves. As she got closer to the noise, she saw a shadow of a person. Before she placed her hand on its back, the figure turned around. Emily grabbed it by its throat and dragged it closer to the window where the streetlight came in through the glass. Emily was shocked who she saw. It was the old man, Gary. Emily transformed back into herself. She let him go and took a couple of steps back, and she started to cry.

"What is going on here? What is happening?" Emily asked him.

Emily was freaking out. Gary came closer to her and told her that it was not over. Emily was confused. She asked him to explain. She asked him how he came across since the portal is closed. Gary took her hand and lifted it up for her to take a closer look at it. He asked her what she sees. She told him nothing, the same ring she always had. He explained to her that even though Aza'el is dead, her soul still remains inside that ring. Her spirit still comes around. Emily stumbled and knocked a couple of books off of a table. She sat down and thought things through. She remembered every time she felt angry, the ring would darken with spots. That is how she had the courage to murder Mitti and Gia. She did not care who died. Gary asked her if anything happened lately. She said, "Yes, I feel her with me."

"We opened the portal so I can come here and warn you, but I see it's too late," said Gary.

"I tried to explain to Mike what was going on with me, but he doesn't understand. I killed like three people. I don't know what to do anymore," said Emily.

"At this point, Emily, that ring does not make a difference. Aza'el is within you and always will be. The ring does not control you anymore. It is all you. The ring did what it had to do, which is release the power inside of you. Even though its creator is as evil as it can get, it is all on you how you use these powers. Plus, the ring can't be destroyed," said Gary.

"What am I supposed to do now?" Emily asked him.

"Come to Arfabele. We will find a solution," said Gary.

Emily told him there is no help for her. She fought and fought and can't overcome the powers of Aza'el.

"The only way to finish Aza'el off is to kill me and melt the rings, bury it together with me into the grave. There is no other way," said Emily.

Gary did not know what to say to that. "There have to be other options. I am sure we can find something," said Gary.

At that moment, they heard a knock on the door. "Open this door, Emily. I know you are in there," said the voice.

Gary walked to the door and opened it. When Allen saw him, he said, "I knew it. I just knew it. It's not over is it?" Allen asked, and Gary shook his head.

They both walked over to Emily, and Allen saw her sitting there, helpless.

"What can we do?" he asked Gary.

Gary told him they had to go back to Arfabele. Emily looked up at her dad. She told him she was sorry and cried.

"I killed Mike," she said to her dad in her crying voice.

"He will be okay. He is in the hospital," said Allen.

Allen told them he was going home to pack up some things, and they would leave in the morning to Arfabele. Gary agreed. Everyone went back to Allen's house and slept there for the night.

The following morning, Mike was feeling better in the hospital. He asked the nurse to be discharged, but she told him he had to stay for another two days. When the nurse left, he unplugged everything, got dressed, and left the hospital. He knew he had to help Emily. Meanwhile, Allen, Gary, and Emily were ready to go to the portal. Gary and Emily were already in the car waiting for Allen. Emily was in the passenger seat, when she felt a hand on her shoulder as the door was open.

Emily looked up thinking her dad needed something, but instead, she jumped out of the car and hugged him.

"I am so sorry. I thought I killed you," said Emily.

"I thought you killed me too," said Mike.

She told him she was very sorry and that it was better if he stayed away from her until they have figured out what to do with her. He told her he almost died because of her and there is no way he will miss out on the rest of the journey. Allen came out of the house, walked over to the car, and told them to get in. They did. All four were on their way to the portal.

Right before they arrived at the woods, Alex appeared out of nowhere from behind a tree. Allen slammed on the breaks, and the car stopped right in front of him. They all stared at Alex. Alex raised his gun and aimed at them. He yelled for Emily to get out of the car. Emily turned to Allen and then looked at Mike. Mike shook his head. Alex pulled the trigger, and the bullet went through the windshield and into Emily's seat. Alex yelled again for Emily to get out of the car. Slowly, all four doors opened up, and they all slowly got out of the car. As Emily stepped out, she told Alex to calm down.

"Do not tell me to calm down. You should take your own advice. Why should you deserve to live when many have died because of you?" Alex yelled at Emily.

"Alex, man, come on, we are friends. How can you do this?" asked Mike.

"We used to be boys, Mike. That ended a long time ago," said Alex.

Alex aimed the gun at Emily again, and when he pulled the trigger, Mike screamed, "NO!" The gun went off. At the same time the gun went off, Alex received an arrow through his head and the bullet missed Emily. All four of them watched Alex fall to the ground and then looked around to see who it was that did that. A Klexon from the Green Village stood on top of a tree holding a bow and arrows.

"You guys looked like you needed help," she told them and jumped off the tree onto the ground. She then told them to follow her. Mike and the rest of the crew looked at one another, and Mike said, "This never gets any easier."

When they arrived at the Green Village, some of the Klexons were happy to see Emily, but some were not. Emily felt the negative attention, and she felt unwelcomed. Emily asked Eliot why some of the Klexons were mad at her. "I will tell you the truth. They are tired. They are tired of Aza'el, and they are tired of you. We can't sit around and hope that you can control this or hope you don't do anything stupid. They are scared Emily." said Eliot.

Eliot left Emily standing by herself. Emily balled up her firsts and wanted to fight Eliot right there, but then, she heard Mike calling her name. Emily looked at Mike to see what he wanted, but then decided to ignore him. Emily walked over to Eliot and tapped her on her back. Eliot turned and faced Emily. "I am also tired of all the blaming on me. You don't know what it's like to be in the situation I am in," said Emily.

Before Eliot was able to say anything, Emily walked away.

Later that night, everyone was sitting outside around the fire discussing what they could do to keep their village and their forest safe.

"How can we get rid of it?" Emily asked them.

They knew what she meant. Everyone looked around at each other hoping someone would answer her, but nobody did. Gary stood up and started walking around the circle.

"There is no going back to being a normal human again. We have to find a way to kill Aza'el's soul or you just have to learn how to control it better. The last option is," said Gary, but before he finished his sentence, he stopped talking.

"What? What is it?" Mike asked.

"I know what needs to be done," said Emily. She stood up and excused herself from the meeting.

They watched her leave and walk into her cottage.

"What did she mean by that?" Mike asked.

"She is talking about taking her own life. The only way to destroy Aza'el's blood that runs through Emily is Emily's death," said Eliot, the warrior leader.

Allen jumped up and told the crew that would not happen. He told them to use their magic and do what they need to do to find another way. He was not losing Emily. Allen had enough. He did not want to hear another word so he left. Mike followed. Eliot turned her attention to Gary. "You shouldn't have said that," said Gary

"What was I supposed to say?" asked Eliot.

Gary exhaled and walked away. Eliot knew she didn't say anything wrong but tell the truth.

Chapter 22

THE REAL IS NOT REAL

The following morning, Emily got up and ran as fast as she could. The closer she got to the open field, she whistled, and there he came from high in the sky. Maxi was flying as fast as he could because he knew who was whistling for him. Maxi landed, and Emily jumped right on his back. She wrapped her arms around his neck and told him how much she missed him. "Lets fly!" she said. He took her around the mountains, the waterfalls, and high into the sky. Emily enjoyed Maxi's company. She forgets about everything when she is with him. Meanwhile, Mike was looking for Emily. He walked into Gary's cottage and asked Gary if he has seen Emily. Mike indicated he has not seen her since this morning. Gary told him she probably went to see her Visionair. Mike nodded and asked Gary what he was doing. Gary told Mike he was working on some spells trying to see if he could find an alternative way to save Emily.

"Good, because you know we cannot kill her," said Mike.

Gary looked at Mike straight into his eyes. "I know that, but if we don't find another way, then I don't see any other options," said Gary.

Mike took a couple of seconds to comprehend what Gary just told him. "I love her, and I can't live without her," said Mike.

When Emily returned back to the village, she found Mike and her father practicing fighting with the Klexon warriors outside on the open field. It was a late evening but still enough sunlight. Emily was walking by them as Maxi flew away. As she walked up to Mike, he was not paying attention to the arrow coming for his head. Emily caught it with her hand right in front of his face. Mike quickly turned his attention to the rest of the crew and realized he could have gotten killed.

"You might want to pay attention," said Emily.

Mike looked at her again and smiled. "Yeah, I do, but when something like you passes me by, I can't help it but look," said Mike.

Emily smiled, gave him the arrow, and left. Mike watched her leave.

"Come on, man, focus. You almost got killed!" Allen yelled out.

Mike turned his attention back to the field and smiled.

When Mike returned back to his cottage, Emily was sitting on the bed in her rope, showered. Her long wet hair fell down her back. Mike was all dirty and sweaty. He tried to hug her, but she told him to go shower first. They both laughed. When he came out of the shower, Emily was holding a picture of her mother. Mike asked her if she was okay. Emily told him she missed her a lot and she also missed Mayla. Emily watched Mike walk to the bed in pain. She told him she was sorry for trying to kill him. When she was upset, she couldn't control the anger and she admitted that. Mike told her he will sleep with one eye open just in case. Emily smiled.

"We will end this soon. I promise," said Mike.

"Mike, I know what needs to be done to end this," said Emily.

Mike walked over to her and grabbed her hand. "Do not talk crazy like that. We will figure it out. Gary is trying to find other options as well. You have to be strong for yourself, Emily, not for others," said Mike.

The next morning at the cottage, Emily went into the bathroom to brush her teeth. When she spat the water out and lifted her head back up, Aza'el's face appeared in the mirror. Emily screamed. Mike ran into the bathroom and asked her what happened. Emily was crying and telling him that she saw Aza'el in the mirror again. She walked out of the bathroom, and Mike followed.

"I cannot keep living like this, Mike," said Emily in a worried voice.

Mike hugged her and told her it would be okay. The next thing they heard was a scream coming from outside. Everyone was coming out of their cottages to see what was going on. Two Klexons were running into the village saying everything is destroyed.

"What is destroyed?" Gary asked the two Klexons.

One of the Klexons responded by saying, "The forest, it is rotting, it is burned, it is spreading toward the tree-flower. The fairies and the rest of the creatures will be killed if we don't stop it."

Gary had an idea. He ran as fast as he could into his cottage, grabbed a potion, and poured it over his cane. He walked back out and told Eliot to get a Grounder and give him a ride on it to the forest. Eliot did. Emily, Mike, and Allen followed as well and so did the Klexon warriors. The rot was spreading quickly, and the creatures that live within the forest were trying everything to stop it, but nothing. The rot was spreading fast destroying the forest nature and everything that lived in it. The Grounders ran fast into the forest, and they stopped right in front of it. As they watched the rot continue to spread, Eliot asked Gary if he knew what caused this.

"This is magic. Someone used magic to create this," said Gary.

The rot was coming at them like a big wave in the ocean. Gary faced it and behind him stood Eliot, the Grounders, and everyone else.

"Do something now!" said Eliot.

Gary lifted his cane in the air, said his spell, and slammed the cane into the ground. The trees shook, and a strong wind blew. A shield popped up from the ground shooting upward and away from Gary. Everyone else had to cover their eyes and take shelter because it was very powerful. The force and magic Gary used stopped the rot from spreading, and it killed the evil magic. Everyone surrounded

Gary and thanked him for stopping it, but everything that has been destroyed has died. There was nothing they could do about it.

"We can only hope it can be regrown again," said Gary.

Everyone cleaned up as much as they could; however, the rot stayed. It caused a lot of damage, but at this point, they did what they could. As they walked back to their village, Emily approached Gary.

"I feel her presence, Gary. I feel her everywhere I go. I can smell her. I can hear her think. I feel like I am her. It is driving me nuts. Every day, I fight to be myself," said Emily to Gary.

"I know, Emily. There is not much that I can do to help you with that," Gary replied.

He walked away from her, and she watched him. Gary was starting to feel that Emily was not strong enough to fight Aza'el off, and everyone else was suffering for it, but he still held onto hope. As he walked away, Emily watched everyone around her. They all looked at her angrily like she had something to do with the rot. They knew Aza'el ran through her blood, and there was always that possibility that Emily could have done it. Emily did not feel comfortable being with the Klexons anymore and decided to go back to the human's world. She hurried back to her cottage and grabbed some of her things. At that point, her father walked in. Allen asked her where she was going, and she told him back home. Allen explained to her she was not ready to be out in the human's world without the Klexon's supervision. After her dad told her that, she got even more upset.

"So you don't believe in me anymore either?" she asked her dad.

He told her that was not true, but she did not want to hear it anymore. She grabbed her things and walked right past her dad. As she sped off to the portal, Mike saw her and followed her. Allen saw Mike going after her, but he stayed behind.

As Emily and Mike were on their way to their house, they argued the entire time. Emily was complaining about how she did not belong with the humans or the Klexons and she might as well be better off with Aza'el. Mike told her to stop talking crazy. When they finally arrived at their home, they walked in and both stopped at the front door. Everything inside of their house was destroyed.

"Who did this?" Mike asked as he walked further into the living room.

Emily told him she had no idea. Then, they heard someone running around in their house, and Emily got ready to attack as she transformed into a Dark Zal. Mike looked at her and got worried because of how quick she was ready to fight. From around the corner of their living room, Pete stepped out. Emily quickly transformed back into human. Mike asked him what he was doing here, but before Pete could answer, Mike noticed how angry Emily got just by seeing Pete, therefore, he pulled Pete by his shirt guiding him outside. "What are you doing here? Did you do that to my house?" asked Mike. Pete told him that he did not destroy the house, but he wanted to explain himself. Mike told him he did not want to hear it and told him to leave.

"Okay, let me just say that I saw something unusual here. I tried to follow it, but it was too fast. It did not look human," said Pete.

Mike looked at Pete and said okay. Pete saw Mike still wanted him gone, so he said he was sorry and left. Mike walked back into the house and told Emily what Pete said.

"We both know what that means," said Emily, and Mike nodded.

Later that night, Emily went to the gas station down the street from her house. Since they had everything destroyed, she needed to get a couple of things for the house, like some food. Emily was at the register getting ready to pay. She looked out the window and saw four boys bullying on another boy. She could hear the four boys calling the one boy ugly, fat, freak, and other things. These boys looked to be in their teens. They started pushing the one boy around. Emily was waiting on the cashier guy to hurry up because the bullies were really starting to upset her. She finally took the bag and left her change. She walked out, and right when one of the boys tried to kick the kid, Emily grabbed him by his shirt. The other three boys yelled at Emily and told her to let him down. She looked at all of them in their eyes and made her eyes turn from normal to all yellow. The three boys got freaked out and ran away. Emily held the fourth boy and threw him against the concrete, and his arm broke. The boy screamed in pain. Emily told him to get up and run before she breaks a leg too. The boy did. The kid that was getting bullied on was scared of Emily too, but he did not move. Emily turned to him, looked down at him as he was sitting on the ground, and she gave him her hand. She helped him get up and whispered in his ear that he was not a freak and never to let people talk to him that way. She told him to do what he needs to do to protect himself and not to be scared to fight. The boy watched her get into her car and leave. She watched the boy in her mirror as he disappeared. As she continued to drive down the long street, something slammed on top of the roof of the car and created a dent. Emily turned the wheel and almost crashed. The car stopped, but Emily did not get out of the car. She sat in her seat, quietly. Thump! There it was again, another hard stomp on top of the car. She quickly jumped out and looked around. Nobody, nobody was there. She walked around the car and looked everywhere, nothing. "Someone or something wants to mess with me, okay," she said to herself, sat back in the car, and drove off. When Emily got home, she told Mike what happened with the car. He had no explanation for it either.

That night, Emily and Mike went to Gary's bookstore to see if they would find anything new about the Dark Zals. As they were finishing up with their reading and locked the bookstore behind themselves, they saw from a distance Nikki and Jack walking with a child. Emily and Mike approached them.

"Hey, Nikki, it's been a while," said Emily.

"Hey there guys, how have you been? Let me introduce you to our daughter Kayla," said Jack.

"Your daughter?" Emily replied back with a question.

"Yes, isn't she adorable?" asked Nikki.

"Yes, she sure is," Emily replied with a soft voice.

Mike did not have anything to say. Emily got quiet as well. Nikki gave Emily a blank stare and asked her if something was wrong. Emily told her nothing, "But it just seemed like it's been only a couple of months ago when you announced that you were pregnant," said Emily.

Nikki looked at her confused. "Oh, I must have not known I was pregnant until later on. Had my dates wrong," said Nikki.

Emily gave Nikki a smile and told them she had to go and will catch up some other time. Jack smiled and said okay. Mike and Emily left. When they got home, Emily told Mike she was feeling some sort of connection to that child. Mike told her to stop it and not start one of her craziness again. Emily looked at Mike.

"I'm serious. There is something about that child," said Emily.

"Emily, you need to stop. Not everything is abnormal just because you are," said Mike.

Emily got upset that he viewed her as abnormal because she's half and half. She ran past him and to the bedroom.

"Emily, I'm sorry. I didn't mean it like that," he said to her, but she locked the door. Mike left her alone for now.

Emily was falling asleep as Mike unlocked the room and walked into the bedroom. He lay down next to her and went to sleep. In the middle of the night, Emily started feeling pain and a hard time breathing. She felt like she was dreaming that she was dying but could not catch her breath. She finally woke up and opened her eyes to see a black figure standing over her choking her. Emily started to fight back but for some reason was having a hard time to escape from those hands. She swung her arm and hit Mike. He woke up and saw the figure on top of Emily. Mike jumped on the figure, but the figure got away. It ran toward the window and jumped out. Mike ran to the window and looked out, but nothing. It disappeared. Emily was coughing and gasping for air. Mike returned to comfort her.

"Who and what was that?" Mike asked her.

"I do not know," Emily replied.

Mike held her in his arms. She calmed down and told him who-ever it was, she would find them and make them pay for what they just did. Emily managed to go back to sleep, but Mike did not. He sat there on the bed, freaked out.

"What the hell did I get myself into with this girl?" he asked himself as he continued to sit on the bed wide awake.

The following morning, Emily walked to the library. Before she entered into the facility, she bumped into a boy and his mother. The woman started yelling at Emily for breaking her son's arm. At first, Emily did not know who this woman was until she looked at her son. Emily remembered the boy from when he was bullying on the younger kid. However, as the woman continued to yell at Emily, Emily told her that she did not know what she was talking about. Emily tried to convince the woman that she did not touch her son. However, the woman would not let it go. She came closer to Emily's face and yelled more. Emily grabbed the woman by her throat and told her to fuck off and next time she catches her son bullying on someone again, she will break his neck. The woman did not say any-thing anymore. As Emily held her by her throat, she looked passed the woman into the windows of the library and saw her again. She saw Aza'el. The reflection in the mirror was not Emily. Emily let the woman go and walked passed her closer and closer to the windows. She realized the way she moved, the reflection of Aza'el moved as well. Emily got so close to the window. She touched the face of Aza'el with her hand. The woman grabbed her son and as she was walking away she said, "You are insane." Emily did not pay her any attention. Emily continued to look at the reflection in the windows and realized that she was Aza'el. Emily realized she was doing all the dirty work for Aza'el. Emily backed away from the window, and the reflection of Aza'el went away and the image of Emily appeared.

When she returned back home, she told Mike what happened.

"Emily, I feel like we will never be happy or have a peaceful relationship. I do not know how much more of this I can take? What can I do to help you solve this?" he asked her.

Emily was a little upset because of what Mike said. She told him he did not understand her and never will. She was tired too, always needing to fight with herself.

"What do you think we can do here?" Mike asked her.

"I don't know. Do you think Aza'el will win?" Emily asked him.

"I don't know. I guess that depends if you are getting weak," said Mike.

Mike told her to come with him to see Gary, maybe he discovered something new that could help them. When they arrived at the Green Village, they saw the rot in the forest was still there. As they walked from the portal toward the cottages, Emily tripped on something and fell. As she got up, her and Mike saw it was a Klexon, dead, just lying there on the ground. It was a female, and it looked like she was stabbed about five times and left there to rot. Mike picked the Klexon up and carried her to the cottages. When the other Klexons saw Mike carrying one of their kinds, they ran to him and asked what happened. Emily told them that they found her by the portal already dead. Eliot looked at Emily with anger.

"Did you do this?" asked Eliot angrily.

Emily looked at Eliot but did not respond. Mike told Eliot not to talk to Emily like that. Emily then looked around at the rest of the Klexons, and she felt as they were looking at her the same way Eliot was. Emily asked everyone if that was how they all viewed her now, if they looked at her as a murderer and not one of them. Nobody answered. Mike gazed at Emily. He did not say anything to her either. She back away from everyone and ran back toward the portal. Mike called after her, but she did not return. Mike handed over the dead body to Eliot and left to catch up to Emily.

"Wait, Emily. Where the hell are you going?" Mike asked her.

"I am out of here. I am not welcomed here!" she said as she continued to walk toward the portal.

Mike ran up to her and grabbed her arm.

She stopped walking and turned to him. "You know, I thought you guys believed in me. Mayla was right. This will never end, and since I'm a witch, humans won't accept me. But since I am a Dark Zal and not a Klexon, they won't accept me. I guess I'm on my own!" she yelled at Mike.

"Emily, that is not true. You just have to prove yourself to them and understand where they are coming from. You have killed before. I think you know why they would question it," said Mike.

Emily did not say anything. She looked at Mike and couldn't believe what he has said. Emily started to walk again but then stopped and quietly turned to face him again.

"You have felt the same way the entire time, haven't you? You never had the nerve to say anything until now!" said Emily.

"What are you talking about? I am here for you, and I'm trying to help you understand where they are coming from. If Aza'el is dead, who could have done that then? You keep saying that her soul is still alive through you, but how? Nobody has ever seen her image through you. How do you expect others to believe that?" Mike asked her.

"We both just found her dead. When could I have killed her?" Emily asked him, but he did not respond. "It is better if you do not follow me anymore until all this is resolved," said Emily.

As she started to walk away again, she started hearing voices in her head. She grabbed her head and squeezed. She yelled out in pain because the voices were loud and they were telling her to kill Mike and finally get rid of him. But she tried to ignore it and continued to tell the voices to go away. Then, she heard only one voice, laughing in her head, laughing at her. The voice was Aza'el. The voice finally faded away, and Mike walked up to her trying to help her. Emily dropped her hands down, and Mike saw the veins in her face. Emily saw how he looked at her with scare in his eyes, and she waived her hand using her force to throw him away into the bushes. She then ran off toward the portal and jumped in.

Chapter 23

THE TURNAROUND

When Emily returned back to the human's world, she was very upset. She stayed in the woods by the portal and did not know what to do with herself anymore. She felt like she was going to go crazy, insane, or lunatic all at once because she couldn't handle it anymore. She walked back and forth in those woods. She was going crazy, hearing the voice of laughter in her head again. Emily held her head and screamed for the voice to go away. She finally calmed down and looked around in the woods. It was getting dark, and she saw the tree, a specific tree. She slowly walked closer to the tree, touched it, and the memories of getting raped returned. She quickly pulled her hand away from the tree and ran out of there. At this point, she just wanted to be alone. She was so overwhelmed and was not sure how much longer she would be able to control herself, her emotions, her anger, or people in general. Sometimes, she felt like giving in to Aza'el and do what Aza'el wanted just to make her own life easier.

As Emily walked away from the woods and passed the town, she was walking between two buildings. All of a sudden, something fell right in front of her. She stopped walking. She was trying to see what it was, but it was too dark outside. She walked closer and closer and then saw it was a dog cut open. Emily placed her hand over her mouth and looked up to see where the dog came from. She saw a shadow disappeared into the night jumping from one building onto another. Emily transformed into a Dark Zal and followed. Emily tried to catch the shadow, but it got away. She stood on top of a building looking into the night. She had to find out what that was because no human was capable of doing what that shadow did.

Emily looked over the city and toward the woods. As she gazed around the town and the forest, she noticed the tree branches moving in the woods. She jumped off the building and ran as fast as she could back toward the woods. She hid behind a rock and watched. There was nothing but blackness around her. She did not take her eyes off of the woods. She knew there was someone out there. As she closely listened to the sound of the wind, and watched the tips of the trees, she saw it. Quickly she ran deeper into the woods and followed the trail of the moving branches. Her yellow eyes lit up in the night. "Got you," she said and slammed right into the shadow. Emily pushed the figure into a tree, and the figure turned to face Emily. They were facing one another, but Emily was still not able to see who it was. It was too dark, and the person was dressed all in black with a hood over their head.

"What are you?" Emily asked the individual. Emily did not receive a response. The person stood there with their head down not saying a word. Emily ran toward the person to fight, but right before Emily got too close, the individual turned away and ran up a tree like a monkey and disappeared. Emily did not follow.

"We will cross paths again," said Emily to herself.

Emily was not in the mood to face neither Mike or her dad. She walked to a park and slept on a bench. Meanwhile, back at the Green Village, Mike and Allen hoped that Emily was okay. As Allen was getting ready to go to bed, Mike left the Green Village to look for Emily. Mike knew he had to find Emily, not to protect her, but to protect others from her. Mike left the village, went through the portal, and into the human's world. When he saw she was not home, he walked around the town yelling for her name but received no response. He kept looking and looking even through windows trying to see if maybe she went inside a building for the night, but no sign of Emily. As he passed another building and was calling for her name, something grabbed him quickly and held him against a brick wall. It held Mike by his throat and squeezed. Mike kept gasping for air but nothing. He tried to kick it, but he missed. He was not able to see who it was or what it was. It had a dark hoodie over its face. Mike thought that was it for him. He thought he was going to die. He raised his arm and tried to take the hoodie off, but when he grabbed the face, the person moved back. The person then punched Mike in his face, and Mike fell on one knee. When his knee hit the ground, the blue rock fell out of his pocket. The rock rolled closer to the shadow's feet, and the shadow backed away from it. It did not attack Mike anymore. Mike looked up seeing the figure looking down at the blue rock and then turned and ran away. Mike got up to his feet, walked over to the rock, and picked it up.

"Only witches are afraid of this," Mike said to himself and wondered if that was Emily trying to kill him. If not, then it's another witch.

After he searched for hours and still no sign of Emily, he decided to go home and wait for her there hoping she would return. The following morning, Emily did arrived at Mike's house. She thought Mike was at the Green Village, but instead, there he was sitting on the couch waiting for her. She saw he was beat up and asked him what happened to him.

"I was looking for you last night. Where were you?" he yelled at her loudly.

"I had to get away for a little and I did not know where to go, so I slept in the park. What is your problem?" asked Emily.

Mike stood up from the couch, walked up to her, and told her that he got the shit kicked out of him and was almost killed last night while looking for her. She asked him what happened and he told her.

"The only reason why I am still alive is because of this," he said and pulled out the blue rock.

Emily backed away. She grabbed her stomach and was telling him to put it away. Mike put it back into his pocket.

"Exactly," said Mike.

"What are you doing?" she asked him.

"It dropped out of my pocket last night and that thing, whatever it was, backed away from me. It was scared of it. Only witches are afraid of this, Emily," said Mike.

"Are you asking if it was me?" she asked him.

Mike looked at her angrily and exhaled heavily. "Of course not," he said to her in a softer voice and walked over and kissed her. "It has been crazy lately, and it scares me. It was different before. Before, you were your own body; but now, it's like there are two people inside of you and it's a little freaky," he said to her.

"You have no idea how it feels for me. I get this rage of wanting to kill and sometimes even you, but I fight it because I love you. I am scared too, because it gets harder and harder every time," she said to him.

They both were quiet for a moment.

"Anyways, about this thing that tried to kill you, where do you think it came from?" Emily asked him.

Mike told her he was not sure especially because he can't remember any of the Dark Zals surviving when Aza'el was destroyed.

"We need the Klexon's help," said Mike.

Emily right away told him she was not going back there anymore. Mike told her to stop acting like that and to come with him. She told him no and walked away. She went into their bedroom and closed the door. Mike went after her and yelled. "You cannot stop now. We are in the middle of everything. We have to finish it, Emily. Nobody else will help us besides the Klexons!" But when he entered into the room, the window was open and she was gone. "Damn it, Emily!" Mike yelled.

Emily left the house and did not want to go back to the Green Village. She was so tired of everyone doubting her, but at the same time, she knew they had good reasons to doubt her. As she walked, she saw a nice fast-food spot. She got a burger and fries and took it to go. She did not know where to go, so she went to Gary's bookstore.

She sat at his old desk and started to eat. About halfway into it, Emily dropped her burger on the table, looked at it, and started to cry. She wrapped her food back up into the bag and moved it to the side. She placed her hands over her head and continued to cry. She could not even eat normal. She lost all her appetite for regular food. "I do not know what else to do with myself. I am so lost in this world. I can't trust anyone because they don't trust me," she said to herself. "I trust you, and you should be able to trust me," a voice came from a distance. She quickly stood up from the chair and saw him standing there.

"I thought I would find you here," said Mike.

She was happy to see him, but she pretended not to be. "What are you doing here?" she asked him.

Mike walked up to her, grabbed her hand, and told her to come with him. "There are others who want to help you too. Trust me," he said to her.

She hesitated at first but then agreed to go with him.

When they arrived at the Green Village, Allen was happy to see his daughter. Emily was not too happy to be back. Eliot and Emily exchanged looks but didn't say anything to one another. Eliot turned her back to Emily and walked away. Emily watched her leave, but she didn't care anymore what Eliot thought of her. All of a sudden, they saw Maxi flying left and right. He was not able to keep his wings open straight. He was bumping into trees and cottages on his way down and then slammed onto the ground. The Klexons ran to help him. Maxi was hurt badly. Emily quickly ran toward him. She stood by Maxi and placed her hand over his chest. She felt his breathing. It was heavy. His wing was shot with an arrow, and he had cuts on his leg and chest. He was bleeding badly. Emily was upset. Maxi was the only thing she admired so much. Gary ran into his cottage and came back out with medicine, gauze, and some liquid for the creature to drink. Gary told Maxi not to fly anymore until the bleeding stopped, and he was all healed up.

Maxi was in so much pain, Emily couldn't watch anymore. She turned away from Maxi and ran toward the portal not looking back. She was mad as hell and wanted to find whoever did this to Maxi. Before she jumped into the portal, Gary stepped in front of her using his magic. She stopped and faced him.

"Whatever you are going to do, you need to think twice before you do it," said Gary.

"Whoever did that to Maxi will pay," said Emily.

"Let me help you," said Gary.

"There is something following me, and I don't know what or who it is. I will find it, and I will destroy it. Keep an eye out on Maxi," she said and jumped into the portal.

Gary watched her disappear into the portal, and he shook his head. "That girl will get us all killed one day if she's not careful," he said to himself and went back to the village.

Mike, who was next to Maxi, saw Gary walking back into the village. When Gary got close enough, Mike said, "She left again, didn't she?"

Gary nodded.

As Emily was out in the darkness looking around the city for the figure that was following her, she stumbled into a man who was sexually harassing a woman. The woman was screaming for help, but nobody was around. Emily right away remembered when she was raped and rage took over her. Emily jumped from the top of the building behind them two. The man heard some footsteps, let the woman go, and turned around to see who it was.

"Hey, asshole, why don't you mind your own business?" the drunk man asked.

The closer he walked toward Emily, the better he was able to see her. Emily was transformed into a Dark Zal, and when the man realized what he was looking at, he tried to run. As his back was turned to her, Emily lifted her arm up and used her force to lift him off the ground. She carried him in the air toward her. He was floating right in front of her. Emily looked up at him, and he looked at her. He told her to let him go. Emily smiled. With her other hand, she unzipped the man's zipper and grabbed his penis.

"You are really proud of this one, aren't you?" she asked him in a deep voice.

The man did not respond. Emily ripped his penis right off of his body. There was blood everywhere, and the man screamed in pain. She dropped him to the floor and started eating on his neck. As Emily continued to eat the man's flesh and suck out his soul, the hooded shadow saw the whole thing. It was not until the man stopped screaming and stopped moving that Emily lifted her head up, her eyes went from yellow to normal, and she realized what she was doing. She quickly spat out the flesh and wiped her mouth. She transformed back into human and backed away from the body. She looked down at her bloody hands, then at the dead body and ran home. Once she entered her house, she locked the door behind herself, sat on the floor with her back leaned against the door, and she cried herself to sleep. Next thing she knew, she felt a hand on her shoulder and she woke up. She laid there, dirty and bloody on the floor by the door. As she opened her eyes, she saw Mike. She slowly stood up and Mike asked her, "What have you done?"

Emily looked at herself again and saw the blood. "I am sorry. I don't know anymore. I tried helping a woman who was attacked and rage took over me," she said.

"Damn it, Emily, not again!" Mike yelled. He tried to get closer to her, but she backed away.

"No, get away from me. I am disgusting like this, and there is nothing I can do about it. I can't fight it anymore!" she said to him as her voice started to change.

Mike tried getting closer again, but now, she yelled, "Go AWAY!" Mike never heard her talk like that before. Dark lines formed on her face. Her eyes filled with the color of yellow. Emily saw the way he looked at her, with disgust, so she turned away from him and ran out of the house. He followed her. She walked faster and told him to leave her alone. He said he would not do that and told her to stop running away and face him.

"I am gross and you deserve better," she said.

"Stop talking crazy. I love you and will do what I have to do," said Mike.

Emily stopped walking and grabbed her head. She was hearing voices in her head again and she screamed. Mike grabbed her and asked her what was going on. She lifted her head up and stared straight into his face. He felt her breath on his cheeks. It was cold. She was breathing heavily, and the colors of her eyes were changing.

"Run!" she yelled to him.

Her voice was breaking between hers and the evil sound. Mike could tell she was trying to fight it, but Aza'el was too strong.

"Run, damn it!" she yelled at him again.

Mike ran as fast as he could. A couple of blocks down, he stopped to catch his breath. He slowly turned toward the direction he was running from, and as soon as he turned around, she jumped on him and knocked him to the ground. She was transformed into a Dark Zal and wanted to kill him. Mike realized that loving her would not save him now and he had to fight back. She was sitting on top of him trying to bite his neck. He punched her a couple of times but nothing. She was too strong. She scratched his face with her long nails. Mike held her face away from his to prevent her from plunging her teeth into his flesh. He managed to throw her off of him and quickly pulled out the blue rock. He held it close to her face, and she started crawling backward away from him. Mike slowly got up onto his feet and continued to hold the blue rock in front of her.

"Emily, come back to me!" said Mike.

Emily was laughing. Her voice was so deep and creepy.

"She is gone," Emily responded, but it was not really Emily, the voice was not hers. "That rock won't always be with you. It won't save you next time," she said and ran in the opposite direction.

"Fuck! This shit is crazy. She's lucky she turns me on," he said to himself.

Back at the Green Village, Gary and Allen were researching how to save Emily without killing her. At that moment, Mike storms into Gary's cottage and says, "Guys, we have a problem."

Allen stopped doing what he was doing and gave Mike his full attention. Gary continued to work on his potions.

"Speak. What happened?" Allen asked him.

"Emily tried to kill me. I think we are too late," said Mike.

"Where is she?" Allen asked him.

"I don't know," Mike responded.

"I am not giving up on her, and I will not lose her," said Allen.

"We have to find her," said Mike.

"Finding her will not be hard. However, when we find her, we will have to finish her. That time has come," said Gary.

"No! There has to be another way!" Allen yelled. He grabbed Gary by his shirt and pulled him close to his face.

"I will save her," Allen said and pushed Gary to the side.

Gary watched Allen walk out of the cottage and said, "It's too late."

Mike was standing outside, leaning against his and Emily's cottage watching Gary walk outside and order Eliot to gather the warriors and start looking for Emily. Mike walked over to Gary and said, "You are really doing this."

Gary ignored him as he was walking away. Mike grabbed him by the back of his shirt and turned Gary around to face him. Allen happened to walk by and saw them two arguing.

"What is going on?" Allen asked them.

Mike took a couple of steps away from Gary and said, "He ordered Eliot and the warriors to find Emily. They will kill her."

Allen looked at Gary and asked him if he really did that. Gary nodded.

"How could you do this? She helped you with your dead wife, she saved all of you, and now that it's time to save her, you are raising your hands in the air?" Allen asked angrily.

"I can't continue to allow her to kill innocent people or any Klexons. She has become weak. I tried other ways, but we have come to our last resort," said Gary.

"I will go with the warriors. I can try to bring her back to us," said Allen.

"Good luck," said Gary.

Gary wanted to save Emily as much as Allen and Mike did, but he couldn't risk anymore lives. Allen followed the warriors as they were leaving the village. Eliot was riding a Grounder and so was Allen. She looked back and locked eyes with Allen. She smiled at him and then turned back around facing the front. Allen was irritated.

Emily was running in the woods. She ran as fast as she could, and when she got to the deepest end of the forest, she stopped. She looked around. It was quiet. The quietness of the woods helped her to finally calm down. She looked down at the ring, and saw the darkness floating inside of it. She sat down onto the dirt and leaned against a tree. She looked up into the sky and gazed around into the darkness. "This world seems to be so quiet and peaceful and yet so evil," she said to herself. She felt so tired. She leaned her head against the tree and closed her eyes. As soon as she closed her eyes to relax, she heard her again. Aza'el's voice was getting louder and louder inside her head. "No! No!" Emily yelled as she grabbed her head. The voice wouldn't leave. Aza'el was laughing inside of Emily's head. Emily could not take it anymore. She turned her head to the left and pulled out a pocket knife. "I cannot do this anymore," she said to herself. She held the knife in her hand and lifted it. She held it in front of her chest, grabbed it with both hands, and was ready to stab it straight through her heart. Tears fell down her face as the voice in her head continued to laugh. "It's over," said Emily. Right before the knife went through her skin, someone screamed her name. Emily stopped. She turned her head toward the voice that called out for her. There he was along with Maxi. Mike stood there, scared, but still walking slowly toward her. Emily dropped her hands and watched him and Maxi. Maxi slowly walked up to Emily and lowered his head onto her lap. Mike asked her not to do it. He told her he loved her and he needed her in his life. Emily did not say anything. Maxi still laid in front of her. Right away, Emily started hearing Aza'el's voice again.

"Please leave now before things get worse," she said to Mike as she still sat on the ground leaned against the tree with Maxi's head on her lap.

"I am not going anywhere unless you come with me," said Mike.

Emily let out a short laughter. "You know, you never listen. I am tired, I am crazy, right now, I am mad as hell, and who knows what else is going on inside my head right now? So for your own safety, I am asking you to LEAVE!"

She yelled as the Dark Zal's features were coming in. Maxi felt Emily's presence fading away. He slowly lifted his head off of her lap and backed away. Mike knew something was about to happen. Her long dark hair fell over her face. She lifted the knife up and was going to end her life. Mike yelled, "NO!"

"There is no other solution," said Emily.

"Maxi brought me here to you, because he can sense you, which means you are still in there somewhere," said Mike.

Emily listened to what he said, and she lowered her arms down to her waist still holding the knife in her hand. Emily turned her head to face Mike as tears slid down her cheeks.

"I hear her all the time. I see her in the mirrors all the time. The only way to get rid of this whole thing is to kill me," said Emily.

Like she was in a hurry, she lifted the knife again; and this time, she went for it. Mike screamed and ran toward her to try to stop her, but it was too late. Right when the knife poked her flesh leaving a small mark of blood, Emily was hit with a rock, knocking her over to her side and she dropped the knife.

"Emily!" Mike yelled and ran over to help her. He was on one knee helping Emily as he looked around to see who threw the rock. Mike looked up at the figure dressed in all black but could not see who it was. Its back was turned to him. Emily slowly stood up. It was dark in the woods, and all they heard were wind and leaves moving in the trees. The figure slowly turned to face them and took its hood off. Emily could not believe who she saw.

"What the hell is going on here?" Mike asked.

Emily did not say a word. She did not take her eyes off of Nikki. Yes, it was her friend Nikki. She was a witch, a Dark Zal. Nikki then transformed herself back into a human.

"Surprise," said Nikki as she walked around Emily and Mike. She smiled at Emily, but Emily couldn't believe what she saw.

"I know this is shocking to you. But don't worry. I am here to help you," said Nikki.

"You, how could you do this? The entire time I thought you were my friend. I told you almost everything about me," said Emily. Emily transformed into a Dark Zal and attacked. Emily jumped high into the air and Nikki transformed into a Dark Zal and followed. They met in midair, grabbed each other, and came back down on their feet. Emily was throwing punches back to back, but Nikki was dogging them.

"I will kill you!" said Emily.

"I came here to show you that you should be on our side," said Nikki as they continued to throw punches at each other.

Emily backed away and stopped fighting. Nikki stopped as well. They looked at one another, and Mike was in the background watching to see what was going to happen next.

"Our side?" Emily asked confused.

"Yes!" said Nikki.

She ran up to Emily grabbing her by her throat, dragging her across the grass, and slammed her against a tree. She held Emily against the tree for a minute and Mike tried to run up on Nikki to help Emily, but Nikki used her powers to lift Mike and toss him across a river. Nikki turned her attention back to Emily. Nikki let Emily go and took a couple of steps back. Emily grabbed her own throat for comfort and looked at Nikki.

"How do you have those powers? Only major witches have those powers," said Emily.

Nikki tilted her head and smiled.

"Emily, Emily, why can't you use that brain of yours. I am the daughter of Aza'el. A very long time ago, my mom fell in love with a human. But none of the Klexons accepted it. They left my mother like an outsider just because she had me with a human. Of course, the human did not want anything to do with my mother because he found out later that she was a witch and left us. My mother was crushed. She loved him and he left her with a child, and the Klexons never accepted my mother or me because of it and my mother had nowhere to turn to. The Klexons always said to keep us and the humans separate. You see, my mother tried to combine us; but instead, everyone turned their backs on her. And then some years later, her sister, Alona, fell in love with a human, you know, Gary, and for some reason the Klexons had no problem with that. Oh, that did it for my mother," Nikki said with laughter. "So you see, my mother had no choice. They made her evil. My mother started her own army and became a Dark Zal, but then Alona placed a spell on her and I never saw her again. Then one day, I saw you in school with that ring. I knew it was time. I have been looking for that ring my entire life," said Nikki as she walked over to Emily's knife that was on the ground. Nikki picked it up.

"What about your parents here. Who are they?" Emily asked.

"Those are not my real parents. They adopted me. Before Alone placed a spell on my mother, she sent me through the portal into the human's world. She thought I would be better off here, but I was not. None of the Klexons came looking for me. None of them cared what happened to me! I searched and searched for that ring everywhere so that I could bring my mother back, but I never found it. Then, you came along and there it was. I knew the time would come for me to see my mother again and for us to complete what she started. But you are making this very difficult. Oh, you really pissed me off when you killed her. You know I still loved her," said Nikki.

"Now what?" asked Emily.

"Look around you, Emily. In this world, every hour, every minute, there is some sort of disappointment, hurt, or betrayal. Aren't you tired of it?" Nikki asked Emily and gave her the hand to join Nikki.

Emily did not take her hand.

Nikki dropped her hand and asked, "How many times will you get hurt, Emily? Do these people really love you? Or is it just a matter of time until they disappoint you again?"

Emily looked around. She saw Mike struggling to get over the rushing river to get to her side. Maxi was not around. Emily was not sure where he went. Emily took her time to think. What Nikki said was true. Maybe it was meant for her to join Nikki. She looked down at the ring and remembered how much pain it brought her. Emily took a couple of steps forward and extended her hand to Nikki. Nikki smiled and grabbed Emily's hand.

"You don't have to end your life. Join me, and we will be so powerful. You will never have to worry about getting hurt again," said Nikki.

As the two girls were walking away, Maxi flew in with Allen on his back. Maxi landed, Allen jumped off, and Maxi flew across the river to help Mike.

"Emily, don't do it," said Allen.

Emily stopped walking and faced Allen. Allen saw the sadness in his daughter's eyes.

"Are you telling me that you are going to join the evil that killed your mother?" Allen asked her.

"She cheated on you. Why do you care?" Emily asked him.

"It does not matter. I still love her. She is your mother and the love of my life," said Allen.

Emily started hearing Aza'el's voice in her head again. She closed her eyes and placed her one hand onto her forehead for support. "Shut up!" Emily yelled at the voice in her head. "Come on Emily, fight it," said Allen. Emily lowered her one arm back down but kept her eyes closed. She muted everyone out. She focused on the silence inside her head and she remembered the happy childhood she had with her mother. She also replayed the vision of Aza'el stabbing Gabby. At that moment Emily opened her eyes and quickly snatched her other hand away from Nikki. Nikki saw the change in Emily, and therefore, she raised the knife she had in her hand and swung it at Emily's back.

Mike screamed, "Watch out, Emily!"

As Emily turned around to face Nikki, the knife was coming straight at her heart. Emily did not fight it. She knew it was too late. Right before the knife ripped her skin open, an arrow knocked the knife out of Nikki's hand. Emily then quickly backed away. Everyone looked around to see who shot the arrow. Then, there he was, Pete, standing between two big trees holding the bow and another arrow ready to go. Mike smiled.

"You? What the hell are you doing?" asked Nikki.

"You are not the only one with tricks up your sleeve," said Pete.

Nikki turned her attention to Emily. Emily was pissed. "You know the one mistake I made was turning my pain into weakness when instead I should have turned it into strength," said Emily.

Emily grabbed Nikki by her throat and lifted her body up with one hand. Emily slammed her against a rock with her hand still around Nikki's neck. Nikki had one hand on the rock and one around Emily's hand that was squeezing her neck. Emily released her hand off her throat and punched her in her face. Nikki managed to slip away. She ran toward a tree and used her strong nails to climb up like a spider. She was fast. Emily followed. Mike, Allen, and Pete watched them jump from branch to branch, and disappearing into the dark woods. Mike tried running after them, but Allen stopped him.

"What? Come on, let's follow them," said Mike.

"Right now, we sit here and wait. We can't keep up with that," said Allen as he sat on a rock.

Nikki jumped from tree to tree until she did not see Emily behind her anymore. Nikki finally stopped jumping and quietly listened to see if she could hear Emily anywhere, but nothing. Nikki turned her head to the left to take a peek behind the tree only to be face to face with Emily. Nikki got scared and fell over the branch and down to the ground. She did land onto her feet, and Emily was right there as well.

Nikki was backing away from Emily.

"Mom, I know you are in there somewhere. Please stop her. We can do this together, Mom," said Nikki, trying to get the soul of Aza'el to take over Emily's mind.

"Mommy is not here now!" said Emily, her voice still deep and evil.

Emily laughed loudly. Nikki tried to use her force to throw Emily against a tree, but Emily held her feet tightly onto the ground. Her feet slid backward just a little but that was about it.

"One thing you don't know about me is that I am very strong when mad as hell," said Emily.

Emily used her power of force and moved Nikki's body closer toward her. Nikki tried to hold onto the branches as her body slid closer and closer toward Emily. Nikki tried to pull back but nothing. Emily was too strong. Now, Nikki was so close to Emily's face that she grabbed Emily by her throat. Emily did not move. Emily could feel Nikki's hands squeezing around her throat. But Emily didn't flinch. Emily quickly stuck her fingers inside Nikki's mouth and used both of her hands to pull her jaw apart. She then grabbed her neck and snapped it. Nikki's body slowly fell to the ground and turned into ashes. Emily watched the ashes get blown away by the wind.

"You made me do this to your own daughter," Emily said to herself.

"She was too weak anyways," a voice responded to her, Aza'el's voice.

Mike stood up from sitting on a rock when he saw Emily returning. She was still transformed as a Dark Zal. Mike was not sure if she was going to kill them or if she was in control. All three of them stood there, waiting to see what Emily's move will be. However, she started walking slower and fell to her knees. She grabbed her chest and started screaming. Mike, Allen, and Pete ran toward her. Mike grabbed her and held her tight. She was fighting him off, but Allen jumped in and helped holding her down. Emily's body was shaking, and she was screaming. Pete stood back and watched.

"What is going on?" Mike asked.

"I don't know," replied Allen.

Emily was lying on her back, as Mike held her arms and Allen held her legs. All of a sudden, she stopped moving. Allen and Mike slowly let her go. She then became stiff, her chest rose upward, and her head tilted backward. Her body kept changing from Dark Zal to human over and over again and then it stopped. She laid there, transformed back into human. She looked like she was sleeping. The boys looked at one another, not sure what to do. Mike leaned over Emily's face to check if she was breathing when a black, strong, fog shot out of Emily's mouth knocking Mike backward onto his back. The men watched the fog shoot high into the air, and they heard Aza'el screaming in pain. Slowly the fog disappeared.

"What the fuck?" Mike asked.

Emily slowly opened her eyes and stood up.

"I think she's gone," said Emily.

"How?" Mike asked.

Emily walked over to Pete and said, "I forgive you. I have to or I will never be able to move forward in my life." She then walked over to Allen and said, "You showed me that love can last forever, even when it hurts." She then walked over to Mike and said, "You, I'm still trying to figure you out. You stayed through everything and never gave up on me. Now I know why I'm so crazy over you."

Mike smiled and hugged her. They had a long passionate kiss until Allen interrupted. "Alright, not in front of me," said Allen.

Chapter 24

THE COMING BACK

When Emily and the crew arrived back at the Green Village, the Klexon warriors were hiding in the bushes and waiting to attack anyone that was a threat. When the warriors saw it was Emily and the others, Eliot stepped out of the bushes and yelled at Emily to leave right away.

"You are not allowed to be here. I should kill you right now, right here," said Eliot as she held her weapon pointed at Emily.

"Stop! It's over!" yelled Mike.

Eliot looked at all of them angrily. "Fine. We will see," she said and walked away.

"I will prove to you all that the evil is gone. I have learned to forgive, believe in love again, and believe in family. My heart found peace and I no longer carry anger within my heart and that is what has set me free," said Emily. Eliot stopped walking away and faced Emily. Everyone watched to see what Eliot was going to say, but before Eliot spoke, Emily closed her eyes and her body lifted off the ground. Her skin complexion became very pale, her ears got pointy, and blue veins ran through her cheeks. Long eyelashes formed, and ruffles formed on each side of her face. She transformed into a Klexon. Everyone was surprised.

"I am one of you guys now. I can't get rid of the witch blood cells that run through me, but my heart has changed the witch I have become," said Emily as she smiled.

Eliot dropped her weapons and was surprised at what she saw. "How did this happen?" Eliot asked.

Emily walked closer to her and said, "I just had to find peace with myself."

Everyone was happy that finally, they did not have to worry about Aza'el or her dark force any longer. Gary watched from a distance, smiled and walked to his cottage. Later, Emily and Mike arrived at his cottage and they asked Gary what he was doing.

"Cleaning up the potions. We won't be needing these anymore," said Gary.

Emily ran up to him and hugged him.

"What's this for?" Gary asked her.

"Thank you for helping me," said Emily.

"No, thank you for not giving up. I am so sorry that I was about to give up on you. I honestly thought we ran out of options," said Gary as he lowered his head.

"You were ready to do what you had to do to save your people. I would have done the same thing," said Emily.

Emily walked out of the cottage. Mike and Gary watched her leave.

"You sure picked a good one," Gary said to Mike.

Mike smiled. "I knew I did," he said.

Emily was outside whistling for Maxi. She missed him so much. As she waited, Eliot walked up to Emily and told her she was sorry for everything.

"I wish there was more I could have done to help you," said Eliot.

"It is fine. I would have done the same thing if I was in your position," said Emily.

The girls hugged and Eliot left. Emily heard Maxi's wings and she looked up. He flew above and landed in front of her. She jumped on his back and hugged him. She felt so free and happy. Maxi flew high into the sky and stood in midair as Emily looked down at Arfabele, at the Green Village, and how beautiful it looked.

"I will miss it all," she said. Emily yelled out in joy as Maxi flew very fast downward, between trees, and back up between the mountains. Emily was laughing and enjoying the feeling of being free. Then, she remembered the tree-flower. Maxi flew her there to see how bad the damage was. When she arrived, she saw all the creatures and fairies working hard to take care of the tree-flower. Everything looked so magical. The forest was healing. Emily slowly walked over to the tree-flower and placed her ear on it. She heard the heartbeat and softly touched it.

"Take care of this land," she said to it and then left.

When Emily returned to the Green Village with Maxi, Allen and the rest of the crew were ready to head back home. Emily said her goodbyes to everyone and told them she would never forget them.

"Do you really have to go? Why can't you stay here?" Eliot asked her.

"I am all my father has and he needs me," said Emily.

Eliot nodded, and they hugged. As they all stood at the portal to say their goodbyes, Gary told Emily that the ring she was wearing has no more power over her or the portal.

"I have something for you," said Gary.

Emily listened.

He walked up to her and poured a blue potion over her ring. The ring turned from silver to gold with a blue line around it.

"What is this?" Emily asked.

"You don't have to say goodbye forever. Now, that the ring is owned by a good witch, you control it. With this ring, you can re-open the portal. This way, you can come visit us whenever. But, you can't let the humans find it," said Gary.

"This is a great gift. Thank you so much," said Emily.

"You are welcome," said Gary.

"I was going to keep the ring anyways but this is better," said Emily.

"I know," said Gary.

Allen, Mike, and Pete went ahead and jumped into the portal. Emily looked at Maxi again and tears fell down her cheeks. This time, they were happy tears.

"I will come and visit you, boy," she said.

Gary stayed in Arfabele where he knew he belonged. Emily was happy for him. Emily left, and the Klexons watched the portal close.

When Emily stepped out of the portal, they watched the portal get smaller until it disappeared.

She looked down at the gold ring and knew she would be back visiting Arfabele. All four of them started walking home. Right after they exited the woods, Emily stopped walking. All three men looked at her. "Are you okay? You look like you saw a ghost," said Mike.

"Jack!" she yelled.

Allen, Mike, and Pete were confused.

"What about Jack?" Mike asked her.

"Nikki and him had a daughter, which means she is half witch, a Dark Zal," said Emily.

The men looked at one another.

"Oh, man, this shit is crazy!" said Pete.

Mike grabbed his head and asked Emily what they were going to do about it. She told them they had to tell Jack the truth.

"All right, we will do it tomorrow. Let's go home and rest," said Allen.

The following day, Emily and Mike arrived first at Jack's house. Allen arrived next and then Pete. Before they knocked on Jack's door, Pete pulled Mike to the side and said, "I know that we are not on great terms yet, but I am very glad that Emily forgave me for what I did and I was wondering if there is any chance you could forgive me too."

Before he said another word, Mike interrupted him. "You saved Emily's life. I am pretty sure we are back on good terms," said Mike.

Pete thanked him, and they joined Emily and Allen. All four stood at Jack's door, and Emily knocked. When Jack opened the door, he was holding his daughter in his arms. She was already growing fast.

"What are you guys doing here?" Jack asked them.

"Can we talk?" Emily asked him.

"Yeah sure, come in," Jack replied and walked into the living room placing his daughter into a playpen.

Everyone sat on the couch. Jack asked Emily if she has seen Nikki. He told her that he was worried about Nikki because she did not come home last night. Emily asked Jack to sit down. "I have something to tell you," said Emily. Jack sat down, but before Emily could say anything, Mike started talking. He told Jack everything, about the Klexons, the Dark Zals and about Emily being one of them. As Mike was filling Jack in on everything, Emily kept her eyes on the child. The child took a couple of glances at Emily as well. Emily felt connected to the child. After hearing everything Mike had to say, Jack got up from the couch and paced around the living room. He was trying to comprehend what he just heard. Emily turned her attention back to Jack.

"I need proof of all of this," said Jack.

Emily stood up and transformed into a witch. Jack jumped back and almost fell to the floor. He could not believe what he was seeing.

"Okay, so what you are saying is since I have a child with Nikki and she is what you say she is, that means that my daughter is half and half, right?" he asked them.

Emily nodded. "Now that you know everything, it is important for you to raise your daughter with the Klexons because the evil blood is already in her and she has to be taught to use her powers as a good witch," Emily explained to Jack.

Jack ignored her. He was not ready to do that.

"I miss her," he said speaking of Nikki.

Emily told him that Nikki loved him very much, and she was sorry that Nikki was gone. As Jack sat back down on the couch, he looked up at Emily and asked her how she felt when she killed Nikki. Emily did not know how to answer that at first. She then told him it felt terrible but it had to be done. Jack did not take his eyes off of Emily.

"I cannot believe this is happening. But what makes you determine that Nikki was the enemy? Is it because she tried to kill you? How come there was nothing else you guys could have done?" Jack asked them.

Emily could feel a little tension from Jack, so she turned back into her human self and did not respond. She had nothing else to say.

"I understand this is all very hard for you to take in, but Emily did not kill Nikki out of rage. She did it to save herself and all of us. Nikki was an evil witch. Her mother was Aza'el, the one who tried to destroy our world. Emily had to do what was right," said Mike.

Jack was listening to what Mike had to say, but he still kept his eyes on Emily.

"I guess you are right. You had to do what you had to do," Jack said in a calm tone as he stared at Emily.

Jack then got up, walked over to the playpen, and picked his daughter up.

"I have to get her ready for dinner soon if you guys don't mind," he said.

Mike, Pete, Allen, and Emily understood and were leaving. Before Jack closed the door behind them, Emily told him if he ever needed anything to just ask. Jack nodded and closed the door. Jack took his child into the kitchen. He placed her on the floor and started to cook. While he was cooking, tears started to fall down his face. He tried to hold it in but it was hard. Then, he heard skillets and pots banging together. He knew it was his daughter and he asked her to stop playing around with the dishes. The banging did not stop. Jack turned away from the stove ready to take the pots away from her. When he saw his daughter, he dropped a plate to the floor and grabbed the kitchen counter for balance. His eyes wide open. He was in shock. He saw his daughter standing there with her hair flying in the air and kitchen items floating around the room. There were plates, skillets, spoons including knives. Jack did not know what to do. His daughter on the other hand was laughing. Jack started running around the kitchen grabbing the knives, the spoons and the skillets. He quickly put them all away and grabbed his daughter. When he grabbed her, her hair fell back down and everything else that was floating fell to the floor. He carried her into the living room and placed her on the floor.

"How did you do that?" he asked her, but she only laughed. "If others find out, they will take you away from me. You cannot do that anymore, okay," he told his daughter, but she was just staring at him. She did not understand what he was saying. He picked her up and said, "I will protect you."

Meanwhile, Mike and Emily were home alone, finally relaxing like normal human beings. They just finished watching a movie on their couch and were walking to their bedroom to rest for the night.

"It feels so good to be happy and free," she said to him.

Mike looked into her eyes. "You don't know how good it will feel to know I am falling asleep with my woman and not some crazy evil witch who might get up in the middle of the night to go and hunt someone down," he said to her.

She laughed, and they both went to bed.

The following morning, Mike and Emily ate breakfast. Mike was getting ready to go to work and Emily was going to check on Jack and his daughter, Kayla. Mike told Emily to be careful. They kissed and Mike left out the door. Emily finished washing the dishes and then left the house. As Emily was walking past the woods across the street, she felt a presence. She started to walk slower thinking that somehow she would see Aza'el's presence again, but nothing. She shook her head and continued to walk. Emily knocked on Jack's door, but he didn't answer. "Maybe he is not home," she said to herself and left.

Later that night when Mike came home, Emily was sitting on the couch. She asked Mike to sit next to her. She wanted to talk to him. He sat next to her, but before she spoke, he told her to hold on and not forget what she had to say, but first, he wanted to give her a gift. He handed her a box, and she opened it. It was a nice long black dress.

"We are going out tonight and actually enjoy a normal night out. Go try it on," he said to her.

She looked at him and said okay. When she stood up to go to the bedroom to try the dress on, he asked her what it was that she was going to tell him. Emily stopped at the doorframe and shook her head. "Nothing," she said. She did not want to bring up witch stuff now and mess up the moment. Emily put the black dress on, and looked into the mirror. The dress has a long split from her ankle all the way up to her hip. It's tight around her waist, and V-cut by her breast. As she was checking herself out, she smiled. Mike was dressed in a suit. He was in the living room waiting on her.

"Oh my God, girl, come on. By the time you get done, I will fall sleep," said Mike.

As soon as he said that, Emily walked into the living room. Mike could not take his eyes off of her. She had on red heels and a red purse. Her hair was pulled back. The red lipstick she had on made her lips look delicious.

"Wow, you look amazing. I mean not that you don't every day, but I have seen you get your butt kicked lately. I missed that clean face," said Mike.

They both laughed. Mike walked up to her, touched her face, and told her how beautiful she was. He kissed her. Mike grabbed her by her hand, and they left the house.

They parked the car in front of the club and walked in. They walked to the left of the club into a restaurant to have dinner first. They talked, laughed, and ate. They also drank some wine. Emily was feeling a little tipsy. She has not felt this way in a very long time. Mike then paid the check and took her to the other side of the club. The club played great music with a huge dance floor. They danced and had a couple more drinks. Everyone at the club was dressed classy. Emily and Mike were standing at the bar, when she told him she had to freshen up. She left the bar and walked to the bathroom. Emily placed her purse by the sink. She wanted to freshen up her makeup, but she was scared to look into the mirror. Slowly, she lifted her head up and saw herself. She misled. "No Aza'el," she said. She took her lipstick out of the purse and applied more onto her lips. All of a sudden, someone bumped into her knocking her lipstick to the floor. Emily picked it up, grabbed her purse and started walking toward the door. But the girls blocked her way trapping her in. Three girls stood in front of the door with their arms resting across their chest. Emily recognized them right away. One of the girls got closer toward Emily.

"Well, look who we got here, the little princess," said the blonde girl, and her friends laughed.

"I remember you from school. You gave Briana a hard time. You know she was one of us. No wonder Briana didn't like you. I mean, look at you," said the blonde girl again as her friends laughed.

Emily did not say or do anything. The blonde girl walked closer to Emily's face.

"I heard you know something about those witches who killed Briana. You know, you should be the one that's dead not her," said the blonde girl.

Emily stayed silent. Another girl asked Emily if she liked it when the football players were fucking her. Emily got mad, punched her in the face knocking her to the ground. The other two girls moved away from the door and Emily walked out.

Meanwhile at the bar where Mike was waiting on Emily, two of his old friends approached him. One of the guys asked Mike if he knew what happened to the girl he used to have a crush on.

"Oh, you mean Emily? I'm still with her. I'm in love with her," said Mike.

The two young men laughed.

"You are joking, right?" they asked Mike.

"No, I am not," said Mike.

Mike was getting pissed off, and he asked them to leave. As the two men were about to walk away, the one guy said, "I would hit that and then drop it."

Mike grabbed the young man by his shoulder and punched him in his face. The other fella jumped on Mike and a fight broke out between the men. A bouncer from the club ran up on them and separated them. At that moment, Emily walked up and grabbed Mike's hand. She was pulling him out of the club, but Mike did not want to leave yet. He wanted to keep fighting. Emily pulled on him harder leading him toward the exit, and they left the club. Outside, Mike snatched away from her hand and walked aggressively to the car. Emily quietly walked behind him. He opened the door for her, she sat in the car, and he closed the door. He walked around the front of the car and sat in the driver's seat. She saw the anger in his eyes. He turned the car on without saying anything and drove off. About three minutes into the ride home, Emily asked Mike why he hit that guy. Mike kept his eyes on the road.

"I don't want to talk about it," he said.

"It is because of me, isn't it? A couple of girls came into the bathroom and harassed me. I don't know why these people treat me this way. If Briana did not start this in the first place, it would have not gone this far. It's all her fault. I hate her for it," said Emily.

Mike slowed down the car and pulled over. He paused for a minute and then turned to look into her eyes.

"You still don't get it, do you? This town is not that big, and when someone is so popular, everyone else wants to be like them. Briana was popular because she had a lot of money. That girl was dumb as a rock. I left her, and you came along. She did not like it and became jealous of you. If she didn't like you, she would destroy you. Briana was good at that. And even though is dead, her mother funds the school so much money that her name will never be silenced. That's just how it is. I have been by your side since day one, and I'm not going anywhere," said Mike with anger and love in his voice.

Emily stared into his eyes. She saw he was hurting for her because he loved her. Emily leaned over and started kissing him. It was a long passionate kiss. Once she removed her lips off of his, she whispered, "I love you too," and then continued to kiss him again. She then sat back into her seat and Mike exhaled. He then leaned over to her, grabbed her face gently and said, "I am here to protect you. I don't give a damn if you are crazy, a psycho or a handful. I fucking love you and there is not a damn thing that can change that." He then grabbed her by her neck and kissed her aggressively. Emily let out a quiet moan and Mike sat back into his seat leaving her feeling hot and wet. He pulled the car back onto the road and continued to drive home.

"Let's keep this mood up. We are almost home," said Mike.

Chapter 25

OLD LIVES NEW BEGINNINGS

The following morning, there was a knock on Emily's door. Mike woke up first and Emily got up after him. When Mike opened the door, Allen let himself in and told Mike to put on a shirt and to come with them. Mike asked him who he was talking about, who was "them." Then, he saw Eliot. She was dressed in all black and wore a hood over her head so people would not see her.

"What is going on?" Mike asked them.

At that moment, Emily came from behind and Mike looked at her. "What's going on?" Mike asked again.

"I opened the portal," said Emily.

"Why?" Mike asked her.

"Because we need to save Kayla," she said.

Allen did not say anything at this point.

"Jack's daughter, but why?" Mike asked.

"She is the same as Emily. She is human and a Dark Zal. If we take her, we have a better chance to raise her as a Klexon. We will teach her how to use her powers as a good witch. She belongs with us," said Eliot.

"Hold up! You guys want to take the child away from her father? Jack won't allow that," said Mike.

"We have to. There is no other choice. If her powers get out of control, the humans will know and it could start another war between us and them," said Eliot.

"She is right," said Emily. "We have to talk to Jack, and hopefully, he will understand. It is for her own safety."

As Allen was walking out of the house, he said, "I agree. I think it's time we talk to Jack."

Emily went upstairs to get dressed and Eliot followed Allen. Mike watched them leave, and he shook his head.

"Here we go," said Mike to himself.

When they arrived at Jack's house, Mike knocked on his door. When Jack opened the door, he said, "You guys again. What is it now?"

"Can we come in? It is important," said Emily.

"It's not a good idea right now. Maybe tomorrow, okay, guys," said Jack and tried to close the door.

Mike slammed his hand on the door and told him to keep it open.

"It's Kayla, isn't it?" Emily asked him.

"I don't know what you are talking about," said Jack.

Jack tried closing the door again, but Mike did not let him. Jack finally gave up and let them in.

"Where is Kayla?" Emily asked.

"Why are you looking for my daughter?" Jack asked her.

"You know why. Has she done anything strange lately?" Emily asked him.

"Like what?" Jack replied with a question.

"Magical, crazy. Has she done anything magical lately?" Mike asked Jack with frustration.

"No! Maybe it's time for you guys to go," said Jack, and he walked over to the door.

He opened the door to show them the way out, but instead, he saw Eliot. Jack backed away from the door and Eliot walked in closing the door behind her.

"What the fuck is going on?" Jack asked.

Emily walked next to Eliot and told Jack to have a seat. They have something important to discuss with him. Jack took Emily's advice and sat down. Emily explained everything to him: how they think Kayla should live in the Green Village to teach her how to be a good witch. This would also prevent the humans from finding out about Kayla. Nobody wanted the government involved. After hearing everything that Emily had to say to him, he could not believe they were asking him to give up his daughter. Jack was shaking his head and asking them to leave. Emily tried to convince Jack to give Kayla up, but he had enough. He yelled at everyone to get out of his house.

Eliot stepped into his face and said, "If you do not hand her over and let us raise her the best way that we know how, you will create a war between us and the humans and it won't be pretty. The last thing we need is for the government to find out that there is a witch living among them. There will be a point in her life where she will not be able to control her powers and humans will find out. If you don't hand her over willingly, we will do what is necessary to keep my kind safe."

Eliot left the house. Jack had nothing to say.

"Please make a decision soon. We are running out of time," Emily told Jack, and they all left his house.

When Jack closed the door behind them, he turned around and Kayla was standing there in the middle of the living room. He walked over to her, dropped to his knees, and hugged her. He broke down and cried. Kayla wrapped her little arms around him. The child had no idea what was going on, but she did not like seeing her daddy sad.

Later that night, Emily and Mike were getting ready for bed.

"Do you think Jack will let her go?" Emily asked him.

"I honestly don't know," replied Mike.

Emily stared at the mirror in the bathroom that was connected to their bedroom. She transformed into a witch and stood there, examining herself, knowing that was who she will be for the rest of her life. Mike walked into the bathroom and she quickly transformed back into human.

"What are you doing?" he asked her.

"Nothing," she replied and went to bed.

Mike followed.

The following day, Kayla and Jack were at the coffee shop. Jack was working and Kayla was playing in the backyard. There was a small playground and a lot of the neighborhood children come and play there as well. One child started to cry loudly. Jack could see the mother of the little girl running toward the crying child. Jack followed to make sure everything was all right since the playground was on his property. The little girl was lying on the ground with a broken arm, and her mother picked her up. The little girl told her mother that someone pushed her, but she did not see who it was. The mother took the child away. Jack noticed how Kayla just stood there watching the little girl cry. She had no expressions on her face. It was like it did not bother her one bit that the girl broke her arm. Jack walked over to Kayla and asked her if she saw what happened to the little girl. Kayla shook her head and went back to playing.

At the end of the day, Jack was closing up his shop and he yelled out to Kayla telling her to pack up her toys. Kayla did not respond. Jack stopped cleaning the tables and went to the back of the shop to check on her. Kayla was standing in the middle of the back room staring at the wall. Her back was turned to Jack when he walked in.

"Kayla, honey, what are you doing? You were supposed to pack your things. It is time for us to go home," said Jack as he was walking closer to her.

Kayla did not say a word. Jack walked closer to her and touched her shoulder. Kayla quickly turned her head only toward her father and Jack stumbled backward falling to the floor. Kayla's face was not Kayla. She was transformed into a witch, a Dark Zal. She slowly started walking toward Jack. The closer she came to him, her face and skin started to change back into a human.

"What are you doing on the floor, Daddy?" Kayla asked, hardly pronouncing the words.

She grabbed Jack's hand and helped him up. He could not believe what he saw. Jack hurried up, packed her things, closed the store and was on his way to Emily's house. When he arrived at their house, Emily opened the door and Jacked walked inside holding his daughter. He placed her on the floor, and she ran off to play in their house.

"What is going on?" Emily asked him.

"I have no other choice but to ask for your help. Earlier today, there were children playing in the back of my shop and one of the girls broke her arm. Kayla was standing there. She was looking at the little girl like she did not feel bad for her at all. And the girl mentioned that she was pushed by someone. Also earlier today at home, all these things were flying in the air, spoons, knifes, dishes, and shit. I did not know what to do. Then, before we left the shop today, I went to check on her in the back room and I saw her staring at a wall. When she turned to look at me, it was not Kayla. She, she looked like one of them," said Jack.

Mike almost dropped his food out of his hand.

"What? This can't be. It's too soon," said Emily.

"You have to help her, Jack. Your child is part of a witch. She always will be. But if you want her to be safe, you have to send her to the Green Village where she will be raised to be good. We don't know what will happen if the humans find out there is a witch living among us," said Emily.

Jack nodded and started to cry. "I don't know how I will live without her. But I have to make sure she is safe," said Jack.

"You can visit her when she is older and knows better, but for now, I think she needs to leave this world," said Emily.

"I know what I need to do, and I am willing to do anything to keep her safe," said Jack.

He agreed to take Kayla to the Green Village and leave her there for the Klexons to teach her how to use her powers as a good witch.

They packed their things, and Jack grabbed his daughter. Mike, Emily, Jack, and Kayla went to the portal. It was twirling in a circle. Jack stared at the portal like he was looking at a monster. He held his daughter's hand and looked at Emily and Mike.

"Are you sure?" he asked Emily and she nodded.

Emily told them to hold hands to make sure they all exited at the same place on the other side of the portal. As soon as they arrived at the Green Village, they saw all the different creatures walking, running, and flying around. Kayla thought they were fun, and she ran off into the field to play with the creatures and the children of the witches. Gary was waiting for them outside his cottage.

"Welcome back. That was fast. Well, common in," said Gary.

As they entered into Gary's cottage, Jack glanced over to check on his daughter before the door closed behind him.

"I would like to start off by saying you have made the right decision," said Gary.

Emily stood against the wall, and Mike was sitting on a table with one leg on the floor. Jack stood in the middle of the room and dropped Kayla's stuff on the floor.

"Well, I did not have other options here," replied Jack.

At that moment, Eliot walked into the room. Jack examined her from head to toe and saw the bow and arrows she carried on her back.

"Wait, is my daughter going to be around weapons like that?" Jack asked them.

Eliot turned her attention to him. "Your daughter is half witch. She will be raised to be a good witch and to know how to fight," said Eliot.

Everyone was silent in the room. Emily walked over to Jack and grabbed his hand. "I understand you are worried. I will be here a lot training myself. She is in good hands. You cannot visit her here because we do not want her to know about the human's world until she is ready. I will bring you pictures all the time until she is ready to get out there on her own," said Emily.

Jack nodded. He went outside to say goodbye to Kayla. Everyone in the room watched Jack walk out of the cottage and toward the field where Kayla was playing with the Klexon kids and the creatures. He grabbed his daughter by her hand and walked her over to the side. He kneeled down to her eye level and told her that he loved her very much. He told her he had to go away for a little bit but would come and visit her when he could. Meanwhile, she would live here and have fun. Kayla didn't say anything. A couple of tears fell down her face, and Jack hugged her. He then looked into her eyes again and smiled.

"Now, we will not cry, okay. You will have fun here, okay," said Jack.

Kayla nodded, and Jack walked her back where the Klexon children were playing. Emily and the others were outside waiting for Jack. As Jack was walking toward them, he turned back to look at Kayla one more time and said to himself, "I will get you back one day." Jack walked up to Emily and told her he was ready to go. She nodded and Mike took Jack back to the portal and into the human's world. Mike informed Jack to make sure he did not reveal the portal to anyone; otherwise, Emily will have to close it. Jack understood. Once Jack arrived back home, he walked into Kayla's room, sat on her bed, and held her pillow. He glanced around her room and cried.

Meanwhile, at the Green Village, Emily was going to stay for a while and help the Klexons train Kayla. She herself thought she could use some training. Emily also wanted to make sure Kayla was comfortable. For weeks Kayla has cried for her father. Emily did her best to comfort her. After years of training and spending time together, Emily and Kayla became very close. It was Kayla's eighteenth birthday, and Emily finally took her to see the tree-flower. Emily explained to her that the life of the forest comes from the tree-flower. Kayla was amazed by the tree-flower and everything around it.

One day, Emily and Kayla were out in the field along with other Klexons practicing with the Grounders. Eliot was giving orders, and there was a specific male Klexon named "Abe" who did not like taking orders, especially not from a female. Every time Eliot gave him a specific order, he always did the opposite. Eliot ordered him to teach his Grounder how to wrap its tail around the Klexon's body, lift him up and hold him in the air without squeezing him to death while the Grounder is still running. But, he totally ignored her. Eliot got upset, jumped off of her Grounder, and walked over to him. She pulled him off of his Grounder, and started punching him.

"What's the problem?" he asked her as he finally grabbed her hands and held them preventing her from punch him again.

Others stood around and watched.

"Well, this is interesting," said Kayla to Emily, and they both smiled.

As Eliot and Abe faced one another, he told her that females were not strong enough to be leaders. Eliot then twisted his hand and kneed him in his stomach, and he fell to the floor. She stomped her foot on top of his chest and said, "Don't underestimate a woman." She left him lying there. Other male Klexons that watched laughed at him. Abe watched her walk away as he was getting up onto his feet.

Abe was the type of warrior who believed men should take care of females and women were not capable of doing things on their own, especially not being a warrior. When the training was over for the day, Abe was still upset. When they returned back to their village, he walked straight into his cottage without speaking to anyone. Eliot saw how upset he was so she went after him. She knocked on his door but he did not answer. She opened the door herself and walked in. He was standing by the bathroom door with no shirt on. He was cleaning himself up. He was very big and muscular and was not as pale as the female Klexons. His back was turned to her. As he was wiping his arms with a rag, he heard the door close shut, so he quickly turned around to face the door. When he saw her, he asked her what she was doing here. The ruffles on her face moved but she did not answer him. They locked eyes on each other and Abe waited for her to speak. He was so mad that his veins popped out all the way from his chest going up his neck.

"I see you are upset. You need to learn how to control your anger," Eliot finally broke the silence.

"Is that why you are here? I mean, let's not forget, I'm the best one on your team. But for you to treat me the way you did out there on the field was humiliating," said Abe.

"You see, that attitude and thinking you're the hardest Klexon walking around will get you killed one day," said Eliot.

"Until then, I am who I am," said Abe.

"All right, I came here to check on you; but if you want to continue being an asshole, you do that on your own time. While you are out there on that field and fighting for your people, you will follow my orders," said Eliot.

Eliot turned away from him and started to walk out, but Abe grabbed her by her hand and pulled her against his body.

"That is not the only reason why you came here," he said to her.

Her breathing was getting heavier. She felt his chest against hers. She could feel his hands around her back. He moved one of his hands to her face and touched her ruffles. His hand moved from the ruffles toward the inner of her cheek. She closed her eyes, and her long eyelashes sparkled. Her tight cheeks felt smooth underneath his touch. She then opened her eyes and pushed his hands away. She started walking toward the door again. He told her to stop before she grabbed the doorknob, so she did. He walked over to her from the back, turned her around, grabbed her hand, and walked her back into the room.

"We are not in training anymore. While we are off the field you listen to my orders," he said to her. He then picked her up, and her legs wrapped around his waist. He started kissing her and carried her placing her body on top of a dresser. He took her clothes off as he was kissing her. Her legs still wrapped around his waist as his hands squeezed around her thighs. She tried to tell him what they were doing was wrong, but she did not have the will power to stop him. As she sat on the dresser, his kisses moved down her neck, onto her breast and toward her vagina. He raised her legs and placed them on his shoulders. His tongue slid inside of her as his lips covered her vagina making her feel hot. He pulled his tongue out and inserted his finger while his tongue played with her clitoris. Her legs locked around his neck, her back arched and her head resting back, she finally released. He came back up to face her. She dropped her legs back around his waist. She looked into his eyes and told him that she did not know he felt like this about her. He told her she never gave him the time to show it. Before she could say anything else, he slowly slid his manhood inside of her. "It isn't over yet," he said. He went in and out slowly at first watching her body move along with the rhythm. He then grabbed the back of her hair and slightly pulled tilting her head back. His strokes became faster and harder. His strong arms held onto her body. He pulled her lower body closer to his manhood allowing him to slide in deeper. She felt pain but good pain. She dug her nails into his back. He was striking her so hard that the dresser broke. The side of the dresser cracked, and it tilted to the side. He picked her up, carried her off of the dresser, and pinned her against the wall. Her arms wrapped around his shoulders as he held her by her legs and butt. His manhood continued to satisfy her needs. She released again. He struck and struck until he released as well. She held on tightly to him. After they both released, he held her longer against the wall with his manhood still inside of her. He relaxed his head on her chest and exhaled. Every time he exhaled, it sounded like a slight growl. Every time he took a breath in, his shoulders rose and then back down. His veins popped out on his chest and arms. As his head was resting on her chest while he held her against the wall, she slowly rubbed his arms up and down. He lifted his head up and looked into her eyes.

"I'm falling for you," he said to her.

She did not say anything. He lifted her up and off of his manhood. Eliot quickly fixed herself, got dressed, and started walking toward the door. He was naked standing in the middle of the room and asked her where she was going. She told him she had some stuff to do and had to go. She turned to look at him and saw he stood there, naked.

"Are you going to get dressed or what?" she asked him.

He smiled at her. He walked over, grabbed her hand, and told her she did not have anything to do today and to get in the bed with him. She did not want to, but he picked her up and carried her to his bed. He took her clothes off and covered her with the sheet. He laid down with her and placed his arms around her, holding her softly but yet strongly. As they both lay there together about to fall asleep, he said to her, "A strong woman needs a strong man and I got you." She loved those words and allowed herself to stay in his arms where she felt safe. They both fell asleep.

Meanwhile, Kayla and Emily were in Emily's cottage. Emily was brushing Kayla's hair as she asked Kayla if she was happy that she finally received her own cottage for her eighteenth birthday. Kayla told her yes, but she missed spending the nights with Emily in her cottage.

"Sometimes, it gets lonely in that cottage. I'm all by myself. At least, you have Mike," said Kayla.

"I know what you mean. But don't worry. I'm not far, and you never know, you might meet a handsome Klexon," said Emily.

"Can I ask you something?" Kayla asked with a sad voice.

"Of course," said Emily.

"I know you guys said my parents died, but how did they die?" Kayla asked.

Emily stopped brushing her hair. She did not know what to say to the girl.

"It was an accident a long time ago," said Emily.

Kayla wanted to keep asking questions, but Emily interrupted her by telling her she was going to sleep. Kayla sensed something was wrong but decided to leave it alone. Kayla said, "goodnight" and left. Emily closed the door behind Kayla and went to bed. Kayla walked over to her own cottage, went inside, changed into her pajamas, and laid down on her bed but was not able to fall asleep.

"Something is missing here and I will find out what," she said to herself.

The following day, Emily took Kayla out on the field to train with the Grounders again. She felt like Kayla needed more practice on how to fight while riding a Grounder. As Kayla was riding one, she was supposed to make the Grounder run fast and then throw its tail into the ground using its tail to lift its body over a pile of rocks. However, she failed and the Grounder's tail gave in and they both fell onto the rocks. Kayla hit the rocks hard and sprained her shoulder. She got mad at the Grounder and used her powers to hurt the creature. The Grounder roared in pain and then ran away.

"Stupid animal," said Kayla as she was cleaning the dirt off of herself.

Emily walked over to Kayla and yelled at her for hurting the Grounder.

"What did you do that for? It was not his fault. It was you. You were supposed to pull on its back when you want it to jump, but you pulled too late. Don't do that again, and next time, get it right," said Emily and walked away.

As Emily was walking away, Kayla yelled out, "Oh yeah, well, what for? What are we training to fight for? Why is everyone so over the edge here? Protective all the damn time. What are we being protective from? And I want to know where I come from, because you and I are not like the others, so you better start talking."

Emily stopped walking away and turned to face her. "What is going on with you, Kayla?" Emily asked her.

Kayla had no response. Kayla looked around the field and into the forest but didn't say anything. She dropped her weapon and ran off. Emily decided to give her some space.

The following morning, Emily decided to go and visit the human's world and warn Jack about Kayla's suspicions. Now that Kayla is older, it was harder to hide from her. Everyone at the Green

Village kept the secret from Kayla about the human's world and the portal. When Emily arrived in the human's world, she went to check on her father, not realizing that Kayla was following her.

"So this is what you have been up to, Emily," said Kayla to herself as she continued to follow Emily.

Later into the day when Emily arrived at her own house, Mike was already cooking in the kitchen. Kayla walked around the house and to the back. As soon as she hit the corner of the back door, Emily was standing there with her arms crossed looking at Kayla.

"You know, I thought I smelled something," said Emily.

"Damn, you caught me," said Kayla.

"You know Green Villagers are going to be worried about you when they realize you are gone. What were you thinking? Come on, I will have Mike walk you back to the village," said Emily.

Kayla told Emily she had some explaining to do.

"What is this place?" Kayla asked.

But Emily didn't answer her. She told Kayla to get in the house before someone saw her.

"Why do I have to keep hiding? Is this where you and I come from because we are different than the other Klexons?" Kayla asked her.

Mike stepped out from behind the kitchen and Kayla saw him.

"You live here?" she asked him.

Mike nodded his head.

"What is going on?" Kayla asked.

Emily took her hand and told her to sit down. Kayla snatched her hand back and told Emily to start talking.

"All right, listen. You and I are half witch half human as you can see. Your parents did not die in an accident. Your mother was murdered because she was evil and wanted to destroy the Klexons and this world. Your father is still alive," said Emily.

When Kayla heard those words come out of Emily's mouth, she took a couple of steps back and was in shock.

"Who are you people?" Kayla asked them with disgust. "My whole life was a lie, and it is all your fault," said Kayla.

"I am sorry, but this was not supposed to happen like this. We were all just trying to keep you safe," said Emily.

"Keep me safe from what?" Kayla asked.

"The humans and the Dark Zals. Your grandmother had her own army and created a war among us and the humans. The humans think we vanished. If they find out that we still exist or if they find out about Arfabele, there will be war. Humans are not the only reason why we were hiding you. Your grandmother was the queen of evil. The queen of Dark Zals, and your mother followed her footsteps. We wanted different for you," said Emily.

"That's why I look different. I'm not a Klexon, I'm a Dark Zal," said Kayla.

"Yes," said Emily.

Kayla was thinking for a minute, trying to wrap her mind around it all.

"We tried to help your mother but it was too late," said Emily. Kayla looked at Emily with disappointment.

"She was still my mother," said Kayla.

"I am sorry," said Emily.

Tears fell down Kayla's face.

"Where is my father? Why has he not searched for me?" Kayla asked.

"We convinced him to let you go and live with us for your own good. He loves you very much. You have to believe that," said Emily.

This whole time Mike stood back and watched. He did not want to get in the middle of two witches.

"Where is he?" Kayla asked.

Emily looked at Mike and then back at Kayla.

"I will take you to him," said Emily.

Chapter 26

DAUGHTER'S REVENGE

The following day, Jack pulled into his driveway after a long day at work. He stepped out of his car and walked toward his house. Before he put his foot on the first step, he dropped his keys. Jack bends down to pick them up and when he looked up again Emily and Kayla stood in front of his door. "Dad?" Kayla asked.

"Kayla?" Jack asked.

She nodded her head and Jack ran up the stairs and hugged his daughter. He held her in his arms and cried.

"I am so sorry. I should have never let you go," said Jack.

He let her go and turned to Emily. He thanked her for bringing Kayla to him and asked them to come in. The three of them sat at the dining room table and talked. Kayla was not too happy about the whole situation, but she was happy to finally see her father.

"I do not like that you guys took a very important part of my life and hid it away from me, but I am glad that I finally got to see you, Dad," said Kayla.

Emily told Kayla she could go ahead and spend the night and she would pick her up tomorrow before they return to the Green Village. Kayla said okay.

As Emily was driving back home in Mike's car, she saw someone standing on the side of the road. When Emily drove right by it, she saw it was a Dark Zal. Emily quickly hit the brakes, and the car stopped. She jumped out of the car and saw the Dark Zal run away.

She was already far ahead. Emily did not go after her. She got back in the car and stared into her rearview mirror. The Dark Zal was already gone. She put the car into drive and drove off.

When Emily got home, she told Mike what she saw. She walked upstairs and started changing clothes.

"What are you doing?" Mike asked her as he followed her around the house.

"I have to go find her," said Emily.

Mike grabbed her by her arm and told her to calm down.

"Why don't you wait for her to find you? I am sure she wanted you to see her," said Mike.

"I cannot sit here and not do anything," said Emily.

She kissed him on the cheek, put a black shirt on, and rushed out of the house. Mike let her go. Emily was walking through the town, the forest, and the parks looking for this Dark Zal, but nothing. As Emily passed a strip of shopping stores, she saw Kayla. Emily walked up to her and asked her what she was doing out in public. Kayla told her she was just checking out the town, and Jack didn't mind.

"Well, I mind and so do the rest of the Green Villagers," said Emily.

Kayla got frustrated and said, "You know what, I am so sick and tired of you guys trying to control me and what I do. How do you know I don't belong here? How do you know there will be a war between us and the humans? They just might end up liking us," said Kayla.

"You have no idea what happened in the past, so just go home now and in the morning go back to Arfabele Land," said Emily.

"You need to relax. Nobody knows I'm a witch," said Kayla and walked away.

Emily watched her leave and quickly ran to Jack's house. He opened the door, and she stormed in.

"What now?" Jack asked.

"Why? Why did you let her go?" she asked him.

"Look, the girl has never seen this side of her life. Let her explore a little. It seems to me she likes it here, and she has her powers under control. Maybe she does not have to go back," said Jack.

"Do not do this. We worked very hard with her and came a long way. Do not let it go to waste. It took a lot of metal strength for me to fight the inner evil. She is not ready, Jack," said Emily.

"Look, why don't we talk about this later tonight? I have to run to the shop real quick. I forgot something, and I will be back in about an hour," said Jack.

Emily didn't say anything, and instead, she stormed out of the house.

As Emily was walking back home, she heard a woman screaming. Emily ran to assist the woman and saw she was bleeding from her neck and her arm. Emily was putting pressure on the woman's wound that was on her neck and asked her what happened.

"I don't know what it was. It happened so fast," said the woman.

Other people in town heard the woman's suffering and ran to help. Since she was getting the help she needed and the police were called, Emily backed away from the scene. Emily walked between two brick buildings trying to avoid attention. As she walked between the buildings, she saw a big dent on the side of one of the buildings. Emily touched the cracked bricks and knew that no human did that. All of a sudden, she heard another scream. Emily followed the sound and saw the Dark Zal dragging a woman by her hair. Emily transformed into a Klexon and ran to help. Emily kicked the Dark Zal, and she fell. The woman was free and ran away. The Dark Zal stood up onto her feet and looked at Emily.

"I know you, Emily. I heard a lot about you. I am sure you are wondering who the hell I am. Well, let's start with names. I am Saga. You see, I used to work close with Aza'el until you destroyed everything. We had big plans, but then, you messed everything up for us. You may have destroyed Aza'el, but you have no idea how many of us are left behind. I learned a lot from her mistakes, so don't underestimate me," said Saga.

Emily looked deep into her eyes. Emily could tell Saga had no fear. Emily ran to attack her, but Saga turned and ran away as she yelled out, "I am not ready, but I will come back for you, Emily!"

Emily watched her disappear down the road and into the darkness. Emily went home and told Mike what happened.

Meanwhile, Kayla and Jack were having a nice dinner at Jack's house. Jack told her that he was very sorry for missing so many years of her life. Kayla asked him why he sent her to the village while he stayed here with the humans. He explained that he was just trying to keep her safe. Nobody was allowed to find out that she was a witch.

"I was not allowed to visit you because they said it would be better if you did not know about the human's world," said Jack.

Jack explained to her that the Klexons were the ones who knew how to teach her to use her powers. Kayla understood, and the two of them finished their dinner.

Later on into the night, Kayla saw a picture of a woman hanging on the living room wall. She asked Jack if the woman in the picture was her mother, and Jack said, "Yes." Kayla took the picture down and held it in her hands. She took the picture out of the picture frame and asked if she could keep it. Jack told her yes. She asked him if he missed her mother, and he told her he did. Kayla walked over to the sofa and sat down. "Could you tell me more about her," asked Kayla. Jack walked over and sat next to her. He told Kayla stories about the things he and Nikki did together. Kayla listened to her dad go on and on about her mother to where it made her cry. Jacked leaned over and hugged her.

"Don't cry. She loved you very much," said Jack.

"Mom does not sound as evil as Emily said she was," said Kayla.

"Your mother was not as evil as they say she was. We don't even know for sure what happened to Nikki. I know your grandmother started this whole destroy-the-Klexons thing, but Nikki was not like that. She would never hurt me or you. She loved you. Your mother was only trying to protect your grandmother, which anyone with a good heart would have done the same. Good or bad, Nikki would have done anything to save her mother, wouldn't you?" asked Jack.

Kayla listened to what her dad said, but she was quiet. He then asked her if she wanted to watch a movie. She told him yes. After the movie was done, she walked upstairs to her bedroom and went to bed. In the middle of the night, Kayla felt cold. She woke up and saw the window was open. She walked over to it and closed it shut. When she turned to go back to bed, right in her face stood a Dark Zal, Saga. Kayla was about to scream, but Saga placed her hand over Kayla's mouth and told her to be quiet she was not going to hurt her. Kayla slowly calmed down, and Saga took her hand off of her mouth. Kayla asked her who she was and what was she wanted. Saga sat down on Kayla's bed and started talking.

"I knew your mother Nikki and your grandmother Aza'el. Aza'el was envied by the Klexons for having a child with a human. Nobody accepted her with a human child. Nobody wanted to love her with a human child. You can only take so much emotional pain before you flip your shit. Aza'el wanted revenge for being left in the dirt. As far as Nikki, she wanted to finish what her mother started. If I was you, I would blame Emily for the reason why you don't have your Mama," said Saga.

"Why Emily?" Kayla asked.

Saga looked up at her.

"Oh, you didn't know?" Saga asked her.

"Know what?" Kayla asked her.

Saga stood up, walked over to the window, and opened it; but before she jumped out, she said, "Emily killed our mother. Why don't you look into the mirror sometimes? You will see you look just like me and not a Klexon. If you want to know more, meet me tomorrow around midnight at the forest. If not, then I will be seeing you around."

Before Kayla was able to respond, Saga jumped out the window and disappeared. Kayla felt tears coming down her cheeks. She slowly walked over to the mirror in her room and transformed. Saga was right. She was not a Klexon. She was like her mother. Kayla slowly walked down the stairs. Her father was washing dishes in the kitchen. He then heard Kayla ask him if it was true. He stopped washing the dishes and gave her his attention.

"What you mean?" he asked her.

"How did my mother die?" she asked him.

Jack did not answer at first.

"How did my mother die!" She yelled this time. Jack saw she was angry.

"Okay, hon, I think you should calm down. We can talk about this," said Jack.

"They all lied to me my entire life, about me, about you, and about mom; and you allowed it. I finally see you, and you continued to lie to me too," said Kayla. Her voice sounded very crackly from crying. "It was Emily, wasn't it, Dad?" she asked him.

"Who told you this stuff?" he asked her.

Kayla did not answer him. Jack tried walking up to his daughter to comfort her and calm her down, but she did not give him the chance. She transformed into a Dark Zal and ran upstairs to her room locking the door. Jack ran after her. He was knocking on her door, but no response. A couple of minutes later, he broke the door in and saw her window was open but no sign of Kayla. Jack ran downstairs, grabbed his jacket off the couch, and ran outside. He made his way to Emily's house. Mike answered the door and Jack stormed in. He walked passed Mike and straight to Emily who was sitting on the couch.

"Kayla knows," said Jack.

Emily stood up and asked him what he was talking about.

"She knows you killed Nikki!" Jack yelled.

Emily's face dropped. "How did she find out? Now, she probably thinks we are the bad guys," said Emily.

"You know what Emily? You are the one who got me in this bullshit. Now, fix it," said Jack and left.

Kayla, however, ran into the forest where Saga said she would be waiting for her. Kayla then walked quietly deeper and deeper into the forest, but there was no sign of Saga. A couple of minutes later, Kayla heard a, "Stop," from behind. Kayla turned around, and there she was, Saga, standing with a smile on her face.

"I thought you would come," said Saga.

Kayla walked closer to Saga. She was as a human at this point. "I want to know more. Tell me everything you know," said Kayla.

Saga laughed. Saga walked between branches coming closer toward Kayla. "Trust me. I cannot wait until you hear everything," said Saga and then jumped onto a tree and used her sharp fingernails to climb up yelling for Kayla to follow her.

Kayla transformed into a witch and followed. Saga continued to jump from one tree onto another until they saw the portal. Saga jumped down in front of the portal, and Kayla followed.

Saga grabbed Kayla's hand, and they jumped into the portal. When they exited the portal, they ended up on a dirt road, not too far from Aza'el's castle.

"How did we get here?" Kayla asked her.

"You can travel wherever you want if you focus strong enough," said Saga.

As they walked down the dirt road Saga said, "There are many other portal destinations. If one opens, they all open." When they arrived at Aza'el's castle, Kayla looked at the castle and then at Saga.

"This place is abandoned," said Kayla.

Saga looked at Kayla, shook her head, and walked into the castle. Kayla followed. As they were walking through the castle, Saga said, "This is where your grandmother Aza'el lived. You see, many years ago, there used to be an open portal between us and the humans all the time. That is how Aza'el met a human. She got pregnant by him, but he didn't want to marry her because she was a witch. He left her and the child they were having. The Klexons, so-called the good witches, helped her raise the child. But, since Aza'el had a child with a human, other male Klexons didn't want her; therefore, she never found love again. As years passed by, her heart forgot what love is. She joined the dark side and created us to be her army. Right before she was put under a deep spell, she managed to leave your mother in the human's world thinking she would have a better life there. One thing led to another. Emily found your grandmother's ring, which holds the greatest powers, which brought Aza'el back to life. But then Emily killed her and your mother. There, that's the full story."

When she was done telling Kayla the story, she opened a large door in the basement of the old castle and Kayla saw many other Dark Zals.

"I did not know there were others," she said.

"We were created out of Aza'el's blood, we carry her inside of us, and we are here to finish her duty. The reason of your birth is because of Aza'el. That makes you our queen," said Saga.

All the Dark Zals faced Kayla and kneed in front of her, but Saga did not. She did not want to work for anyone, but she knew she had to get Kayla on her side. Kayla stood there, looking at all the Dark Zals bowing down to her. She did not know what to do.

Saga walked over to her and told her, "You are their ruler and you are powerful. They will obey you."

Kayla nodded.

Later that night, Kayla was sitting outside of the castle looking deep into the field. There was nothing around, no life, no creatures, nothing. She took her mother's picture out of her pocket and looked at it. Saga came from behind her and asked her if she was all right.

"Yes, I'm just hurt. I cannot believe my whole life was a lie. The people I thought was my family are actually my enemies," said Kayla.

Tears came down her cheeks and Saga rolled her eyes.

"Look, kid. Do not start crying on me here, okay. Now, love kills. It really does, but this is the time to be strong; and if you can't do it for yourself, then do it for your mother," said Saga.

As Saga was walking away, Kayla turned her way and said, "I want revenge for my mother."

Saga faced Kayla and nodded her head.

Jack just arrived home from the grocery store. He walked over to the kitchen and placed the groceries onto the counter. He walked back to the living room and turned on the lights.

"Holy shit! You scared me," said Jack when he saw Kayla sitting on his dining room chair.

"Where were you? I was looking for you," he said.

Kayla did not blink or move.

"Listen, I am not good with all this witch stuff, okay. I am sure whatever questions you have, Emily can answer them," said Jack.

Hearing Emily's name pissed Kayla off. "Fuck her! I have some questions for you!" she said and stood up from the chair.

"Okay, I will answer all your questions," he said.

"Eighteen years later, I find out that Emily killed my mother and everyone kept this a secret from me and I want to know why," said Kayla.

"Listen, I do not know much about what happened with Nikki. I think it is better if you ask Emily. She knows more about this," said Jack.

Kayla laughed. "Do you know anything? Did my mother mean anything to you?" she asked him.

"Of course, she did. I loved her and I still love her," said Jack.

"Then, how did you let Emily do this to us, Dad? You didn't do shit about it. You just went along with Emily's plan!" Kayla yelled at him.

Her dad was getting mad and said, "You watch your tone. I am still your father. You think I don't feel the pain? I miss her every day, and I regret every day for letting her go and leaving you in their hands. But I can't go back and change what happened."

He walked closer toward her, but she transformed into a Dark Zal and her father stopped.

"You are pathetic, Dad. Did you even try to look for Mom and find out what really happened?" Kayla asked him.

Jack hesitated for a minute. "No," he answered.

"Figured you didn't," she said.

Kayla lowered her head downward facing her shoes, but her eyes were looking straight at her father. Jack has never feared his daughter the way he did now.

"Kayla, are you okay?" Jack asked her because she was not moving.

Her eyes locked on Jack as she used her force to choke him. Jack felt pressure around his neck and he tried to gasp for air. He fell to his knees trying to get his words out asking her to stop. Kayla stood there, not thinking twice about it. A tear fell down Jack's face. He knew he was going to die. But then, the doorbell rung and Kayla lost her focus. A voice came from the other side of the door telling Jack to open up. Kayla ran out the back door. Jack watched her run out, but he was too weak to follow after her. He slowly walked over to the door and opened it. It was his neighbor Charlie.

"Is everything okay, man? I heard some yelling and banging," said Charlie.

Jack said everything was fine. Charlie tried to look inside the house, but Jack blocked his view.

"I really have to go now," said Jack.

"Well, while I'm here, I was wondering if you had some milk I could borrow?" asked Charlie.

Jack looked at him and told him if he knocks on his door one more time asking for milk, eggs, or anything else, it will be the last time he eats and drinks that shit. Jack then slammed the door in Charlie's face and ran out the back door to look for Kayla.

When Kayla arrived back at the castle, Saga was sitting in a corner sharpening her knife.

"I am ready. I want you to teach me how to be a heartless Dark Zal. I want to get rid of Emily for good," said Kayla.

Saga looked up at Kayla and smiled.

"Be ready tonight around midnight," said Saga.

At around midnight, Kayla met Saga at the nearby forest.

"Go kill something," said Saga.

"The Klexons taught me how to use a bow and arrow," said Kayla as she raised her bow and arrow and aimed it at a deer that was running by. The arrow went straight through the deer's head and it tumbled to the ground. "See, I told you," said Kayla with excitement.

"Now, go eat it," said Saga.

Kayla's smile went away. "What? I don't want to eat that," she said.

"Oh yeah, how will you survive? Here with us Dark Zals, nobody will cook you a nice warm soup, sweetheart. We hunt our own food," said Saga.

Kayla held a disgusting facial expression.

"What type of a witch are you? I mean even the Klexons have tasted flesh before," said Saga.

Kayla walked slowly toward the deer. She stood right next to its head. Kayla looked down at the animal and then up at Saga. Saga nodded her head telling her to go ahead and do it. Kayla looked back down at the deer again.

"You won't get your revenge if you can't even take a bite at the neck," said Saga.

Hearing those words, Kayla dropped her bow and arrow and dropped to her knees. She lifted the animal's head and dug her teeth into its neck. Saga smiled as she watched Kayla eat the flesh of the dead deer.

It was a late and dark night. Saga decided to test Kayla. "Come on, let's go to the Green Village," said Saga. Saga used Kayla to show her where all the hidden traps were and they both made it to the cottages. Saga picked the closest cottage to her and told Kayla to follow her. They both entered the cottage through a window, and walked over to the bed where a Klexon was sleeping.

"Come here," said Saga, and Kayla came closer.

Saga handed her a knife and told her to stab the sleeping Klexon right through her throat. Kayla took the knife but hesitated for a second.

"I don't think that I can do this," said Kayla.

"Do it for your mother," said Saga.

Kayla transformed into a Dark Zal, held the knife in both hands, and raised it above her head. She stuck it so fast and hard the knife went straight through the sleeping witch's throat. Kayla pulled the knife back out and the Klexon woke up holding on to her throat trying to gasp for air. The blood squirted from her throat onto Kayla's face. After there was no more struggle coming from the Klexon, Kayla handed the knife back to Saga and said, "I am done for today." Kayla jumped out the window, and went back to the castle. Saga followed.

The following morning, Emily and Mike went to Jack's house to find out if he heard from Kayla. He told them no. Emily told him she probably just needed some time to cool off.

"This is not like her. I am very worried," said Jack.

"We will find her. Do not worry. She cannot be far," said Emily.

Jack walked over to his front door, opened it, and asked them to leave. They did, and Jack slammed the door shut.

"Well, that did not go well," said Mike.

"Let's go see Gary," said Emily. As Mike and Emily were on their way toward the portal, Pete happened to be driving nearby and saw them walking into the woods. He decided to follow them.

Mike and Emily were getting ready to jump into the portal when they heard someone.

"Why is this open?" asked Pete.

"Something came up, and we have to take care of it," said Emily.

"Well, count me in," said Pete.

"Now is not a good time," said Mike.

"Look, whatever it is, I'm pretty sure you could use me. Plus, I have to do this for Mitti," said Pete. "What exactly do you need to do for Mitti?" asked Emily. "Oh, I'm sure the witches had something to do with her death," said Pete.

Mike walked closer to his face and asked him what the hell he was doing.

"Just looking for answers. Why is that a problem?" Pete asked.

Mike didn't respond. He turned his attention back to Emily, and they jumped into the portal. Pete stayed behind.

When Emily and Mike arrived at the Green Village, there was a huge commotion. Emily ran up to Eliot and asked her what was going on. Eliot turned to Emily and slapped her. Emily was caught off guard.

"Hey, what the hell you do that for?" Mike asked Eliot as he grabbed Emily into his arms.

"This is probably her fault," said Eliot and walked away.

Emily caught up to Eliot, grabbed her by her arm and said, "I am a part of this village if you like it or not. I will give you a warning this time but next time you won't get off that easy." Eliot looked down at Emily and said, "I don't have time for your shit. Something came in here last night and killed a Klexon. Whoever this was knows about our traps. The only one who leaves this village and comes back is you."

"That is no longer true," said Emily.

"What are you talking about?" Eliot asked her.

"Kayla is gone, and we can't find her," said Emily.

"God damn, Emily. When did you plan on telling me this?" Eliot asked angrily.

"Today. That is why I came here," said Emily.

"Where is she," Eliot asked.

"I don't know. She ran away," Emily replied.

Eliot slammed her weapon against the ground, pointed her finger at Emily and said, "This is why we did not approve mixing forces with the humans in the first place."

"Did you ever think that just maybe that was the mistake to begin with? I mean, if the Klexons didn't disown Aza'el for falling in love with a human none of this would have happened. You can't control emotions. The heart wants what it wants, but that does not make an individual bad because they are different," said Emily.

Emily took a couple of steps closer to Eliot.

"Maybe it's time we show the humans who we really are. Maybe we are the bad guys," said Emily.

Eliot stepped even closer into Emily's face and said, "Life is just not fair and we all have to find ways to deal with it. We did not forbid Aza'el to be with a human cause we didn't like her, we forbid it because the humans will do anything to demolish us! Just because you don't get your way does not mean you become a Dark Zal and turn against your own people."

Eliot called out for Abe and the other warriors. They lined up in front of her, and she ordered them to find Kayla. Eliot told them to be careful and do whatever is necessary to survive.

Emily interrupted Eliot and said, "Let me find her. She is just a young girl."

"I am sure she can fight her own battles. From here on, I am handling things my way," said Eliot.

ABOUT THE AUTHOR

D ragana Stjepić was born in Bosnia and raised in Croatia. At the age of five, she was present in the 1992 war when Croatia fought for its independence. Very lucky to be a survivor, she appreciates the smallest things in life. In 2000 she moved to the United States and made it her new home. She obtained an associate degree in criminal justice and a bachelor degree in technical management. As a single mother she always made sure her daughter had a smile on her face. Dragana stays busy with work and writing but nothing comes before her daughter. Together they are always looking for new adventures. Dragana was a felony probation officer when she finally decided to put her dreams into action. She loved writing about, drama, love, murder and sex in a way that takes our imagination to another level. So be ready to read more of her amazing stories and let her take you into an imaginary world.